THE LAST CALL

NIKKI BELAIRE

PLAYLIST

Issues—Julia Michaels

Strip That Down—Liam Payne, Quavo

How You Remind Me—Nickelback

Let Me Go—3 Doors Down

Blow Your Mind—Dua Lipa

Paralyzer—Finger Eleven

Whatever It Takes—Imagine Dragons

I Like Me Better—Lauv

Never Be the Same—Camila Cabello

Nevermind—Dennis Lloyd

8 Letters—Why Don't We

You Say—Lauren Daigle

She only has three rules

1. No husbands
2. No drugs
3. No commitments

THE
LAST CALL

PROLOGUE

THE INSTRUCTIONS I'VE HEARD—THAT I'VE RECITED MYSELF IN our meetings with the new pledges—circle around and around in my mind.

Preserve evidence by placing belongings such as clothes in a paper bag. I shove my bloody panties and ripped skirt down to the bottom of the trash can and cover them with a wad of paper towels and stale cupcakes left over from Jordan's birthday that no one's ever going to eat, tossing the empty box in the recycle bin.

Don't shower or bathe. I gather my damp hair into a pile on top of my head. Not bothering to comb out the tangles.

Go to the nearest emergency room and ask for the sexual assault advocate. I tiptoe to Margaret's room. Grateful to see the light still on. A sweet, studious girl who everyone loves. Although I always wonder if she knows how much people make fun of her behind her back for never drinking. But now I realize that all along she's been the genius. Never having a drop of alcohol in her life, she sits at her desk typing away. Free from harm. Safe and content. Without any guilt or pain or fear.

She doesn't seem surprised when I knock on the cracked door. Maybe a lot of people bother her this late.

"Hey Sydney. What's up?"

I'm terrified out of my mind and don't know what to do. "I'm sorry to bother you but I was wondering if you could take me to the drug store." I smooth down the sleeve of my sweatshirt. Trying to hide the shaking in my body and my voice. "I mean if you don't mind. I really, really need to go."

Worry reddens her freckled cheeks, and she runs a curious gaze down my body. Almost as if she senses something's wrong. I guess wearing jeans and such a heavy top does seem strange when it hasn't been less than eighty-five degrees since the summer semester started.

"Sure. Let me get my keys."

"Thank you."

My whisper must be loud enough for her to hear because she nods and grabs her phone off the dresser too. I follow her mutely down the hallway and through the common area to the back door. Realizing when I traveled this same path hours earlier I thought all my dreams were coming true. So different from the nightmare destroying me now.

The interior light of a red Hyundai sedan blinks on when she pushes the button on her fob. Practical, sensible, and efficient just like her. I forget how tender I am until I drop onto the seat. My mental anguish worse than the physical pain until this reminder. She doesn't say a word but I'm sure she hears. How can she not notice when I gasp like a furnace kicking on?

She looks straight ahead as we drive while I stare at my hands. Fingers scratched from fighting with his. I gag a little from the dark pink lines under my nails. Not sure if it's his blood or mine.

Neither of us attempt any small talk. I don't think I

could manage a conversation even if I tried. We don't even play music which is kind of weird. But good too. The club where we were at tonight ruined my favorite song anyway.

Only three other cars fill the parking lot. Flooded with artificial light, bright and welcoming for shoppers anytime of the day or night. Or exposing them to all their sins they want to hide from in the darkness.

I guess I sit for too long since she puts the gear in park and turns off the engine. She clears her throat and pats my trembling arm. The amethyst stone in her high school class ring so innocent and clear. Just like I used to be. "Do you want me to go with you?"

Yes, please. I don't want to be alone. "No, I'm good. But thanks."

We both know I'm lying but she doesn't argue and I don't let myself beg her to come along. I keep the mask on, portraying the flawless straight-A sorority girl cheerleader I've always been, and slide out of the seat. Forcing myself not to cringe or whimper. Because no one can ever know that I'm not perfect any more.

CHAPTER 1

I TOSS THE BLACK CRYSTAL FOB INTO THE VALET'S OUTSTRETCHED hand. Not even bothering to threaten him about what I'll do if my One-77 comes back scratched. No need. Although I've never seen the kid before, the young guy's already trembling.

He nods furiously. Wild brown curls bouncing from the force. His wide-eyed gaze flits from me to the Aston Martin and back again. Afraid, like I've actually spoken the warning out loud. Warned, I guess, by his boss to fear me. Everyone here frightened of my wrath. As they should be.

"N-no worries Mr. Sabatini. I'll take good care of her…" He swipes at the sweat beading on his forehead with the back of his hand. Embarrassed by his misstep. "…I mean it…the c-car for you."

Funny how much I used to love that shit. Stuttering and stumbling to appease me. Which stoked my already inflated ego. Fuck yes he should be scared. But right now I'm too furious to answer or care. I've got much bigger issues to deal with. Zeke's fucked up, and he's going to realize how much when I find him.

I stride between the massive pecan doors, winding between the four floating fireplaces in the expansive lobby, and down the wide, gray-toned hallway to the bar. Pride wells up in my tight chest despite my irritation. My first hotel and still my favorite after all these years. A complete dump when I bought the property. Stalled in sales and travel site rankings. With a lame ass bland 80's atmosphere that no one had ever bothered to update. So that was my primary priority, and I sunk every penny I had at the time into the project. Taking an enormous risk with all the money I actually earned myself rather than inherited from my father to create an experience that actually makes staying at my place better than your own house.

Ignoring the advice of the haughty decorators arguing for a neutral décor, I went with my gut instead. All chrome and glass with blasts of red, silver, and black. Overstuffed sofas and abundant leather ottomans instead of plastic tables and metal chairs. All the open areas just an extension of your room. Grab a whiskey, prop up your feet, and relax. Even if it's only for fifteen minutes while your boss checks his messages or the kids nap or your wife blows out her hair. You're away from home, and because of me, you're going to fucking enjoy every second of the trip.

Only took six months to earn the reputation of the premier resort in the area. I have the magic touch. So I bought another and another until I was competing against myself. Now my properties hold the number one spots in the business, romance, and family categories. All of which provide the perfect cover for my family's real business. Thousands of people visiting my lodges every day. Bringing in and taking out everything we need to rule this fucking city.

And I'm not going to let my formerly best captain ruin my success. I pause in the doorway of the bistro and glance around the warm space. About half of the club chairs are filled as happy hour quickly approaches. Not at all pleased. Stupid fucker's late. Again. And some dark-haired goddess sits in my usual spot at the bar.

I'll admit she's spectacular. Sophisticated in her white dress that's completely modest yet sexy as hell. Silky fabric covers every inch of her full breasts and narrow thighs down to her knees. Yet the luxurious material smooths over her luscious curves more sensual than lingerie. Standing out like a siren even in this opulent setting.

Yet, her confidence draws me to her even more than her body. Unlike most women who would be restless in their insecurity from sitting alone, she conveys an assured ease. Relaxed and carefree, sipping a dark wine. The claret as rich as her lipstick. She doesn't look around for company or attempt to alleviate her uncertainty by playing on her phone. Just enjoys her drink.

I march up to her like a tyrant. She must not know who the fuck I am. "You're in my seat."

Now that I'm closer I can tell what a classic beauty she really is. Sure, make-up covers her flawless face, and loose curls, perfectly coiled from some kind of styling tool, spiral down her slender back. Bare except for a hint of sparkle floating over smooth skin. Fucking stunning. But underneath all that, she's naturally gorgeous. Smells fucking great too from some expensive perfume wafting over her.

A lazy gaze drifts from her glass to my face. A long linger studying my expression before she takes me all in, sweeping downward, lingering on my crotch with a defiant smirk before she lifts to meet my eyes again.

"Wow!"

Yeah, I'm that guy. The man who impresses the ladies with just one look. I don't spend over an hour a day in the gym for my fucking health. Just wait until I get her on her back. I stifle a groan. Or on her knees.

"Do you actually get fucked using lines like that?"

Fuck me. She's incredible. The epitome of elegance with the mouth of a sailor. "Not a line. My hotel. My restaurant. My chair."

Dainty hands flatten on the ebony speckled counter, leveraging her sweet ass in place as she twists her torso in the stool. Black leather creaking when she strains to check over each slim shoulder.

"I don't see your name on it. Maybe you should have a sign made. Or better yet, just piss on it. You know mark your territory…" A saccharine smile curls her plump lips, and she twirls a short burgundy fingernail in the air. "…since you own all of this."

Her condescending tone flames my desire and stirs my dick. Fine. She's not impressed. I like a challenge, and the night is young. With Zeke fucking flaking on me, I've got all the time in the world to prove to her who the boss is. And who she should submit to.

I lift two fingers to the bartender, who pretends to ignore our conversation while he stocks the garnish tray with olives, cherries, and thick slices of lime. Although smart enough to hover in preparation for my demands. "Another one for the lady."

Spindly hands smooth over his crisp, white apron double tied at the waist. "Yes, sir. A Syrah and a Macallan coming right up."

My gaze bores into hers. Proving to her the respect I command from my employees. Unmoved by my prowess, she rolls her eyes. Fucking rolls her luminescent ice green eyes at me.

"He knows you drink scotch. Yep, you showed me. You're definitely in charge."

Insolence rolls off her body and her tongue. What in the goddamn fuck? I've just met this lady, and she can't stop busting my balls. Even fucking worse, I can't seem to stop letting her. I've got to get my shit together and get back on my game.

I smile. Sweet and contrite. Which. Fucking. Kills. Me. I'd rather twist a rusty dull blade through my gut than show any weakness. But I've got to figure her out. Try and comprehend why the fuck she's not fawning over me like every other woman I've ever met. "Listen, I think we got off on the wrong foot. Let's try this again. I'm Julius Sabatini."

Delicate fingers softer than silk curl around my outstretched hand. Sparking a current through my pulse. Stirring a rare sensation in me to pull her closer. Some kind of crazy, fucked up primal desire flares deep in my belly to scoop her up and never let her go. I can already tell this is going to be way more than just a fuck. Which means I am totally fucking screwed.

"It's nice to meet you Julius."

An amused grin twists her lush mouth. Matching the humor brightening her expression. Her grip tightens as she sets a silver, red-bottomed heel on the swirled sable carpet and slides out of her seat. Her slight body skims across mine. Button nipples straining against the thin cloth of her ivory sheath. Fuck yes, this is what I'm talking about. She's ready to head upstairs with me and put one of my rooms to the best possible use.

"I'm...leaving."

Rare shock blasts through me as I watch her glorious hips sway back and forth. Swinging with the rhythmic sensuality of a dancer while she glides away from me and toward some douche bag with a comb over swimming in a baggy, wrinkled suit talking to the hostess.

A woman has never walked away from me.

Ever.

I do the walking. *They* do the chasing. Begging. Seducing.

What in the actual fuck? Too astonished to move, I stand here like a bitch ass pussy. Completely unable to fathom what in the fucking hell just happened.

A muscle head bigger than me hops up from a sofa near the entrance and follows about one hundred feet behind her. Not interfering yet not completely inconspicuous either. I'm too fucking busy to keep up with Hollywood, but she's not any celebrity that I can remember. And, I know all the wives, girlfriends, and daughters from the other families so she's definitely not mafia either.

The asshole waiting for her lights up like he's just won the fucking lottery as she approaches. Because of course he fucking has. She's on his fucking puny ass arm. Leaning in with her graceful head only inches from his, listening intently to whatever bullshit spiel he's laying on thicker than a cement grave. Her glossy hair flutters over her gently defined bicep as she laughs softly in agreement. Cuddling so close like someone's fucking paying her to hang on his every stupid word.

An amazing woman with a hulking bodyguard dating a nerdy loser. Nothing about this adds up. Until the realization hits me harder than my damn head. She *is* being paid. A fucking hooker. Albeit high end and discreet, but still a goddamn hooker. Now I'm fucking furious. Someone's fucking running game in my hotel. Hell the fuck no.

Another one of Zeke's fucking failures. I control every goddamn racket in this city, and somebody's fucked up if they think they can move into my territory. I yank out my phone and pound the digits for my best tech guy so I can figure out who the fuck she works for and shut this shit down.

Now it's my turn to smirk at the confidence radiating from her svelte frame as she allows the old man to guide her away from me. Although I swear to fucking god the light in the room dims from the loss of her radiance.

At the last second, she looks back over her shoulder. Her succulent mouth parts in surprise when her beautiful eyes meet mine. A marvelous pink flush spreading over her glowing cheeks. I'm an arrogant bastard and can't refrain from dropping my chin and winking at her. As much as she pretends to loathe me, I can tell I've affected her too.

Good. Because it's the last call, angel. That magnificent ass is mine now.

CHAPTER 2

STUMBLE, HYPNOTIZED BY JULIUS'S BURNING GAZE. Mesmerized by his dominance. His commanding persona invading the room. His broad stance. His demanding tone. His imposing confidence.

Thankfully, Arthur curls me closer to his bony body. Always such a gentleman, he wraps a protective arm around me, preventing me from tumbling forward and embarrassing myself even more than I already have.

"Are you okay, Sydney?"

Worry deepens the heavy creases that already line his broad forehead. So much for the poise and grace I try to exude. I meet his anxious eyes and offer an apologetic nod. "Yes, I'm sorry. My heel must have snagged on the carpet. But I'm fine."

"Good. I'm glad." Thin, dry lips brush my temple, although he doesn't release me. "I didn't mean to walk so fast, but Robert wants to meet with me before my presentation, and I've got to put my note cards on the lectern…"

Smiling in agreement to the words tumbling out of his mouth that I can't really hear or understand with my heart thudding so hard in my chest. Which is crazy. I'm with men all the time. Hell, I fuck men all the time. But something about Julius…his possessive touch…rages an inferno through me that I've never experienced before. With anyone.

Especially an arrogant prick like Julius. I mean really. His ego's so huge I'm surprised he even fit through the door. He probably thought I was going to drop to my knees right in front of him the way he

"What do you think?"

Arthur's exuberant tone yanks me out of my thoughts. Shit. Shit. Shit.

With his white bushy eyebrows lifted, he looks at me expectantly, and I have absolutely no idea what he just said. Fifty-fifty chance, but I guess I've never been a woman afraid to gamble. Please God let me be correct. "Yes, I would have to agree."

A satisfied laugh blows on my cheek, and he squeezes me again. Still chuckling as he nuzzles my hair. "I knew you would. You're a very smart lady."

Thank goodness. Luck might be with me, but I refuse to risk another faux pas. I've got to focus on Arthur. He deserves my full attention. He pays for my complete devotion.

To reconnect with him, I tug down his tweed jacket, hanging on his wiry frame. Poor guy. Never clues into the hints I make about the professional image he would convey in a well-fitted suit. Oblivious to my suggestions with his mind too deep in his research to worry about his appearance. Maybe our next date can be to the tailor. "Thank you for inviting me tonight. I'm excited to celebrate with you. It's wonderful to finally see all of your hard work paying off."

He beams down at me, his pale face flushed and shiny. Genuinely happy. I won't ruin his evening with my distraction. I refuse to minimize his exhilaration

"Ready?"

No. *"Yes, let's go."*

With my confirmation, he grasps my hand and leads me to the lobby. One foot in front of the other for a nice evening that he's paid a lot of money for. That I know I'll enjoy too. That I should appreciate as an easy job. That I should be grateful for and not be distracted. By Julius or the strange sensation of loss rippling through my chest from walking away from him. That I don't like or understand.

"I told everyone you've been out of town visiting your sister who's been ill, and that's why you weren't at the last event."

A sudden shyness overtakes his tone, pink circling his gaunt cheeks from his admission. While a flicker of guilt heats my own heart. He worries his co-workers will figure out I'm not really his girlfriend. But I've played this role before, and know just how to appear dedicated but not disingenuous. A very fine line to be convincing. I entwine his sweaty fingers tighter with mine. *"Luckily, she's all better now, and I'm happy to be back home with you."*

I play along, not even saying the words to him admitting that I'm an escort. No chance of anyone overhearing or intensifying his embarrassment by discussing our arrangement. We took care of the business side of things for rates and agreements a long time ago. Now we're just a couple enjoying his awards ceremony.

Last minute preparations bustle in the banquet room, with a tall blond lady wearing a headset directing two young men in black suits where to place tall vases overflowing with yellow and purple hydrangeas, the corporate colors from Arthur's pharmaceutical company. While an older woman in a charcoal dress uses a ruler to ensure the silverware stems lay in perfect alignment.

Arthur ushers me to the round table closest to the stage, and I offer him a reassuring smile to ensure him I'm fine alone. I actually prefer to be solitary. Pleased to see a steak knife in my place setting. Arthur thinks my appetite is sexy. Always amused I'm not too shy to skip the salad and decline the chicken and go right for the good stuff. Although I can only allow myself a few bites, I know they will be amazing. The chef here really knows how to grill a filet. My stomach already growling as I glance toward the service door.

Julius.

Another arrogant expression lights up his face as he strides toward me. I hop up trying to cut him short. To keep him as far from Arthur as possible. Warmth flames through my body that's not just from worry when we're only a few inches apart. "What are you doing?"

His demanding gaze bores into me despite my terrified whisper. No mercy at all for me or my fear.

"I have business to discuss with you."

A violent shudder vibrates through me from the way he says 'business.' In the six years I've been doing this, I've never been confronted. Maybe suspicious inferences or doubtful expressions. But not once actually discovered to be anything other than what I claim to be for the evening. That cannot change tonight. "Not here."

"Then later." He slides out his card and grasps my trembling hand. Caressing my thumb with an intimacy I haven't experienced in a long time before he forces the thick paper into my palm. Curling his strong fingers around mine to make a fist. "Call me when you get home."

As terrified as I am, I refuse to let him see me as weak. No man will make me do something I don't want to ever again. My head shakes as I match his stare. Just as defiant as mine. *"No."*

"Don't deny me Sydney."

My body betrays me. Clenching between my thighs from his menacing tone. A deep ache pooling low in my belly and tingling in my nipples from hearing my name on his lips. That he shouldn't know. Proof he's even more powerful than I suspected to have already learned who I am in just a few short minutes.

"I always get what I want."

Luscious scents of black pepper and rich leather waft over me when he speaks directly into my ear. The scruff of his late day shadow tickles my already sensitized skin. His sultry tone makes me want more than just his voice surrounding me.

"Is everything okay over here?"

Julius leans back, giving me a traitorous wink, as Arthur's hand slides onto my lower back. Cold, thin fingers thrusting into my skin with his apprehension. Before I can answer, Julius extends his hand to Arthur. Forcing him to release me lest he be rude.

"Of course. I'm Julius, an old friend of Syd's." Another grin lifts his cheek. *"Surprised even more than she is to run into her again after all this time."*

"Nice to meet you."

Anxiety swallows Arthur's protective tone. Worried as I am Julius will reveal our secret.

"You as well." Julius' eyes remain locked with mine. An underlying warning for me to comply with his earlier request. *"I'll catch up with you later. After you enjoy your party."*

Fury burns through me from his threat. Well aware how

helpless I am to argue against his intimidation and jeopardize Arthur's celebration. With no other choice, I acquiesce to the implication and force myself to smile. "Yes, I look forward to our discussion too."

When I tell you to go to hell. The smirk slides off his face when I tuck myself against Arthur. Snuggling into his side with the familiarity of a couple in love. Reminding him he doesn't control me. No one controls me.

Anger flashes in his face more dazzling than lightning, and I can't hold back the shiver that engulfs me. Not sure from fear or lust. Probably both. Insanity too. I shouldn't give a damn about irritating a man I just met. But I do. And I like the rush of power I have over him despite how much he wields over me. And I want more. So much more than I should.

Mired in ambiguity, we remain silent watching Julius as he walks away. A stride—almost a swagger—that exudes confidence and charisma few other men can convey. Well aware of our scrutiny, he never glances back before he marches through the swinging door. Too slick to even have to push the handle as the server on the other side is quick to grab the edge and nod in deference to his boss. Must be a real asshole for everyone to be so subservient to him.

Once he's gone, Arthur's body sags with relief while mine pulses with dread. And disappointment, if I'm honest with myself. Although I'm not sure exactly why. Uncertain for the first time in a long time of what I want. Which scares the hell out of me. I know. I always know. I've always known. Myself. My goals. My plan. None of which includes someone like him.

"Are you cold?"

The concern in Arthur's tone shames me for the second time tonight. Not waiting for me to respond, he turns us, escorting me back to the table with a tight grip around my waist. Which is good because my legs can't seem to stop wobbling. Shrugging off his jacket when I'm seated again, he wraps the scratchy fabric around my shoulders. Despite the added layer, my muscles tremble from what almost happened. From what is going to happen later. Because even though I don't know him at all, I know men like Julius. He won't let this go. He won't give up. He won't give in. No matter how much I fight or protest or argue.

"Cabernet ma'am?"

My head bobs more enthusiastically than it should from the waiter's question. "Yes, please."

Alcohol never solves anything, but I sure as hell need something stronger than sparkling water to soothe my shaking hands and calm my pounding heart.

I murmur my gratitude to the server and greedily sip the rich liquid. Downing almost half the glass before I remember myself. Realize that I'm Arthur's doting girlfriend rather than a lush who cares more about the free booze than him and his success.

Wrapping my hand around his bicep, I give his arm a gentle squeeze and look up to him. Smiling my appreciation and pride to him. Which rewards both of us when some of the tension releases from the taut lines of his pale face. "Thank you. I'm much warmer now."

"From the wine or my blazer?"

A relieved laugh bubbles in my throat and softens my shoulders. Both from the proof that the trepidation Julius generated has waned, as well as from Arthur's relentless curiosity. Inquisitive enough to want to know the difference and ask me. The clinician within his personality shining through despite us sitting at a dinner table rather than a lab bench. "Both."

He nods slowly. Probably performing calculations in his head analyzing my weight and the heaviness of the coat and the alcohol volume of my drink. Forever a math nerd in his sweet, gentle heart. I release him as he stands for his boss and her husband. Warm smiles from each of them as Arthur reminds them again of my name since I haven't seen them since the Christmas party. Granted I'm sure neither one has forgotten. Both of them cordial and welcoming every time I see them regardless of how infrequent.

Although, unfortunately, I can't say the same for the other couple joining us. Intolerant of each other and everyone else, they revel in the discomfort of their colleagues. Especially when they're the ones to inflict the anxiety.

"Jim, Annette, you remember Sydney."

I earn only a terse nod from Jim before the stout man plops into his seat, seemingly relieved to be sitting down after crossing the expansive hall to reach us. Not surprisingly, Annette's demeanor isn't as indifferent. "You weren't at the spring gala. I thought maybe you decided our Arthur was too boring for you."

The mischievous tone belies the insinuation underneath, and her antagonism stirs my protective streak. Not because Arthur's paying me. But because he deserves to have someone defend him, despite his mild disposition, since I know he would never assert himself. "You must not know him very well if you think Arthur could ever be boring."

Feigning a teasing chuckle, I wink at her. Rosy circles pop on Arthur's narrow cheeks from my proclamation, and I can't help but genuinely smile at this docile man. Wishing deep that he realizes how sincere and genuine I am in my feelings for him.

She leans forward, tapping her fingertip on the cream

tablecloth. Accepting my challenge. Good. Because I don't intend to lose this battle over my friend.

"Exactly how well *do* you know him?"

Even her spouse is shocked by her blatant vulgarity. Shaking his head at her boorish demeanor. Yet, she ignores his silent reprimand, and so do I. Since neither of us appears ready to back down, I grin. My smile as phony as her saccharine tone. I read her for who she is and what she wants to know. The real meaning behind her implication. The suggestion really code words for 'aren't you just a gold digger?'

"Very well."

I allow the inference to hang between us. Relishing in her discomfort. She waves an impatient hand at me as if I'm the one to misunderstand her meaning.

"I mean how did you two even meet?"

Perfect. A well-tuned story with just a few specific details to be believable. "Well, I'm a nervous flyer, and he was unlucky enough to be stuck next to me as I was returning from visiting my sister who has a lot of health challenges." I peer at him again and tilt my head as if trying to remember another detail. "You were coming back from that biotech conference I think…"

Arthur nods, quick and urgent. Approving my performance, which bolsters my confidence even more. I let out a self-deprecating laugh. "Anyway, we hit some turbulence, and I grasped his hand like a crazy woman. Poor guy couldn't wring himself loose if he wanted to. But always the gentleman, he let me cling to him without complaint and talked to me the entire flight, even after we landed, to keep me calm. I'd never met a man more generous and thoughtful than him. We stayed in touch after we left the airport, and he's been my best friend ever since."

The drop of her bottom lip seems almost cartoonish from the exaggeration. She's literally and actually speechless. I snuggle against his shoulder in triumph. No one can argue against best friends. Or the truth. The real circumstances of the first time we met may be different but there isn't any duplicity regarding my description of Arthur's personality. "We just have so much in common. We read the same authors, enjoy the same artists, and can waste away an entire afternoon playing chess."

Jim jumps on that remark. Slamming down his pinot in his eagerness to call my bluff. I'm ready. More than ready to take him on.

"Arthur's terrible at chess."

Smug in his insinuation, he leans back in his chair. The self-righteous grin marring his already ruddy face even more.

"Oh, believe me. I know." I wink at Arthur, letting him in on the joke. Confirming I'm teasing because I know he's good natured enough to let me. "At first I thought he was letting me win to be nice, but then I figured out he doesn't know an exchange from an endgame."

I nudge his shoulder with mine. Encouraging him to accept the playful slight against his strategic skills, which he does with a shrug and impish smile.

Laughter chimes from the other couple with us. Well aware I've won. Effectively shutting down Jim and Annette's rude behavior for the remainder of our evening. Hopefully forever. As much as I want to, I refuse to gloat. Message sent and received. I doubt they'll harass Arthur again, which really is my ultimate goal.

The enormous crystal chandeliers flicker, kicking off the gala and quieting any lingering conversations. With a few soft taps against the microphone, all the attention turns to the podium and my thoughts turn inward. Easy to ignore my apprehension regarding Julius, while I defended Arthur. Now I have nothing to impede the emotions flooding through me.

Somehow I survive the rest of dinner without spilling my wine or choking on my meat that I can't even remember tasting. I smile and clap and congratulate Arthur like a robot. A cool exterior of a devoted girlfriend rather than the absolute mess churning under the surface.

Almost eager to get home and face the consequences from the earlier confrontation. Reminiscent of when I was a little girl and I knew my momma was going to spank me. The threat made in the solemnity of a quiet church or a bustling store or crowded restaurant. Intimidation left to linger and increase the torture until we were home and she pulled her brown belt out of the well-organized closet and bent me over the scratchy fabric of her handmade pink flower quilt. The material deepening to red from my tears. The anticipation so much worse than the actual blows.

My body shudders with a chill I can't contain. I doubt that's the case this time. For as much as I want to kid myself, deep down I know Julius's punishment for my insolence will somehow destroy me. The only question will be when and for how long.

CHAPTER 3

TURN THE DEADBOLT, AND MACK'S DOUBLE TAP RAPS ON THE
door. His goodnight message to me after confirming I'm
safely inside. Yet tonight the ritual isn't as comforting
as normal. I swear I can feel the tension in his knuckles as
they strike the wood. Or maybe that's just my own anxiety
seeping into my thoughts. Yet I know guilt consumes him as
deeply as my apprehension engulfs me.

Although he has nothing to feel ashamed about.
Despite my arguments, he blames himself for being too lax.
Assuming as usual nothing to worry about because I was
with Arthur. The most harmless man we both know. Never
any reason he could have suspected a threat. Julius surprised
all three of us.

My toes rejoice when I kick off my heels. Normally,
after I leave a client, a long hot shower is my first priority.
Eager to wash away the remnants of my evening. I don't
bring men home physically or mentally. Refusing to allow
them to linger in my mind or on my body.

With Arthur I don't have that issue since he's never actually fucked me. Although he pays my sex rate, he can't—or
won't—touch me. I tried once on our second date to pleasure him. Attempting to alleviate his uncertainty by dropping to my knees after indulging in his homemade chocolate

cake. But he was so flustered, so embarrassed, I felt like I was torturing him. Struggling to push me away from unbuckling his belt while fearful of frightening me with use of any physical force. Painful and awkward for both of us. I let him take the lead from then on. Accompanying him to his work obligations. Dinner with his friends at the club. Easily apparent we're the only couple not married for over thirty years. Maybe a walk along the harbor followed by a few cocktails at the hotel bar afterward. Before we settle back into his condo to watch a movie or play chess until he yawns me to drowsiness too and Mack drives me home.

So sweet and generous, I can't help but indulge him with at least a little bit of physical enjoyment. A relaxing shoulder massage as we chat about his projects or the tender stroke of his hair while we cuddle. The only affection he's ever allowed me to offer him in the two years we've known each other.

After spending time with him, I usually end the evening ready for a long soak and a good book. Yet, tonight somehow my feet lead me to my sofa rather than my tub. Before I can argue with myself, I slide my computer onto my lap and type his name with urgent fingers. My heart and pulse pounding as images and articles burst onto the screen.

I should click the stories with headlines proclaiming his wealth and success and prowess—the stereotypical epitome of eligible bachelor. Peruse the reports hinting of organized crime, rumors of him being a mob kingpin that make my stomach swirl. But I can't stop scanning the photos. Shocked yet still pleased, more than I want to admit, from the lack of women accompanying him. Solo in about ninety percent of the shots. The other ones with just the kind of girl you'd expect. Overdone and obvious with fake everything. Figures.

Unsurprising, he looks as menacing in the pictures as he does in real life. Dark eyes burning into the camera just like his calculated gaze bored into me. No smile. No smirk. No smarm. Just a lifted chin, proud and confident, instilling a foreboding sense of dominance and possession. Reflecting more than just ownership of the hotel lobby he stands within. Displaying a genuine nonchalance in the photos capturing him exiting a bar reputed to be mafia owned. Powerful yet unconcerned as he climbs into a huge silver Infiniti SUV. The seats empty beside and behind him. Which why I give a damn about his lack of passengers, I have no idea. And, I don't want to figure my curiosity out. I'm way past worrying about Julius Sabatini.

Shoving the laptop off my thighs and onto the beige ottoman, I hop up and stride back to the entryway, snatching my silver clutch off the ebony foyer table. His card remains stuffed inside. Still crumpled from my earlier fear. More of my normal composure returns when I rip the thick paper into quarters and toss the pieces into my kitchen trash. Exactly where they belong and how I feel about him. Done. He can fuck himself if he thinks I'm really going to call him.

With increasing bravado, I tug down my side zipper and slip off my sheath. Looping the hanger straps over the hook in the laundry room for my dry cleaning pick up on Monday. I'll add the clothes from tomorrow, if they survive.

Brunch with David requires much more exposure than dinner with Arthur. Rifling through the hangers, I chose a pink sparkly crop top tee shirt adorned with *Princess Attitude* swirled around a giant iridescent heart and a coordinating pink and red checkered skirt. At twenty-seven, I'm embarrassingly old for this outfit but I know he'll love it.

Which means I'll probably come home in only his suit coat and my heels again.

Behind closed doors the conservative judge likes bare skin, belly button jewelry, and bouncing tits. Luckily my pert breasts don't jiggle too much yet, or I couldn't pull off going out without a bra. He pays for naughty underneath the sensual. The irony not lost on me of his moderate platform on the bench conflicting with a dirty streak in the bedroom. His psychological issues worse than mine. Which is fine. The more broken the better. Who am I to criticize? No one's more fucked up than me.

Another anxious frown reflects back at me while I wash my face. I force myself to release the stress and lines, which will turn into wrinkles sooner than I can stop if I let the tension invade me. I promised myself three more years. Because no matter how much I want to, I can't do this forever. Regardless of diet, exercise, and endless spa treatments even I can't win against gravity. And thirty will be the beginning of the end. When a man pays more than some people make in a year to fuck you, he demands perfection. Plenty of nineteen year olds ready to be groomed to take my spot.

Besides, I've been smart with my money. All the way back to when I first started with Belle's. The agency kept their fifty percent, and I banked mine. Until I realized I could do this on my own. With Mack's help of course. Ten thousand for an event. Twenty-five for the night. Or even fifty for the occasional weekend. Which with Sergei has turned into a week. Not a bad way to earn two hundred grand, being spoiled on his luxurious island retreat despite servicing a boring dictator every night.

A thunderous bang reverberates from the living room,

and I jump, fumbling with switching out the silver hoop at my waist for the sapphire stone David likes. Pounding again and again until goose bumps erupt on my naked body.

Definitely not Mack.

Another thud.

Surely not Julius.

Three more booms.

Julius would never dare come here.

The walls shake around me from the force.

Oh damn.

CHAPTER 4

I BEAT ON THE DOOR FOR THE FOURTH TIME. IRRITATION BURNING in me as much as the side of my fist from her ignoring me. So fucking much I have to teach her, starting first with never keep me waiting when I want her.

I slam the surface again. I know she's home, and I know she's alone. Under surveillance since Kenneth traced her credit card from her bar tab. Second lesson to learn is not to use her real name when she's doing something illegal. My woman's smart but not slick.

Her thick necked bodyguard escorted her to her apartment around one a.m. before departing about fifteen minutes later. No one coming or going since. Including her.

Fuck this. I don't have time to jack around anymore with this angel. The heel of my foot drives through the thick wood, splintering with a jagged crack as I kick in the damn door. My guys can come back later and fix the damage.

A black Glock greets me when I step inside. Fuck she's magnificent. All intense and earnest in her stance and expression. Gorgeous too. No make-up and a black silk robe wrapped tight around her small body. More fragile than before without her heels boosting her height and her confidence. She's tiny and scared. Even though she pretends not to be.

"Get the fuck out of my house, and I won't blow your head off."

Totally adorable. "Okay baby, put the gun down before you hurt yourself."

"It's not me getting hurt that you should be worried about."

I'm so fucking hard I have to lean forward to relieve some of the pressure of my cock straining against my boxer briefs. Fucking this fireball is going to be amazing. Her gaze and the tip of the barrel follow my hand to my crotch.

"I'll blow that head off too if you're not careful."

Damn. I'm going to fucking come in my pants if she doesn't stop being so fucking glorious. "You won't shoot me."

That assertion riles her up and her plump lips twist into an angry sneer. "Because I'm a woman?"

Sure, I'm chauvinistic as hell sometimes. Women deserve to be protected and worshiped. But I'm no fool. I've known plenty of deadly women. Although she's definitely not one of them. "Because you're not a killer."

Her eyes widen. Only for a second before her deep frown returns.

"You don't know me. You don't know anything."

Pain, deeper than the argument between us, runs through her tone. Somebody fucking hurt her. And she's too fucking tough to let it happen again.

"I saw how you were with Mr. Effingham. Kind and attentive. Not just because he was paying you to either."

Something shifts. In her body and heart. She knows as much as I do that she's a good person. But for some reason somebody makes her think she isn't. Some fucker makes her hide the truth from herself.

"He's…" Worry smothers the relief beginning to soften her shoulders, and she lifts her taut arms higher. Defensive of the old man. Enough to make her battle the one in front of her. "Leave him out of this."

"No worries." I point to her and then back at myself. "This is only between me and you."

Lust, that rages through me too, flames in her eyes. Just as strong as mine. But almost as if she remembers herself, the desire is gone. Vanishing while her guard returns, building up thicker and stronger than before.

"There is no 'me and you' regardless of what you think."

"What I think is that you want me too and you're too damn stubborn to admit it."

"You're so fucking arrogant." Her head shakes more furiously than warranted. Needing to convince herself even more than me. "Besides, you're wasting your time. I don't do relationships."

She does with me. Only me from now on. "Fine. I'll pay you."

Not really. I don't have to fucking pay for anything, especially not sex. Hell I turned down some easy pussy in my club while I worked, waiting for this one to finish her so-called date. But I'm more than willing to play her game—for now—to get her to settle down.

"No."

I lift my palms in mock surrender. Reminding her I'm acquiescing to her threat before I slide my hand ever so slowly to my jacket pocket and pull out my wallet. I yank out all my cash and toss the bills on the side table. "Three grand?"

Fury shakes her petite body. That I want to strip down to lick and suck so damn bad. Tie that belt around her wrists and fuck her smart ass mouth until she can't stand any more and then flip her over make her take me again on her hands and knees.

"Fuck you."

I unhook the latch on my new Vacheron and drop the watch onto the pile. "Forty grand?"

"You're a bastard."

My last ploy. I slide out my car fob and add the key to my bid. "Two and a half million?"

Humiliation stains her cheeks, and her gaze drops along with her shoulders. Defeat engulfing her from my insulting proposals.

"Why are you doing this?"

"I want you Sydney. No matter what it costs, I'm going to be with you."

Matter of fact but she still shakes her head.

"I will never let you fuck me regardless of how much money you offer me."

More despondency in her tone than I expect from the severity of her words. Now I'm pissed. At myself for letting this argument drag on. And her for fighting me. The decision's been made, and she'll never do anything to make me change my mind. She can never win once I've declared victory. With her being the greatest prize. "No more clients. You belong to me now."

More strands fall from her messy bun when she tosses up her chin. Disputing the claim I have on her. Challenging my ownership of that spectacular body and sassy attitude that needs to be tamed. Of course I'm the man to conquer her.

"I don't belong to anyone."

She doesn't understand me yet. But she will. This isn't

up for debate. I don't demand. Or ask. Or negotiate. I take. "You're mine."

"I "

A gasp shudders between her parted lips yet she offers no resistance when I jerk the gun out of her elegant fingers and slide the weapon next to my other shit on her credenza. Absolutely zero struggle when I pin her against me. Good. I didn't want to have to get physical with her. Not yet anyway. Once she's in my bed, she'll understand what my hands on her body mean. "You're too damn beautiful and smart to be giving yourself away to men who don't deserve you."

An irritated huff blows against my heated skin as she stares up at me. Nothing but disgust filling her expression. "You don't deserve me either."

"Maybe not. But I'm taking you anyway."

Terror replaces the fervor in her expression, and I swear to god genuine fear seeps through the whimper she lets out. Fuck. Trembling fingers shove against my chest. She's really scared. I loosen my grip but refuse to let her go. "I'm not going to hurt you."

"You already have."

Bullshit. Absolutely impossible but the ferocity of her accusation makes me question myself which in and of it-self is a rare accomplishment. I stroke her back and scan her arms. She doesn't flinch from my touch or my gaze. Just stares at me with defiance.

"If you're going to rape me, then get it over with. If not, then just get the hell out of here."

Now I'm more pissed than she is. How can someone so delicate be powerful enough to enrage a man like me. "God damn, Sydney."

"You wouldn't be the first and you probably won't be

the last so stop thinking you're anyone different or special because you're not."

Motherfucker. She doesn't know when the fuck to stop.

"You're just like the rest of them. One in a very long line of many. So believe me when I tell you, I'll never be yours."

Enough. I smack my palm over her beautiful mouth to stop the hideous words she spews at me. Relishing how huge my hand looks wrapped around her slim jaw. Enjoying how easily I can control her. My fingers tangle in her tumbled chignon, cupping the back of her head with a ferocity that lifts her off her feet. Fuck if I'm not hard again from her dangling at my mercy. "Too late. You already are."

I guess I've stunned her with my actions and my words. Suspended from my strength and fury, she swings without reaction. Until I instigate one because I love the battle. "You're fucking glorious when you fight me, and you and I are going to have a lot of fights. So believe me when I tell you, I *am* going to fuck you."

Fire roars to life in her eyes again when I throw her own words back at her. Short burgundy nails claw at my wrist and dainty feet kick toward my shins. Better than I hoped with her robe slipping open from her rage, giving me the perfect view of her magnificent body barely hidden only by some sheer lingerie.

"Boss? They found Zeke."

Damn. She stills from my best enforcer's voice behind me. Reminding me of the other concern weighing on me. Her immense jade eyes flick to Reid. As much as I want to do this all night with her, I've got to sacrifice my pleasure for Zeke's punishment. At least for now. I jerk my head toward the damage I caused. "Get someone up here to fix that and put a guard on her until it's done."

"Yes, sir."

Her gaze returns to me, and I can't help but smile. Although I'm pissed as hell about the interruption and the need to jet, I still have to have one last look. Jesus, she takes my fucking breath away. Holding her for a second after I lower her to the carpet, I ensure she's steady on her feet before leaning down to nuzzle her neck. Damn, she smells good. *"I want to see you tomorrow. Don't leave this apartment until you hear from me."*

A chuckle bubbles in my mouth from her bewildered expression. I've shocked her speechless for the first time since I met her. Brushing a kiss on her smooth, warm cheek, I give her shoulder one last caress. Making me surprisingly happy even on my way to kill that bastard.

And just like that, he's gone. Before I get the opportunity to tell him to fuck off or call the police or smack his beautiful, smug face. He saunters past the proof of his impatience and strides down the hallway. Without an ounce of remorse or regret.

Unbelievable.

I slam what's left of the door behind him. Pointless since he's already in the elevator and probably can't hear the crash anyway, but I don't care. I refuse to let him destroy my home. Or at least think I'm going to allow him to so easily.

I pick up my gun with shaking hands. Careful not to touch his stuff. That I should toss out the window. Throw all of his cash and expensive possessions into the street for any random person to grab. So he could get exactly what he deserves. But I'm not that stupid. Angry and confused but not a complete idiot. I know who he is and what he does. I don't want any more of his wrath. I just want to be left alone.

A sharp ping signaling the arrival of the elevator chimes from the hallway again. Hating myself for looking, I peek anyway. Not Julius, thank god. One of his goons, I assume from his broad body, definitive stance, and the enormous weapon strapped on his waist that makes mine look like a toy. All I receive is a curt nod when our eyes meet. I appreciate the protection even though there shouldn't be any need for protection at all if it wasn't for that asshole.

Heat flames in my chest from the realization, and I race into the kitchen and grab a plastic storage bag. I can't even stand for his things to be in here. Unwilling to have any more reminders of him visible. I shove everything into the Ziploc, not caring if the broad face of his expensive watch gets scratched, and march out to the bodyguard who watches me with disinterest. Just like the first one. Who did absolutely nothing to help me while his boss manhandled me. Zero concern I was at the mobster's mercy suspended from his hands like a rag doll. Bunch of psychos. "Tell Julius I don't want him or his bribes."

He smothers a burgeoning grin but accepts the baggie without any comment. Smart ass or otherwise. Good. Then this is over. With him. With Julius. With all of them.

Back inside, I head for the bathroom and ignore my still trembling fingers as I twist the knob and flip up the drain latch. Saturating the air with sweet flowers as the rich, lavender liquid swirls in the hot water. Bubbles cover my body as I slide lower and lay my head back on the thick pillow. Willing my body to relax. My heart to slow. My mind to quiet.

Impossible.

Because we're fools. Both of us are damn fools. Him for trying to seduce me. Me for enjoying him trying.

Furious at him just as much as myself for liking his force too much. A surreal sensation to be weightless and under his power. Yet, I didn't feel scared. Not then. Not now. For the first time, in a really long time, I feel a little more free. Someone else helps hold the burden I carry. Deciding when he set me down. Choosing when I was allowed to move.

I should've been terrified of his words and his actions. He could've easily snapped my neck or tossed me across the room. Yet he didn't. Somehow, even in that terrifying moment, I knew that he wouldn't. Despite all the danger churning around him, he doesn't seem like the kind of man to purposefully assault a woman.

Proven by the concern that lined his face when I accused of doing so. Of the fury darkening his face from my accusation and what he inferred from my allegation. Ready to defend my honor. Of which I don't have any. Probably never did.

But I'm well aware my reprieve is just an illusion. Attraction that feels this good can't be real. Can't be genuine. Can't ever last. This is just two crazy, intense people caught up in an argument that should never have happened in the first place.

I hate him for making me feel things I know can't ever be true. I hate myself for being such a bitch. For letting my emotions get to me. For letting *him* get to me.

Although I liked shocking him, I was wrong to lie. I know better. I've lived the truth and know how devastating reality is.

"I'm not going to hurt you."

My eyes fly open from the memory Julius' assertion invokes and the tightness in my chest contracts harder. That's what he said too. Acrid beer breath wafting against my cheek as his impatient fingertips clawed at my thighs. Sliding under my panties. I wanted to kick and hit and scream. But I couldn't. Then or now.

Swiping at the wetness burning my cheeks, I hop up from the tub and grab my favorite towel. I need to be dry and covered and strong. Stop being so stupid. I haven't cried since college. Not since that bastard destroyed what I thought was mine.

He lied and he hurt me. Permanently scaring me even if the damage is no longer visible. I thought I was over it. I thought I was healed. I thought I was whole.

Until tonight. Julius unwittingly ripping the wounds open again. Yet, this time it was me who lied about him hurting me. Not physically at least. No, the damage he causes is way worse. Breaking me all over again mentally and emotionally.

My skin burns from rubbing the terrycloth against myself so vigorously, and I force a deep breath and calm cadence. I don't have time for this. I need to get some sleep. Mack will be here sooner than I'd like to take me to David's penthouse, and I'm sure as hell not going to let Julius ruin my date or my business.

I don't give a damn what he thinks or says. He's just some rich arrogant asshole who broke into my house and thinks he knows everything. Well, fuck him. Fuck him and his money and his righteousness. Julius Sabatini can kiss my ass.

CHAPTER 5

I WINK AT MACK BEFORE PUSHING OPEN THE OPAQUE GLASS interior doors to David's suite. Attempting, with the light-hearted gesture, to reassure him that I'm fine despite what happened to me last night. Convince him I'm all right regardless of his seething fury over the break-in to my apartment after he left me for the evening.

As scary as Mack is, we both know he can't battle Julius any more than I can. So we agreed business as usual. I keep my appointment with David today and fly out tonight to spend the week with Sergei. Just like planned. Just like normal. Just like expected.

Although we are both very well aware none of this is planned or normal or expected. Not with Julius storming into our lives.

With nothing else we can do, I leave my friend to wait as usual in the foyer. Maybe ease his mind a little with his newest book. The Lincoln biography interesting enough to pass the time but not enough to engross him too deeply if I need him. Surprising to everyone what a history buff he is. Except to me. I know how intelligent he is under the thick layer of beefy brawn.

The weekend hideaway is as tidy as always. The living room bereft of clutter or personal items. As if no one lives here. Which is accurate Monday through Friday. And the Saturdays when he volunteers at the Boys and Girls Club, following up with his good son persona on the Sundays when he takes his mother to church. Yet every other weekend he makes the three-hour drive to fuck me here without anyone's knowledge. Way too much money to spend for such an extravagant home with such little use. But the penthouse keeps his naughty secret safe.

David stands on the balcony. Enjoying the unobstructed river view framed on each side by mid-size skyscrapers in the growing city. Between us, a gorgeous breakfast covers the surface of the round table and chairs set. Once again spoiling me with my favorite food at the peak of the season. Cherries, sliced and pitted, heaped in the bisque bowl sitting in the middle of a gold edged place setting. Mimosas fill the sparkling flutes. Cinnamon scones nestle on each layer of a three-tiered stand serving as the centerpiece.

My heels click on the hardwood, and he spins around from the clatter in the otherwise quiet apartment. Pleasure brightens his face to see me, and he holds open his arms, welcoming me. I run to him as gracefully as I can in stilettos and launch myself at him. Squeezing him tight with my arms coiled around his neck and my legs wrapped around his waist. My lips brush his ear in a breathy insistence. "I've missed you."

"God Syd, I've missed you too."

Only an act on my part but in this moment there's a rare kernel of truth. At least to the ritual of our greeting. Normalcy compared to last night. Reassured from the familiarity of our relationship. Of the easiness between us from the roles we've played so many times before.

"I don't ever want to let you go."

His fingertips burrow deeper into my back. "Then don't."

A complete improvise from our regular conversation. More emotional than I probably should be. But for some reason I find comfort in his touch and his words. Unfair to him to make this about me, I need to dial this performance back. Giggling as I slide down his thick body. A former college defensive end he's broad and sturdy despite his rounding stomach. "But we shouldn't let all of this to go to waste."

He gestures toward the indulgent spread he's laid out. A hopeful expression pinching his already drawn face. So sweet to try and please me. "You like it?"

"I love it." I give him an innocent peck on his cheek, nuzzling against his morning scruff. Playful and relaxed to ease the transition from my overwrought reaction to our reunion. I select the seat right next to his. Keeping my thigh pressed against his leg to build our connection again after being apart. "Especially the cherries."

An almost childlike grin lights up his face. Giddy that I'm delighted with his offering. Which is pitiful for a man of his prominence and position. Always seeking the approval that he never received as a child from the people he cared about. The thought stirring emotions in me I try to tap down. This is business. A client. A job. Friendly but not friends. Sex but not love. Together but not permanent.

I don't like thinking about him like that when I'm with him. I'm his well-read companion until I morph into his bad girl. I moan over a large bite of the decadent fruit to confirm I really do love his treat and nod toward the file lying on the end table right inside the French doors. "I read the brief on the Rosewood case. Quite unexpected that he chose that argument to lead with, don't you think?"

His knife stops in mid-air and the pat of golden whipped margarine slides off, landing two inches from the pastry he intended to butter. Another impressed expression brightens his eyes. "Caught me by surprise too."

Perfect. He launches into the granular details. Kind of interesting, kind of not. I don't get the luxury of deciding one way or the other. His interests are my interests. At least for the rest of the afternoon.

Once he winds down from his dissertation, I show my concern to reflect the same worry I know he carries. "I hope the visibility will be helpful toward your retention election."

"I hope so too. That gives me the most likely chance to be appointed and not have to deal with the damn partisanship bullshit anymore. At least for ten years anyway."

I curl my fingers over his, squeezing with a genuine encouragement I hope I convey. "Well, I'll be here to support you either way. You know that right?"

My sincerity must be welcomed. He lifts our coupled hands and kisses the back of mine. "I do know. Thank you."

His smile lingers, studying my face for a few seconds. "Did you enjoy your brunch, baby girl?"

His cue. The change is unmistakable in his expression and his tone behind his mischievous term of endearment. He's ready to play. I lower my gaze to my plate, empty except for a few crumb flakes from my croissant scattered across the middle. Feigning a bashful modesty he loves with only a quick glance up at him as I flutter my lashes. "Very much. Thank you."

"I'm glad." He nods toward his phone resting on the textured glass top. "I've got one more call and then I'll join you inside."

And like the good girl I'm pretending to be, I hop up

from his dismissal and place another lingering yet chaste kiss on his cheek before I sweep inside. An enticement of things to come.

The huskiness of his voice remains throughout his discussion. It's been two weeks, and I know how much he needs this. How much he needs me. I bundle my hair into a ponytail with the thin black band on my wrist, and shrug off my dark apricot ruffled dress. Revealing his outfit hidden underneath for him.

He stands in the doorway watching me. Julius would walk right in.

Damn it! I can't be thinking about him now. I've got to get my mind and my body back to David.

My fingers strum over the bare skin of my midriff, tempting him with everything above and below my hand. I look up and shiver, pretending I've caught him checking me out. "Oh…hi."

That earns me a slow approving nod. "You're cute. Real cute."

"But, do you think my skirt is too short?"

I twist around, with enough twirl so the thin plaid fabric flutters. Lifting the hem to reveal my pure white panties embellished by tiny red hearts on the ass.

"No, not at all." Desire strains his voice, and if we hadn't role played this scenario twenty times before I wouldn't have been able to make out his words. "How old are you?"

Feigning hesitation, I fiddle with the turquoise jewel in my belly button. "I just turned eighteen. Barely legal."

He sucks in a deep breath. Not pretending anymore. Not faking at all how much that turns him on. His head bobs again. "Barely legal."

"Yes." I step closer. Licking my lips as his hands clench and release. Over and over. Desperate to touch me. To strip me. To take me. But not quite yet. Savoring the buildup is his choice, not mine. "Is that okay?"

"What do you want from me, little girl?"

Now he sounds frustrated. Almost angry. More at him-self than me. I know how much he wishes this was real. The bulge in his luxurious black dress pants twitches when I reach out and tug his belt. So close to where he wants my hand and my mouth, but too soon. Still not quite yet. "I want you to be my Daddy."

"To always love you and take care of you and never leave you?"

Damn, he really is fucked up over his father. Even more than I am from mine. "Yes."

Unable to hold back from my breathless whisper, he ad-vances. Following the same trail across my stomach that I did. Brushing the waistband of my scrap of a skirt. I flex my abdomen muscles that feels like a flutter in response to his touch. Thanks to years spent in the gym giving me—or more accurately him—a little confirmation of arousal when there really is none.

As always the trick works and he groans, deep and gut-tural, and his fingers slide lower. Breaking the final forbid-den cloth barrier to my smooth pussy. Playing an uncertain teenager from his bold move, I gasp and drive my hand down with his. The perfect opportunity to coat my lips with the hidden lube drizzled on my fingertips. A slick technique I learned long ago since no man has ever been able to get me off. He moans again when together we glide through the wetness and I guide him to my clit, where I lead him through the touches I need to make me really come. Letting him think all along it's him. Letting every man think it's them.

His buzzing phone mingles with his heavy panting. A rare interruption since his staff knows his Sundays are dedicated to the Lord. They just don't know it's me he's worshiping instead this morning.

"David?"

Annoyed with the disturbance, he strokes too hard. His caress impatient and hurried. Ruining the orgasm slowly igniting inside me. Which is fine. Like most women, I've learned to fake my pleasure. At least I'm lucky enough to be paid for my performance.

"Ignore it."

His game, his choice. "Okay, Daddy. Whatever you want."

My body jerks upward. Forcing me to stand on my tippy toes from his sudden harsh yank of my tee shirt. "What I want is to watch you come all over my hand."

The answer growls out through gritted teeth. Making me pretty certain he's going to come first and probably the only one between us unless he lets me take over again. "Then touch me. Fuck me like a baby girl needs to be fucked."

He shoves me backward, and I free fall onto the bed. Sprawling very unladylike with my legs splayed open and my shirt pushed up enough to show the alluring swell of my breast line. The lust flaming in his gaze confirms he doesn't care about the lack of sophistication in my wanton display. Only wants more than the preview I've teased him with. Stalking toward me until he stops, biting out a curse word in reaction to the clatter of jangling flatware from the vibrating cell shaking closer to the place settings. He jerks around.

Flying back to the balcony and swiping the offending technology off the glass.

"What the fuck is this?" His head flies up from scanning the screen. Absolute fury raging within him. "You're fucking blackmailing me?"

A shudder rolls through me. More from his accusation than his anger. The allegation the last thing I ever expected him to say. "What are you talking about?"

"Don't act like you don't know."

I hop up from the mattress, racing around the table to see what the hell makes him think I would ever betray him. Nausea overtakes me from photo after photo flipping from his swiping thumb. Me. Us. Here. On his balcony kissing. In his bedroom with his fist twisting the pink fabric above my breasts and his hand shoved down my skirt.

Someone's watching us. I scan the hotel angled to the left. Most of the curtains drawn tight to block out the bright streams of sunlight. Except on the seventh floor where a long black telephoto lens peeks out from an open window and tracks our every move. I point like an idiot. Too shocked to think straight. Too flustered to realize what I'm doing. "There he is."

Until I see the flicker of his flash popping again and again. Shit! I shove against David. "Get inside. He's still getting shots of us."

He takes a few swift steps but suddenly stops. His head whips up, and I flinch from the glare he bores into me. Proof of how he's earned his reputation in the court room as a hardcore beast. He's never looked at me with such disgust and loathing. Until now.

"It's too late. It's too damn fucking late. He's got what he needs to ruin me."

He's right. God, he's so right. I don't even know what to say.

"My career. My marriage. My "

Surprise explodes into my own revulsion from his inadvertent admission. What the hell? "You told me you're divorced!"

"Like it fucking matters now."

It totally fucking matters. Anything goes with my clients except breaking my three rules. "You know I don't fuck married men."

"Grow up Sydney. You fuck whoever is willing to pay you!"

His insult can't even rattle me as furious as I am at him as well as myself. I should have checked more. But he's a judge for fuck's sake. I thought I could trust him. I thought he was honest. I thought he was genuine. Kinky and desperate, but at least trustworthy. "Oh my god. I can't believe you lied to me."

"Well I can't believe you're fucking blackmailing me!"

"I'm not! I didn't do this. I swear."

He jerks away from my hand on his forearm. As if my touch repulses him. "Why should I believe you? You're nothing but a fucking whore."

Whore.

The label burns my ears almost as much as the back of my father's hand on my cheek. My heart. My soul. My spirit. Broken worse from his embarrassment than the humiliation caused by the man who assaulted me. Paralyzed as my Dad attacks me.

Berates me. Whore. Slut. Tramp.

Questions me. What did I do to make him think he could fuck me? What cheap outfit did I wear to lead him on? What did I drink that made him think I was that easy?

Disowns me. Get out of my sight. Get out of my way. Get out of my house.

The tile cold and hard under my clenched toes. The scent of mom's banana bread still wafts through the room. The deep voices of the announcers analyzing the ball game he refused to turn off when I told them I needed to tell them something. The disgust in his eyes as he shook his head at me for the very last time.

Shame instead of sympathy. Contempt instead of comfort. Ridicule instead of reassurance. I couldn't do anything but run. Out of the kitchen. Out of the house. Out of their lives. Driving all the way back to school barefoot and alone.

Regret as soon as the word leaves David's mouth. Shaking his head and reaching for me. Too late. A blur flashes past me, and Mack's fist pounds his jaw with an unmistakable crack. David hits the floor hard, bouncing from the force of Mack's blow. Moaning as he clutches his cheek. Screeching from Mack's foot slamming into his ribcage.

"Don't you ever talk to her like that."

Fuck! I have to stop him before he kills him. I smack my palm on my bodyguard's heaving chest. "No, Mack. Don't do it. He's not worth it."

He stills and meets my eyes when I cup his blazing cheek. Flushed and ruddy from anger and exertion. "Please stop. It's over."

More than just the argument. Or the day. The entire relationship. I'll never be with David again. Not that he'd ever want me either.

Mack must realize the finality of the situation too and curls me against him. Shutting out David's agonizing moans and cocooning me in his huge arms relaying genuine friendship.

"You okay?"

"Yeah, I will be."

After a long minute, he kisses the top of my head and releases me from his safe embrace. The damn phone pings again, and he swipes the cell off the floor. The smooth wood now scratched from the altercation.

"Fuck! Look at this." He holds up the screen for me to see the message.

Never see Sydney again or these will be everywhere.

The bile swimming in my stomach surges again. Attempting to comprehend how and why and most importantly who. Goosebumps lift on my bare arms.

His wife would want a divorce.

His enemy would want money.

This request isn't about him though. It's about me.

Only one person can be behind the threat. Only one man capable of generating a scheme like this.

Julius.

The dread pulling down Mack's scarlet face confirms he agrees with my suspicions.

"Come on. We better go."

I can barely lift my head to bob up and down. Paralyzed with fear from the terrifying revelation. "What about David?"

He squats down in front of my former client. Thrashing in pain from the assault. "Julius Sabatini is threatening you. I recommend keeping your mouth shut about what happened here and he probably won't kill you."

Watching like a zombie, I hug my trembling middle as Mack dials an ambulance on David's phone before tossing the cell next to him. More in his right mind than I am, he grabs my dress and bag before tucking me against his thick body and guiding me out.

With a final click of the knob, it's really over. I can't lie that it doesn't feel good to be in his care. I rarely give into weakness but today I will. For a few minutes anyway. I've lost a client and a steady gig because of that asshole. I can allow myself a bit of wallowing. Before my head and heart start arguing about how I'm going to survive Julius myself.

CHAPTER 6

"WE'VE GOT A PROBLEM BOSS."

I force the bar down again. Ignoring the irritation rising in me from the interruption and try to keep my form. I'm almost finished with my lat pulls and don't want to stop before I've completed them all. I don't like any of the boxes for my workout list left unchecked. Yeah, I'm anal that way. But if you're going to do something, do it fucking right. When I'm in, I'm all in. "Ten minutes ago you said everything went exactly like I ordered it, and now you're back in here to tell me we've got a problem? What the fuck happened?"

Or, what didn't happen would probably be a more accurate explanation he needs to provide. Phillip doesn't flinch from my surly tone. He's worked for me for a long time and knows I don't tolerate bullshit or excuses.

"Kenneth missed a call she made to the dictator's assistant to move up the flight. Instead of taking her back to her apartment like we thought he would, her bodyguard took her to the airport."

The bodyguard—Joel McDonald. Better known as Mack. Perfect nickname for a man built like a damn semi-truck. I actually do kind of like the guy. He takes good care of my woman. Since Kenneth wasn't able to get audio on the altercation between Mack and the judge after I black-mailed him, I can only guess what was said. But him breaking the bastard's jaw and ribs saves me the trouble. Not like I'm opposed to killing another judge. But murdering a high profile official is a lot of hassle and mess to clean up. Besides, he obviously got the message loud and clear from the way the two of them hightailed their asses out of his penthouse.

So, I guess I'll let him live for now. Mack too since Syd likes him. Unless he crosses me again. When I told her to stay put at her apartment, I fucking meant stay put. I should've known better with her. And, with him. He needs to learn how to fucking obey me too. Especially since he works for me now if he wants to keep guarding her.

I tighten my grip and yank again. The smooth metal slippery under my sweaty hands. Only three more. *"And?"*

"Kenneth tried to interfere with the tower's communication, but he wasn't fast enough to hack into their system. They took off before he could get the plane grounded."

Motherfucker. She's on the way to fuck the other bastard I need to eliminate from her life. I have to smile though at her ingenuity. No doubt that my woman's clever. Didn't take her long to figure out what I'm capable of. Quick to discern what I'll do to protect what's mine. Neither of us will underestimate the other again.

Two more slow pulls, and I'm finished. Phillip waits silently and patiently while I wipe the streams of sweat off my face. Very aware any further discussion on his part will not end well for him. Her either since she's forced me to cut short my training. But tormenting her will be so much more enjoyable than punishing him. If my angel wants to run, that's fine. I love a good chase. Just like I always say, no screams, no fun.

Although Phillip seems a bit surprised by my grin. I guess I'm not usually this giddy. But then again I'm not usually having such a good time with a woman that I haven't even gotten into my bed yet. "Get the team ready. It's time for us to do our patriotic duty."

My lieutenant nods slowly, not completely understanding my order but smart enough not to question me nonetheless. I'll fill him in on the rest after I make this call. "Let the pilots know I'll be ready in thirty."

With a sharp head bob of understanding, he heads back out the door while I grab my cell off the bench. Stripping, walking, and dialing grandmother's number on the way to the shower. With the first ring, I hold the speaker a foot from my ear. Prepared for her shrieking. Which of course her happy words screech through the phone. Rapid Italian that makes me feel like a damn kid again. Even though she speaks English fairly well the language escapes her when she's excited.

"Yes, Nonna. It's Julius."

"Yes, Nonna. I know it's been too long."

"Yes, Nonna. I'm seeing someone." That confirmation almost breaks my ear drum from her squeal. I wait her out, only jumping in when she slows for air. "I'll be bringing her tomorrow. Tell Paolo you're having visitors and prepare for a long stay. We'll be there in the morning."

At least for one of us. I'll keep Sydney there for as long as it takes to break her. Well, break might be too strong of a word. I enjoy our brawls too much for her to give up completely. Maybe bend or bow will be enough.

Still rattling on, my grandmother doesn't get the opportunity to say goodbye as I click off. I feel bad but don't have time for an interrogation about who Syd is and what she likes. Nonna will find out soon enough when she meets her. Besides, she'll forgive me once I get there. Or probably more likely berate and then ignore me once she gets a hold of my angel. Which is as it should be.

I toss the phone on the counter while I step down to the white cedar, enjoying the distinctive woodsy aroma that grows stronger as the steaming water pounds the boards. Still grinning like a dumbass while I lather up. She's going to love Syd as much as I do. I lay out the next steps of my plan to keep my hungry cock in check. Or at least try to. He likes the thought of her naked and wet and backed up against the tile at my mercy too. With nowhere to run or hide. She probably fucks as hard as she fights. Just like me.

That'll be the reward for a war won. But we're not quite there yet. I have to destroy this motherfucker first. More ruthless and barbaric than Sydney probably realizes or she wouldn't be fucking him. I mean her little business plan listing out her three rules is adorable yet eye-opening to her naïveté. More innocent than I thought. Not as tough as she thinks she is. Unaware this bastard slaughters his own people—women and children not spared—in his conquests. With Sydney being another casualty once he tires of her.

That thought fires up my ass all over again. I haven't been this angry since I rifled through her files that Kenneth retrieved. Of which I was going to reward him well for his quick work to access her laptop and everything she stores on the cloud until he fucked up missing her call and letting her get away from me. A reminder to have Phillip take care of him too. No one endangers my angel without consequences.

Which brings me back to my current mission. My only mission. Stop her from fucking him and get her ass back where it belongs. With me.

CHAPTER 7

ATTEMPT TO SHIFT WITHOUT REALLY MOVING TO TRY AND relieve the cramp in my leg. I've been in this kneeling position for thirty minutes with my palms outstretched and my head bowed. Creating a curtain of mystery with my long hair brushing my knees. Perfect submission for the dictator. If I move, he'll punish me.

Well, not really. Neither I nor Mack would allow that.

It's the threat Sergei makes. All part of the game he pays for. Likes to fancy himself a real dom. But he's so eager for me, that any chance of bondage or playing with toys only lasts a few minutes before he's ready to sink inside me. Lucky for him, I've perfected the art of gliding on lube with the condom without him ever knowing. So he thinks I'm wet, ready, and anxious for him too. Although I'm none of those things for him. For anyone. Including Julius. Especially Julius.

Damn it. Why is he in my thoughts when I should be concentrating on Sergei? I can't believe I've let Julius get to me again. Interfere with another client. Jeopardize my job. Ruin everything I've worked so hard to build. Fury that I tried to tap down on the flight here swells again, and I shake my head.

"Ah my pet. Didn't I warn you what would happen if you disobeyed me?"

So lost in my thoughts I didn't hear him enter the bedroom. His bare feet fill my view between the strands, and his finger slides under my chin, lifting my face to meet his. "I'm sorry master. I heard you come in and only moved in excitement to see you."

Lust flames in his eyes. He thinks I'm serious. Chubby hands curl around my biceps, and he jerks me to my feet. Dry lips smashing into mine. I open, letting him awkwardly sweep inside. Too erratic and quick. But I moan in approval anyway. He grinds his small cock into my belly and walks us backward to the bed.

"Remind yourself of your safe word. Just in case."

Not that there is any need. He could never hurt me. His abilities can't go that far. "Root beer."

The safe word is really for Mack. I've only had to use it once. I'm up for rough play. A bit of hair pulling and ass spanking is fine. A hard slap across the face isn't. Mack's surprisingly nimble for a man his size. Beat that asshole unconscious until I was finally able to break through the rage engulfing him. Way more punishment than necessary but still spread the word within our world that mistreatment will not be tolerated or survivable.

"Very good." His thumb grazes my nipple. Hard from the cool air rather than his touch. Thank goodness for turbo air conditioning readily available to overcome the humidity of this tropical retreat. "Are you ready for me pet?"

"Yes, sir."

"You know every time my subjects call me that I think of your sweet pussy."

I'm actually impressed. That's the only time he's ever said anything even remotely sexy to me. I reward him with a huge, eager smile. Feigning my adoration and excitement as he slips the silk ribbon around my eyes. Clutching his hairy thighs with a ferocity that suggests I worry he'll disappear while he ties the ends snug behind my head. "How can I make you happy master?"

"You know what I like."

Of course I do. The same as last time. The same as the first time. The same as always. Nothing different since I've been with him. I have to fight my bored sigh. His game and desire never change. A lavish blow job on his miniscule dick. Where I pretend to gag a few times. Pretend that his size is more than I can take. More than any woman can possibly handle.

Although guilt bubbles up as quick as his come will after I take him in my mouth. Deep down I'm going to get him off like this so I don't have to actually fuck him. Because I can't stop wondering what it would it be like to fuck Julius.

"Pet?"

Impatience tinges his tone. I can't wait much longer. I have to stop stalling and pleasure him like I'm supposed to. Like he's paying me. Like I should want to.

But I don't want to. Not anymore. Not ever again.

I don't know what to do.

Muffled yet brusque voices sound from the other side of the door. We've never been interrupted. Not once. His guards always obeying strict orders that he mustn't be disturbed. His fingers fumble in frustration, and the black scarf drifts down to my lap.

He glances behind him. Confusion lining his face too. Then darkening to fury for his men arguing and interfering with our time together. I flinch from his harsh grip on my wrist when I grab for the sheet. Desperate to cover myself in anticipation of his departure.

"No! You do not move until I say so!"

He's out of his mind if he thinks I'm going to allow myself to be exposed to his security team. Irritation pinches his expression as much as his merciless grasp on my skin when I tug again. Willing to fight him for my modesty. Protecting my pride and preservation. *"Root beer!"*

Agony shoots through my cheek from his backhand across my face. Pain and shame explode in my heart worse than in the past.

"I said don't move!"

Fuck this. For the first time ever in all the times I've been with Sergei that I've felt genuine fear. This so called domination game ends now. I jerk my head back up and suck all the air I can into my lungs. *"Mack! I need–"*

His fingers squeeze my windpipe, stealing my scream and my oxygen. What the hell? I claw at his hands. Surprisingly strong for as stout as they are. Perverse power strengthening his resolve to quiet me. Fuck. Maybe even kill me.

Adrenaline kicks in, and I battle him for all I'm worth. Twisting to try and get leverage off the mattress. My resistance infuriates him, and he only throttles me harder, boring his thumbs into my neck. Grunting and huffing as he pushes me backward and into submission. Which I will never allow. I drive my toes into the carpet to lift up my hips. Refusing to give into him or the black spots clouding my vision. I will not let him win.

Our struggle stalls from the shots exploding in the hallway, and finally he stops crushing my throat. I sputter and cough against his palms, drawing in an enormous breath in case I lose my chance. Until I can rise up from this tangle of smooth white sheets and attack him again.

"What the hell?"

The answer he receives is the doors flying open and gigantic rifles pointing at us. At least seven men, covered in camouflage from helmet to boot, crowd the wide opening. No movement or orders shouted at us. Just resolute stances and unwavering aim. Shit!

"Stand down."

The soldiers quickly part from the familiar voice booming behind them, and I can't hold back the shudder that jolts through my bare body despite the heat blazing within me. My labored gasps are the only sound in the room besides the whirling of the bamboo ceiling fan.

"Damn it Sydney." Another tremor engulfs me from Julius's weapon as well as his furious hiss. "I told you no more."

His gaze and the barrel of his gun sweep away from me and zero in on Sergei. Nothing either of us can do or say to stop him. To avert his death sentence.

A tiny red circle suddenly glows like a ruby on the dictator's forehead.

Then his neck.

And then his chest.

Only a devastated humph before he slumps on me. Sliding downward until his face slams into my breasts in an eerie slow motion that I can't prevent or respond to. I simply watch.

His bulk steals my breath again until he's yanked off me and tossed to the plush tan carpet. Unable to see or hear anything until Julius's face fills my vision and his words pierce the silence. "I told you that you belong to me now."

I don't protest when he scoops me up. Too dazed to argue when he curls me against his chest. His heart pounding almost as hard as mine. Grateful to be shielded from Sergei's naked body coated in blood. So much blood. Scarlet streaked down my freezing skin.

Fighting the lightheadedness threatening to pull me under, I clutch his button down with shaking hands. Unnecessary really with the unforgiving grasp he has on me. His fingers gripping my thigh and shoulder, already tender from the force. Long strands of my sticky, clumped hair blow behind us from his speed, whisking past the soldiers still discussing the attack. Winding around too many corpses mangled and mutilated sprawl down the corridor. Thankful none of them are my best friend. "Where's Mack?"

"He's fine. Under my strict orders for him not to be hurt. Put up one hell of a fight for you though."

A little bit of the dread churning in my belly subsides from knowing he's safe. Believing Julius from the definite approval sounding in his tone regarding Mack's loyalty. Now well aware how much we love each other.

Needing to ignore the brutality of the massacre to keep sane and my stomach from lurching, I clench my eyes shut. Although I'm loathe to rely on a man I can't trust to help me, I have no other choice. Because for everything I don't know or understand about Julius, I know he won't let anything happen to me. I don't have to be afraid.

Except of him.

Besides asking about Mack, she doesn't utter a single word as I carry her out. Definitely for the best. Because I don't want to hear a damn thing she has to say right now.

Stupid bastard touching her. Holding her down. Fucking strangling her.

And she fucking wanted to be with him.

My woman.

Fucking naked.

God damn fucking naked in that motherfucker's bed. Drenched in his blood. Better fucking not be his come on her or in her either.

I'll deal with her defiance next. First, I need to get her clean. I step over and around the bodies littering the beach house. Stupid fuckers for sacrificing themselves for this bastard. At least they were easy to ambush and overcome. Posers just like him.

I shove open one of the doors with my shoulder. My guess was correct—another bedroom. I stride to the adjoining bathroom and deposit her on the wicker bench in front of the vanity.

"You killed him…"

I cup her pale face as she studies me with a frantic gaze. Trying to figure out what the hell just happened. The answer is simple. *"He deserved to die."*

For many more reasons than just thinking he could have what's mine.

"He's dead…"

Anxious sage eyes roll upward as she sways, and I catch her sweet body before she tumbles to the marble. Damn it. I guess we're both getting a shower. I haul her against me with one arm while I twist the knob for hot water with my free hand. Not showing her any mercy despite her weak state. *"Did you fuck him?"*

Her head lolls on my shoulder, and I lift her up off her feet, giving her a hard shake. *"Did you fuck him Sydney?"*

"No."

Thank fuck for that. I treat her with a little more gentleness from her admission and tuck her under the waterfall. Her eyes droop shut when I slick down her hair and rinse off her gorgeous frame. So fucking beautiful. Smooth and pink from the steamy spray. After a few seconds, she blinks several times. Bringing me into focus. Huge droplets coat her long lashes that I'm guessing mingle with tears. Probably relieved to be rid of him and happy to be with me.

"I was going to suck his dick."

Son of a bitch! Fury detonates like dynamite through me. So damn defiant. She really wants to push me. Test me to see what I'll do. Then I'm god damn fucking thrilled to show her. Fuck me if she's not my tough angel. Unlucky for her, I'm tougher. And unbelievably pissed.

I jerk her head back and shove her under the water again as her lips fall open to wash away his name and her filthy words. Revealing a double set of diamonds on her tongue that for damn sure wasn't there before. She put in the piercing for him. To pleasure him. To satisfy him. Fucker.

She wrestles against my grip spewing words at me I can't make out through her gurgling. Although I know full well what she's calling me. "You better be fucking glad his cock wasn't in your mouth or your pussy."

She quiets down when the implication from that threat hits her. No further argument while I clean his fucking touch from her swollen cheek and bruised throat. Fully aware what I'm capable of.

Good. I think we finally understand each other.

I slam down the handle, leaving us standing in the cool air. And at a damn stand-off. She's almost too fucking magnificent to be pissed at with her heaving chest and smooth pussy and pebbled nipples. Making my hands ache to ravish her. However, patience is an attribute I pride myself on. I don't mind fucking her in anger but I want her mad too, rather than frightened. She may think her indignation conceals her terror. But, her fear's evident regardless of how much she tries to hide her panic.

I'm not good at making nice or making up since I usually just eliminate the men I argue with. If I hate you, I murder you. Pretty straight forward. But with her, I need to move us past fighting to fucking. Or at least do them simultaneously. I hate that she flinches when I lift my hand. Stumbling backward and bumping her luscious ass into one of the plastic shelves. So I move slowly, brushing the strand dangling over her left eye and clinging to her wet skin, behind her ear. "Don't defy me, and we won't have this problem again."

She bristles from my palm on her cheek and jerks her chin up in disobedience.

"Don't tell me what to do, and we won't have this problem again."

Fucking incredible. I'm instantly hard for her again. But I don't want to fuck her here or like this. So I hustle her out of the stall, rub over her damp body a few times with the white towel from the nearby rack, and yank the bedspread off the bed, wrapping the peach comforter around her trembling damp body. Smart enough not to resist me taking care of her. Or taking her out of here. Sullen yet obedient as I march her through the house to the waiting helicopter.

She scans my rows of men. Almost as if she thinks one of them might help her. Like any of them would even consider speaking to her without my permission. They keep their gazes averted and their hands on their guns. Protecting us just like they're paid to do and to prevent themselves from being killed. No one dare crosses me.

I grasp her dainty hand and help her maneuver the step and climb inside. Slightly indelicate, and definitely awkward trying to keep the quilt tucked tight around her, as livid as she is at me. She doesn't have to worry. With twenty minutes on the chopper to reach my jet and then seven more hours to her new accommodations, we've got plenty of time to settle the argument between us.

CHAPTER 8

HE THINKS HE'S MAD, BUT HE'S NOWHERE NEAR AS ENRAGED as I am. He slaughtered a house full of men in cold blood. He almost fucking drowned me. He blew up an entire island. And now he just sits there relaxed and nonchalant. Sipping on an expensive scotch. Conversing with one of his goons without any fear or worry.

He should have both. Tons of it. Just like I do. But I'll never let him know that. I only care about one thing right now—getting the hell away from him. Then I can figure out everything else. "You'd better be taking me home, or I'm going to call the police."

Finally, he looks over at me. Both him and the guy I think he called Phillip chuckle. Him louder and way more obnoxious and annoying than the bodyguard. Who shakes his head and clears the humor from his throat. Pretending to be engrossed in his phone while Julius stares at me.

"You're not that stupid Sydney."

I guess his insult is the bodyguard's signal to leave because the man suddenly hops up and strides to the rows of seats closest to the cockpit. Sitting with the seven other gigantic men filling the two lines of black chairs. Now that we're on his plane I guess we have to have an entourage accompany us wherever we go. "That I won't call them?"

"That you actually think they'll do anything."

I'm not really sure how this organized crime world works. As definitive as he sounds, I have to guess he isn't bluffing. He probably bribes or bullies everyone else just like he has me. "You're not God as much you want to believe you are."

His head tilts to the side considering my disparaging comment before he nods slowly. Accepting his own conclusion. "Yeah, but I'm about as close as you can get."

This man is unreal. So unbelievably egotistical. "You're fucking insane."

He laughs again when I roll my eyes. "You're fucking beautiful."

Damn the fire sparking inside me from his compliment. I hate him. I. Hate. Him. Why do I have to keep reminding myself of that fact? What the hell is wrong with me? Probably shock. Yes, that's it. I must be hysterical from the stress. I've been traumatized, and I need to see a therapist. Almost as much as this lunatic does. "You can't get away with this. You killed—kiiiiilllled—all those people." I draw out the word for emphasis, not as if he doesn't remember. But I *want* him to realize how dire this situation is. Or that at least one of us is of sound enough mind to understand it. "They aren't going to just ignore a massacre."

His face hardens. I guess he doesn't think I'm funny anymore. I shiver even though I'm not cold and wrap his gigantic jacket tighter around me. Terrible to be forced to wear his clothes, but at least better than the blanket he thought was acceptable to parade me around in. Or being naked as the only other choice he offered when I reminded him I needed something better than a bedspread to cover myself.

"Sergei was a brutal tyrant willing to sacrifice anything and anyone for his regime. No one's going to miss him or be sad he's gone. They're probably fucking celebrating in the streets that he's dead and they don't have to live in terror anymore. So don't try and make me feel guilty or even fucking think about mourning for him."

Which of course I feel incredibly guilty that I'm not grieving over him. While I didn't have any feelings for Sergei, he was still a human being. He probably had friends or family who cared about him. Or maybe he didn't, the way Julius describes him. My head and heart swirl in utter confusion from the overload of conflicting information. Except for one simple, embarrassing fact. "I didn't realize that he was that kind of man."

He sighs from my honest admission. Some of the disgust darkening his face dissipates. Replaced with a softer expression that makes me relax a little bit more too.

"I know you didn't or you wouldn't have been with him."

He's right. I wouldn't have been. I shouldn't have been. When I met Sergei he made me believe he was the de facto ruler of a small, proud country in eastern Europe. A leader in title only. A prince without any real power. Just wealth and ancestry keeping him in his position.

Damn. I was so utterly wrong about him and about David. Unaware of the real truth about either of them until now. I hate that Julius is the one to make me realize how ignorant I've been. But he isn't oblivious or innocent himself. "Well it's not like you're any different. You murdered all of those men!"

I sound stupid. Stating the obvious and behaving like a petulant child. Blaming him for my faults. Turning the spotlight on his flaws to hide from mine. My immaturity is confirmed by his satisfied grin. Proving how seriously deranged he truly is not to be offended by my accusation.

"Yes, Sydney. I did." God how I hate his patronizing tone. "But it's not like they were innocent or weren't expecting an ambush. I'm sure you saw their weapons and the fortress Sergei built to protect himself. He knew eventually he would be attacked." The arrogant smirk returns. Beyond pleased with himself. "He was just too clueless to realize it would be by me, and the devastation would be absolute."

Some of my fury fades from the genuine fear engulfing me. Anxiety bubbles in my stomach because I know Sergei's crimes are not the real reason for his death at Julius's hands. I may not know much about him but I know he has absolutely zero concern for international relations or a desire to be a savior to the oppressed. For my own sanity, I need to hear Julius admit his intentions. "Why did you really kill him?"

The truth flames in his eyes before he answers. Possession. Obsession. Delusion. For me. I squeeze as far back against the cushion as I can when he rises and towers over me. Seeming even more gigantic in this confined space. His huge hands grab the lapels of his coat, and I stiffen. Bracing myself to be hauled out of my seat.

Instead he slowly spreads the fabric apart. Baring my abused body to him. I thought he was unaware of the torture I endured before he rescued me. Maybe not from the intensity of his stare taking in my wounds. A long, thick finger trails down my tender throat. A softer touch than I expected him to be capable of. Conflicting with the rage erupting in his unblinking gaze, and I can't hold back the genuine quiver vibrating across my torso.

She trembles when I stroke her silky skin. But not the good kind of tremors, where she's crazy with ecstasy. Begging and clawing at me for more. No, this is an instinctive response, full of terror and doubt. Caused by me and that bastard and all the other assholes who've let her down. Who've only used her and taken what they wanted. When all I want to do is spoil her and give her everything she needs. Including the patience I'm slowly losing with her magnificent body sprawled below me.

Shock parts her pink lips when I wrap my blazer snug around her again. Keeping a barrier I fucking hate between us. Only allowing myself a caress of her elegant cheek marred by a burgeoning purple contusion. Motherfucker. "I killed him because you defied me."

Thin fingers clutch the armrests, lifting her raging little body closer to me. "You're blaming me?"

There she is. My fighter. My lion.

I can't help but smile when I drop back onto the bench. Enjoying the perfect view of the muscles flexing in her smooth thighs. Wondering how tight those toned legs would squeeze me when I'm pounding into her. "Just stating a fact. You're lucky I'm not killing every man who you've allowed to touch you. But I will if you don't stop testing me."

A shadow flits across her expression that I can't read, although I know for certain it's not the anger she normally hurls toward me. Instead she takes a deep breath and focuses her attention on the hem of my coat. Tugging the gray fabric down to cover as much of her as possible. Which is pointless because if I want her naked, she will be. For now, I'll let her think she has some say in the decision.

I'm more than willing to give her time to process and accept my promise. No need for anything but candor. This is how it works with me. Between us. Toward her. She fucks up, people die. Very simple.

"I have a business. Surely you can understand that. This is how I make my living. This is my job. *Just* a job."

I like her style. Appeasing me with the idea they don't mean anything to her—which I already know. I also appreciate her ingenuity. Appealing to me as a businessman, an entrepreneur, a peer, rather than using hysterics to persuade me. Except that her fucking a bunch of rich idiots is not the job for her. "I know about your…" I can't help the air quotes when I describe her attempt to build a clientele and hide her duplicity. "…business. Your books are terrible and the audit trail for the interior design studio you're pretending to run is too flimsy."

A gorgeous shocked flush stains her ivory skin. I guess my analysis surprises her. "You accessed my files?"

"Obviously. I have to take care of you. You had no inventory. No vendor receipts. No letters of gratitude from satisfied customers. A few excel sheets aren't going to convince someone who looks deep enough."

"No one is looking. They're not interested in me." She shakes her head. Long hair, still damp from our impromptu shower, sways across her narrow shoulders with the force of her denial. Uncertain if she's attempting to convince me or herself. The crack in her confidence growing wider as apprehension lifts her voice. "I'm a single proprietor who—"

"Who makes more than one hundred grand a year. What do you think the threshold is for the IRS to trigger an audit?"

Now she's really worried. Her petite body shrinking into herself. A thoughtful expression as she ponders the implications. "I—I don't know."

"You currently have three customers, no advertising or marketing, no proof of–"

"Okay, okay. I get it."

I grin despite myself. At her slight hand flying up to stop my words. At her realization she's screwed. At her desperation for my help. Which I'm more than happy to give her. "Good. So my best accountant is working to make your records look legit, and then she'll submit the paperwork to dissolve the corporation since you're officially out of business now. She's already moved your money into offshore accounts."

"How dare you?"

Totally not the gratitude I was expecting for saving her sweet ass. Even two of the guys up front turn around from her sharp tone and glance at us. I'll deal with their impertinence later. Right now, she's my only focus. Apparently, I'm hers too as her boiling gaze burns into me.

"You have no right. You can't do this!"

"I do and I did. Since you have no idea how to make a phony business look real, they've cleaned up your documentation and protected your assets. You don't have to worry anymore. You won't go to jail."

Not like I'd ever let that happen. Enough people owe me that I could shield her from any prosecution. Including against charges levied by the federal government. She doesn't need to know that though. I like her feeling indebted to me. Apparently she doesn't enjoy it as much as I do and flies to her dainty feet.

"I wasn't worried."

The uncertainty lining her face says otherwise. "You should've been."

I let my insinuation hang between us. Giving her time for the realization sink in. When she finally understands the jeopardy she put herself in, her slender arms wrap around herself. Hugging herself in hollow comfort. Only I can provide the solace she needs. Only I can save her.

Her frantic gaze glances toward the cockpit and back to me before she suddenly glides out of our row and stomps toward the back. Guess we're taking our discussion to the bedroom then. As good of place as any to hash this out. Without an audience or any interruptions.

After racing down the tight hallway, she suddenly stops. Maybe from the huge platform bed filling up most of the space. Not sure what she was expecting to find back here. Certainly not a damn exit. Whipping around, her small body crashes into mine. Bouncing against my broad chest from the impact, she teeters backward, and I catch her before she tumbles to the carpet. "Careful piccolo leone. You should slow down."

"No, what I should have done is shot you when I had the chance."

Sheer fury drips from her threat. Funny for as much as she likes to pretend she hates me, she always seems to end up in my embrace. "I don't understand why you're so upset." I grab her chin with a harsh grip to make sure she's listening to me. Forcing her to look up at me. Because now I'm getting angry from her thanklessness. From the reminder of what she did after I explicitly told her not to. "You never have to fuck anyone for money again."

Her head twists side to side trying to escape my grasp and the truth. With her arms trapped between us, her fingers claw into my shirt attempting to force me to release her. Fuck if she's not sexy in her frenzied rage.

"It's not just about the money."

Hello earnest. Meet jaded. She really has no idea. "It's *always* about the money."

"I mean for me." Her small palms are warm even through the thick fabric of my shirt. Radiating heat from her hard push that gets her nowhere and nothing. "Damn it Julius, let me go!"

After three useless shoves, exhaustion must take over, and she droops against me. Once she stops struggling, I let her slide down to her feet and motion toward the bed. Of course she moves to the black sofa instead. I smother my chuckle but slam the door shut behind me. Not that she can really get away or has anywhere to go but I want to make sure I get my point across. If I have to tackle her to the floor, I'll probably end up fucking her there too.

Stalling for time, she draws out settling onto the cushion, crossing her lithe legs, smoothing down the bunched wool of my coat. I don't mind. I'm patient when I'm enjoying the show. Finally she entwines her thin fingers and lays her hands on her lap. Staring at them instead of me.

"Thank you for helping me with my business. You were right, and I appreciate you protecting me."

Her voice is soft, relaxed, calm. Too calm for as frantic as she was just a few seconds ago. Making me already know that I'm not going to like what she's leading up to. "You're welcome."

My acceptance of her quasi apology seems to bolster her confidence, and she finally looks up. Hope shining in her deep emerald eyes. A fake smile lifts her cheeks. Too sad to be genuine. "I'll fuck you. Here, now." She nods toward where I'm sitting. "Or I can spend the night with you wherever you're taking me. The whole week, even, if that's what you want. However long you want but you have to promise you'll let me go after that."

She's a horrible negotiator. Her offer sounds like a question. A request rather than a demand. A plea rather than an ultimatum. I have so much to teach her. Starting with I don't make deals. I make the rules. The *only* rules. "Nope."

Displeasure steals her phony grin and the familiar exasperation returns. "Why not?"

"Too easy."

"Bu-but back at my apartment…you said…you said you would pay me and then…."

"I lied."

I'm ready for her to attack. To scream and kick and yell. But all she does is stare. Silent and still. Yet her blank gaze can't hide the dread pooling in her expression. Her eyes fall shut and she swallows hard, tucking her head down to her chest.

"Are you going to kill me?"

Damn. She's more fucked in the head than I realized to ask me that. Luckily, I'm going to be the one to fix her broken mind. "You think I assembled a huge team of expensive mercenaries, hunted you down halfway across the planet, and brought you back to where you belong just to kill you?" I hop off the bed and kneel in front of her, holding her small, trembling hand in mine. "No, Sydney. I'm not going to kill you. I'm going to love you."

So fucking crazy that's it's my admission of devotion that finally breaks her. Even with her flowing hair concealing most of her gorgeous face, I can see the single droplet slipping from the corner of her eye and rolling down her cheek.

Which bothers me way more than I expected. Usually I've not had the opportunity to witness that emotion in a woman. Hell I mean I'm sure I've caused shit loads of crying but I've never stuck around long enough to watch the tears flow after their cursing started. I probably wouldn't have cared anyway. But with her, I don't like it. Not from my woman. Not from my little lion.

I attempt to swipe the streak from her damp skin with my thumb but she jerks her head away. Unwilling to let me touch her. To see her weakness. But that's not how this game is played angel. I cup her cheeks and hold her exquisite face in my palms. "You're going to love me too."

Pure abhorrence taints the beauty that radiates from her. "I can't love someone I hate."

"You will." My cock twitches from her tiny fingers wrapped around my wrists. Failing to break my hold on her. Not now. Not ever. "And until then we'll just fuck. Because you want to, not because I've paid you to."

Fuck me if it doesn't take everything I've got not to lay back her heaving body and ravish her until she taps out. Her uncertainty flares too and she stiffens, bracing herself for more. For me. For an assault. Which I fucking refuse to do.

Instead, I kiss her cheek with as much tenderness as I can manage and release my hold on her. Forcing myself to hustle back to the main cabin. Knowing full well she's too upset to follow. Which is for the best. There's no way in hell I could resist her a third time.

CHAPTER 9

I SNUGGLE FURTHER INTO HIS JACKET. LIFTING THE LAPELS TO cover my throat and cheeks. Even though I shouldn't feel ashamed of the bruises I didn't cause and don't deserve, I still do. Old guilt haunting me after all these years.

Taking a deep breath to quiet past ghosts fills my nose with his rich cologne, and I hate how good he smells. How much I like his scent. How much calmer I feel surrounded by the familiarity of him.

He stands right next to me, yet I feel alone. Out of place. In the way. With all his attention on the older woman fussing at him. From the conversation I can't participate in. At the mercy of him and the guards surrounding us as the two of them argue. Sergei's security was nothing compared to this mansion and the protection Julius has installed. Seemingly an unending army of men sporting their massive rifles posted along the twelve-foot-tall white stone fence.

I like his grandmother. She's frail yet fearless. Waving her hands almost as if talking in a second language to emphasize her scolding him. I laugh out loud when she bops him on the back of the head before pointing to me. Uncertain of what she says, but his expression finally changes from indulgent to angry. He barks something back at her, and I can't lie how sexy his perfect Italian is. Her finger jabs in my direction again, and he finally looks at me too.

"Tell her!"

As if I have any idea what the hell they're arguing about. "Tell her what?"

"That I didn't hit you. That it wasn't me who hurt you."

My hand involuntarily brushes my face. To the swelling I failed to hide. Understanding now why she's so furious. Realizing what she accuses her grandson of. I want to lie and tell her yes. Pretend he hit me and strangled me and humiliated me. So maybe she'll help me escape from him. But despite how much I want to, I can't. Despite his numerous flaws, of which insanity tops the extremely long list, I refuse to make her think he's the kind of man who abuses women.

I shake my head. Giving her what I hope is a reassuring and sincere tone. "It wasn't him. Julius saved me from the man who hurt me."

She looks from me to him and back again. Relief softens her rosy face. Then brightens with understanding. Then explodes with joy. The rainbow of emotions streaks across her expression, and she lights up with an enormous smile. Engulfing both of us with her bony arms. Another flurry of words I don't recognize but understand the sentiment just the same. Oh hell. He's brought me home to meet his family.

Finally.

She gets it. From the look on Sydney's face, she understands now too. I just want the women in my life to meet and get along and be happy. Is that too much to fucking ask? I don't understand why this has to be so damn complicated. "It's been a long night, and I'm starving."

Nonna's eyes go wide, and she nods furiously. No one, and I mean fucking no one, goes hungry at her home or in her presence. She kicks it in gear, entwining her thin arm through Sydney's, and guides her into the house. Moving as fast as an eighty-six-year-old can. Which isn't fast at all. But my angel is patient. Maintaining the same slow pace. She's kind too. Smiling and nodding at Gran's flurry of English peppered with boisterous outbursts in her native tongue.

Syd glances back at me. I guess ensuring I'm following them. Pretty much admitting she likes me too. I wink, which earns me a middle finger behind her back. She doesn't have to worry. I've got plenty of plans for that dainty, dirty finger. All of them, actually.

Nonna has plenty of plans for her too. Albeit very different from mine. While my focus is in the bedroom, her's is on the kitchen. Reassuring Sydney she's going to teach her how to cook my favorite foods. Grow the best herbs in her garden. Make her the best little housewife she can be. The horror on Syd's face reiterates we've got a long way to go. Not that I care about her cooking for me. Fuck we can eat out for every meal if we have to. But I do want her to know that she will always be in my house and always be my wife.

The scent of rich coffee greets us inside the house. Reminding me how much I love her homemade breakfast and how fucking much I need caffeine. Syd looks drowsy too. Heavy lids drooping lower as the minutes pass by while they explore the spotless blue and white kitchen. We have to eat before we sleep though. "Give us ten minutes to freshen up, and we'll be back."

Nonna frowns but nods. Concern lining her already wrinkled brow as she slowly peruses Sydney's lack of real clothes. I'll take care of that issue too. For both of them. Bony fingers cup my angel's cheeks, and she studies her sweet face before she kisses each side. Delighted to have her here and even more pleased she'll return soon to interrogate her more. I get a few quick pecks on my cheeks too. Not quite as much enthusiasm but I know she's grateful that we're both here and that's all I need. Especially when she pulls Syd into another embrace. Overcome with joy.

I think Sydney likes the abundant affection too. Returning a strong hug back to my grandmother. Almost as if she's starving for love. Since nothing came up about her parents in the search of her background, there must be some kind of issue between them. I'll have to have Mitch dig into that too.

I skim my fingertips across her thigh to get her attention and hell because I like touching her. I almost hate to find her clothes since I enjoy her naked so much, but I'm not an asshole. Well not completely. Nonna gets a smile while I get the glare of death. At least she accompanies me upstairs without any complaints. Keeping her gaze glued to the whitewashed wood and at least two feet between us. Unbeknownst to her I like her a step above me. I can watch her sweet ass sway while my proximity gets my lips closer to the back of her slender neck. Just one easy flick of my jacket collar and I could taste her silky skin.

She pauses when we reach the landing. I like that too. Waiting for my orders like the good girl I know she is deep inside. Although the bad girl flashes again when I reach for her hand to guide her to the bedroom she'll use temporarily. I can't lie. I like that side of her even more.

Her gaze flits around the airy space. Taking in the pale yellow furniture and ocean blue accessories. She seems to approve from her slight smile. "Your grandmother's house is amazing."

"It's my house actually. But I want her to be comfortable so it's decorated the way she likes. Whatever she wants, she can have. Just like you."

"So you're taking me home immediately then?"

Funny. My girl brings the jokes. I return her smirk. "Anything you want, as long as it's what I want too."

"Of course it is you selfish lunatic." She murmurs under her breath, but I still catch the drift of her insult. "So do you kidnap all the women you want to date or is this a new level of crazy for you?"

She hasn't seen crazy yet. And, if she pushes me too hard, she'll understand how really crazy I can be. But I'll keep that admission to myself. "I do whatever I need to do to get what I want."

A frown pulls down her smooth lips, mulling over my comment. Surprising me that she seems confused rather than angry like usual. "Why do you even want me? I'm pretty sure there are plenty of willing women that you could have very easily."

True. "Because this…" I love her stuttered little gasp when I step closer, forcing her to look up to me. I can't help myself and stroke her graceful cheek bone. "…is fun, piccolo leone."

Furious aquamarine eyes bore into mine. "That's the second time you've said that. What does it mean?"

Always so suspicious. "You are my tiny lion. So small yet so fierce. I love how hard you battle despite knowing you'll never win."

"I will win."

With her tiny hands balled into fists at her narrow hips, for a fleeting second I almost believe she just might. But then I remember it's me she's fighting against. "No."

"Yes!"

Her emphasis makes my coat swing apart again, showcasing the unbelievable beauty underneath. That unfortunately I need to cover. For now anyway. With Nonna waiting for us downstairs, I have to get her and myself under control.

Even without eyes in the back of my head, I have zero doubt a blazing gaze follows my steps to the closet where I yank out a plain black dress. Looks a bit big but it will work for now. "Put this on. We'll go shopping later and you can pick out everything you need."

"I'm not wearing your girlfriend's clothes!"

Always with the argument. I stalk to her and grab her tiny wrist. Damn she's fucking gorgeous under my domination yet still fighting my possession of her. "Fine. I'll put it on you myself."

Our mutual understanding increases again as she yanks the silk fabric out of my hand. I guess she's not ready for me to strip her down yet. Which is fine. Tonight will be worth waiting for. "See you downstairs."

"Go to hell."

All for show. She doesn't even bother to raise her voice with her admonishment so I know she's not that mad. At least not at me anyway. Probably at herself for being so ornery and difficult for no real reason. Unwilling to admit I've won yet again.

I leave her seething and jog back down to the kitchen. Where a warm satisfied smile and a steaming creamy coffee waits for me. A little too sweet for my taste, but I suck the latte down anyway. Got to keep Nonna happy too.

"She's so very beautiful mio nipote, but I worry how angry she seems with you. You have upset her somehow."

A proclamation rather than a question. The cliché of 'upset being an understatement' swirls in my mind. Nonna's still sharp, and she knows I'm the guilty party in this relationship because I'm always the guilty one. Luckily she loves me despite my flaws. Just like Sydney will—once she accepts us. "Yes, but I–"

"You will fix it. You will make her happy."

Definitive and final. No room for an argument or question. Any other person would get a bullet to the head for trying to control me. Or having the balls to interrupt me. But she gets away with too much. Hell, she gets away with everything. I let her because I love her and because she's right. She's always right. "Yes, Nonna. I will. I promise."

A curt nod to confirm she accepts my vow, and then she's on the move again. Busying herself with loading the table in her most favorite way of showing her love—massive amounts of delicious food. All the fixings of a traditional Sicilian breakfast, including her perfect brioscia. I swipe on a smear of peach jam and take a huge bite. Her head bobs again in approval of my enthusiastic appetite, and she returns to the task of steaming milk for Sydney's coffee. Standing next to the dishwasher she refuses to use and ignoring the housekeeper she refuses to allow to assist her with the meal. Shooing her away to go sweep the terrace or something to get her out of the kitchen.

Now it's my turn to nod. Approving the dismissal Nonna issues to the nervous maid. Who I've hired and I know wants to please me as her boss, but Nonna sees the help as an insult. A real woman doesn't allow another woman to mess around with her man or her kitchen, she likes to say. I roll my eyes. This damn woman is more stubborn than I am. But no one's going to change her after all these years. Might as well let her have her way for the time she has left.

I smile from the other stubborn woman now in my life and in my home. She's going to help me give Nonna the other thing she desperately wants—making her only grandchild a husband and a father.

Piccolo leone.

That's so dumb. Not at all sexy or charming. Neither is he. Most of the time anyway.

I squeeze the cute wrap in my hand. Unintentionally wrinkling the delicate fabric from my punishing grip.

I'm a little disappointed. And I fucking hate myself for it. What the fuck is wrong with me that I'm upset he's brought other women here besides me? That I'm actually and stupidly a tiny bit jealous. That I wanted to be special somehow. That I hoped to be different than the others. Damn! I really am in need of serious and intense mental help to have expected to be the only woman he's kidnapped. Booking an appointment with a therapist will be the very first thing I'll do as soon as I get away from him.

If the girl who wore this dress is anything like the ones in the photos, she probably came here willingly and eagerly. Believing that he genuinely liked her. Thinking he honestly cared about her. But if that were true, she'd be here instead of me. And I wouldn't be here acting like a moron. When what I need to be doing is coming up with a plan to escape. But what I'm sure as hell not going to do is give in to what he demands.

I toss the dress on the bed. It's a shame I have to leave because I would love to stay here. Explore the villa and the little town we drove through on the way to his estate. Swim in the most vivid turquoise sea I've ever seen. Then let the warm sun dry me off while drifting on the luxurious gold hammock swaying on the enormous lanai running the entire backside of the mansion.

It's all right though. Despite Julius's meddling, I still have my money and can take a trip any place I want. Maybe rent something like this. Something even better than this because I won't be with him. I'll be alone.

Just like I want.

Just like I thought I wanted.

A wave of rare loneliness washes over me. I shake off the budding morose and rifle through the drawers in the narrow beige armoire. Ecstatic when I find simple white cotton lingerie, a plain red tee, and black shorts, luckily with a draw string since they're a size larger than I wear. I cinch them as tight as I can and then drop to my knees in the closet, rummaging through the neatly stacked boxes.

The running shoes are too big too, but I double a pair of socks before I yank them on and bolt to the French doors. I push aside the billowing sheers and breath in the fresh, salty air while I allow myself a few seconds to scan the magnificent view. Not just of the perfect ocean, but of the unfettered access from the huge tile patio to the beach. At least two hundred feet between each of the black and copper pillars framing both sides of the terrace. Signifying the ends of the surrounding stone wall.

If I can make it to the sand, I know I can make it to town. An easy run only a few miles from here to catch the ferry back to the mainland. I don't have any euros, but I'll figure out a way to get on the boat somehow when I get there. Right now I just need to worry about getting out of here.

The patrolling guard traverses back and forth for about thirty yards in each direction of the section he monitors. I count each pass, so I can estimate approximately how much time I have to drop off the balcony and race to freedom.

I swipe at the sweat hanging off my eyebrows, threatening to drip into my eyes. Blazing from the adrenaline buzzing through me despite the moderate temperatures. Nothing is going to keep me from my goal. Once he turns and marches toward the driveway, I fly to the handrail and silently loop each leg over the slick metal before twisting to face the house.

The wrought iron swirl edging the bottom is perfect to grasp onto so I only have to drop about six feet to the ground. Sharp pain radiates up my heels and through my calves from the impact of hitting the unyielding travertine, but I suck up the stabbing ache and race toward the aquamarine water.

Too scared to look back regardless of how much I want to, I keep my gaze on the horizon and my feet pounding forward despite the thick, soft sand. Grains kick up on my shins from the force which only spurs me to push myself harder. To run even faster. To sprint until I can't catch my breath.

Past the giant pink brick estate next door. Across the lush green lawn still sparkling with morning dew. Through fragrant rows of olives and lemons in the small garden edging the property. Onto the weathered asphalt reflecting the bright morning rays. I jog in place, glancing down each road at the intersection trying to guess which way leads back to the docks that I spotted as we left the airport. Damn! Uncertainty beats as hard in my chest as my pulse in my ears. Neither way looks correct.

Thick bundles of gorgeous white flowers with fuchsia centers fill window boxes decorating a teal and brown apartment building at the end of the lane. Since pink is my favorite color I take the blooms as a good luck sign and swing to the left. Much easier running on the concrete. I'm almost smiling with relief. Once I cross over the strait into Italy, I can call Mack to overnight my passport, book a plane ticket, and be back in my apartment in just a few days.

My regular pace kicks in, and I feel like myself again loping down the narrow road. Pretending I'm just out for a run rather than racing for my freedom. I shake off the anxiety and lengthen my strides. Pumping my arms. Feeling brave and strong and confident. I know I'm really going to make it.

Until I'm yanked backward from the sudden fierce tug on my borrowed shirt. Almost falling from the force. Only his merciless grasp on my arm prevents me from slamming to the cement. I can't understand the uniformed man's shouted words as he jerks me around to face him, but his tone makes his message abundantly clear.

I'm not going anywhere except back to the villa.

I count to twenty before I push off my chair after Christian drags her into the living room. Huffing and puffing with her ridiculous resistance as she continues to struggle under his grip. Almost as furious as me. I'll put up with a whole lot of shit from my lion. But disrespecting Nonna isn't one of them.

I chin lift him in dismissal, and he steps back. Happy to scurry out of the room. Averting his eyes to avoid catching sight of the confrontation between us. He hasn't worked for me long enough to know I don't hit women. But I'm not sure if I can say the same for her. Her elegant fingers ball into a fist, and I intercept her wrist and lock her down with a tight grip on her bicep before she tries anything stupid. Shoving her up against the wall. Boxing in her small body with my much wider frame. Scratching my palms on the rough plaster from my hands planted on each side of her head.

She feigns fury with her little nose upturned at me as she snarls but I know she's frightened. Very well she should be. Very, very frightened. "You upset my grandmother. She thinks you don't like her. That you don't want to eat her food."

"It's not her or her food that I don't want!"

My girl's ingenious, thinking I'm distracted by her insults, and tries to slide sideways. Attempting to slip her hands down the wall from under mine. Forcing me to press myself against her to hold her in place. I can't lie how good she feels trapped under me. Her perky tits shoved into my chest. "Do not test me by fucking with Nonna. I won't tolerate you hurting her feelings."

Shame fills her huge eyes and her body softens. Which isn't bad either as she squirms up and down. Giving me a small glimpse of how fucking magnificent she'll look like when she rides me.

"I didn't mean for that to happen."

"Well it did."

Her head droops even lower. Making me miss seeing the fire in her dazzling eyes and incredible flushed face. Although I'm pleased she feels guilty from her defiant behavior. Proving she's exactly the kind of woman I need in my life.

"I just don't understand you. You love her and defend her like a good man. But then you turn around and kidnap me and hold me hostage. You don't make any sense."

"I don't know what you find so confusing. I take care of her the way I take care of you."

Finally she looks up. Meeting my gaze and showing me the inferno always simmering under the surface. "Destroying my business, ruining my finances, and keeping me from my friend is not taking care of me!"

Fine. I will explain this to her one final time. I give her an inch of breathing room before I release her arms from my hold and slide out my phone. One of the images of her escape still fills the screen. Irritating but nonetheless sexy as hell to see her determination as she swings from the balcony. Her lithe body suspended for a few seconds before she sails to the patio and sprints like the athlete she is. Fucking gorgeous.

I swipe through a few more apps to get to the document I want her to see and rotate the screen to make the words as clear as fucking possible. "Look. I've deposited double your estimated earnings for the next three years…" I glance at her surprised face, chuckling at her cute little o shaped mouth. "…since that's when you were retiring, according to your ten-year plan, into your account. I did the same for what you pay Mack. Neither of you are suffering any financial detriment from our relationship."

"Holding me against my will isn't a relationship!"

Ignoring her outburst because I know she mistakenly believes she has to maintain the façade of being angry with me despite how much she likes me. I tap on the glass, highlighting her name and account number before scrolling down to the total at the bottom. "Not that you're going to need the money because I'll provide you with everything you'll ever want, but I'm tired of you fucking questioning my intentions. You, my tiny lion, are set for life. A glorious, luxurious life without a worry or care because of me."

Good thing I've got her smashed against the wall, or I think she would fall on her sweet little ass from shock. Or maybe relief even if she's too stubborn to admit it. "You're welcome."

"I can't…I don't…"

My generosity has her tongue tied. Shocked to realize, and more importantly accept, that I *am* a good guy. Well, at least to her. She should be much more grateful for all I did and will continue to do for her.

"It's just…"

With my point proven and my stomach growling, I toss my phone onto the overstuffed bookshelf next to us and glide my hand to the small of her back. The cotton slightly damp from her impromptu run. No worries or rush. We'll take our time showering later. "Come on. It's time to eat."

Mute and agreeable, she walks like a zombie next to me and into the kitchen much to Nonna's returning delight. Grandmother hops up from the table and yanks on her long red oven mitts to retrieve Syd's breakfast from the warming drawer. Despite her perplexed expression, she remembers her manners and thanks Nonna for the plate. Who basks in the warmth flowing between them. While I enjoy another one of her perfect pastries, this time covered in raspberry flavored custard. Damn this woman can bake.

Syd's a fool to shake her head from the brioscia Nonna offers her. "Thank you but I can't have all that bread." She pats her flat stomach and offers her a smile full of regret. "Too many carbs."

This time Nonna argues with her. Her head shaking furiously at the claim. Pleasure always overrides caution in her mind. I would have to agree, especially when it comes to Sydney. "They are too delicious to worry about calories."

Her wrinkled hands motioning for us to eat up. Enjoy. Savor. Relish. Yet hesitation still lines Syd's stunning face.

Easy for me to reassure her. "Don't worry. We'll burn them off later."

Scarlet tinges her cheeks while she acts indignant from my innuendo. Angry wide eyes as she shakes her tilted head. I don't want to fight in front of Nonna, so I smooth over my insinuation. "I have a gym here. You can work out all you want."

As long as I don't have her occupied with something else. Which will burn even more calories than a weight lifting session. After a few seconds, she nods. Settling down before taking a small bite. Stirring up my cock for the millionth time this morning from her absolute sexiness with her eyes sinking shut and the little purr of delight vibrating in her throat. Fuck me.

"See? I knew you would love it!"

A genuine smile I rarely see—or I guess generate—lights up her face as she agrees with Nonna's proclamation. "I do. It's absolutely amazing. Thank you."

Nonna's grin fails to fade while she eats, micromanages what Syd and I eat, and clucks at the housekeeper for sneaking in to try and clean up. All the while a happy matriarch finally presented with what she's always dreamed of. The future of our family clearly visible.

Her frail hand pats Sydney's. "I can go shopping with you today, if you would like. So you can pick out your own things."

"Yes, I would love that." The pleasant tone and expression morphs to bitter antagonism when she turns to me. "Since I prefer not to wear your old girlfriend's clothes."

One of the few subjects—few people—who actually make guilt churn in my gut. "They were my sister's."

"And, where is she? Locked in the attic?"

She's mad and teasing and doesn't know, but I still can't play with her. Not about Joslyn. No one fucks around with me regarding that topic. "She's dead."

Nonna crosses herself, murmuring soft prayers in Italian. A mournful intercession for the granddaughter she lost because of my stupidity.

Both Syd's face and hand fall. Returning her pastry to her plate and clasping her fingers together in her lap. "I'm so sorry."

I appreciate yet don't deserve her sympathy. Fucking hating her heartfelt condolences and pitying tone and kind expression toward my grandmother as well as to me. I have to shut this shit down. "Me too."

They both startle from my chair legs scraping across the slate. Escaping from the compassion I haven't earned, I stride to the sink and set my plate in the basin. Nodding to the hovering housekeeper to approve of her resuming her duties before Nonna even finishes her food.

"Julius, I was kidding. I had no idea. I would never disrespect–"

"It's fine." This is why I love my lion. Her strength as fierce as her sweetness. She knows when to battle and when to back down. "I know."

Grandmother watches between us, unhappy about the sudden shift in our demeanors. Which I hate more than I can stand. But I can't pretend when it comes to my lost twin. "Let's get some sleep."

I brush a kiss on Nonna's cheek. Hoping to reassure her that I'm fine. We're fine. Everything's fine. "Let Giada clean up."

I don't believe her nod of agreement for a second. She'll kick the lady out as soon as I reach the steps. But I'm too tired to argue and Syd looks almost as weary as I feel. Proven by her declination to protest my arm wrapping around her waist and ushering her back upstairs.

The truce budding between us dissolves once we step inside my bedroom. All of the amicability evaporating as her protective shield returns. Thicker and more solid than ever. Suspicious of me and my intentions. Which are even more dirty and delicious than she imagines.

"I don't want you in my bed."

Her plump mouth lies. Conflicting with the lust flashing in her gorgeous eyes now that we're alone together with so much damn temptation surrounding us. "It's my bed."

I stalk toward her, fucking loving her stumbling backward and bumping into the mattress. She stiffens her breathtaking body to keep from falling. To show her courage. To prove her resistance.

Which I believe—I fucking know—I will overcome. "And you'll be wherever I put you."

Fear spikes in her expression. And as much as I like that too because sometimes I truly am a sick bastard, I restrain myself. We have plenty of time for fun and games later. "Where I want you now is the shower. You stink from your little escapade earlier."

Now she's the one to fucking surprise me from her laugh. Damn she must be tired. But I can't lie I love the sound. Refreshing for her to be relaxed enough to let go a little bit.

"So is this how you take care..." Her small fingers turn into air quotes, and I can't help but chuckle at her sarcastic tone. "...of me? By insulting me and then treating me like a child who needs a hot bath and long nap? Is that your kink Julius? You want to be my Daddy and me to be your little girl?" Her gaze flits across the dresser. "You have hair bows and teddy bears hidden away in here?"

Fuck if that doesn't gross me out and piss me off. "I don't fuck kids—real or pretend. I may be a lot of shitty things, but being a fucking pervert isn't one of them."

The grin slides away. Not that either of us was that humored to begin with.

"Then what? What turns you on? Do you want me to call you Master? Sir? God?"

I shake my head from her smart aleck attempt at sass. Well aware the bullshit games she used to play with her clients, and I'm not interested. What we have is real. No imagination required for our sex life to be amazing. "If a man has to force a woman to call him something, he really doesn't have any power at all, does he?"

Surprise lines her face from the response I guess she wasn't expecting. Doubt clouding her expression. "They seem to think so."

"Then they are wrong."

She shrugs from my definitive tone. Pretending

indifference although I've finally made her realize how dominance should really work.

"Maybe so."

Always so unwilling to agree with me.

"So what do you want Julius. What's your fantasy?"

Electricity bolts through my cock from my name on her lips. You, piccolo leone. "My fantasy, huh?" I give her my sexiest grin as I absently stroke my chin. Feigning deep thought and consideration since she seems so intrigued. Completely obvious she's eager to discover what pleases me in bed so she can be the one to give me what I desire. "I want to wake up the next morning and not have to figure out how to get rid of the woman lying beside me without having to speak directly to her."

To my surprise, she laughs again. Not at all shocked. Her eyes rolling so hard it looks like it hurts her forehead. "Classy."

"I'm kidding."

Well, not really but I have to at least make an effort to sound chivalrous. Of course, she doesn't buy my attempt to redeem myself at all. Shaking her head with her own knowing smirk.

"No you're not."

I shrug. Might as well tell the truth so she recognizes why I chose her. "I want a woman who talks as well as she fucks. You know, someone I can actually have an intelligent conversation with outside of the bedroom. Whose brain can comprehend something beyond just shopping and lattes."

"Well I've seen the women you've gone out with. Probably would help to raise your standards a bit."

Fuck yes. I knew it. "So you've checked me out then."

Not a question since she just admitted the truth. The

blush she tries to stop stains her cheeks. Nothing but absolutely adorable.

"No. I…I just…"

I let her off the hook because I don't want her to shut down. I'm more curious about hearing her response than teasing her about stalking me. "So what about you? What gets you off?"

"My own hand."

God damn, I can't get enough of her. I love when her confidence reigns through her uncertainty and she challenges me. "Besides that. What's your fantasy?"

Another glare of death. "To be kidnapped by a deranged, delusional mobster who only wants me for my vast intelligence and witty conversational skills."

Disappointed with her mean spiritedness, I cock an eyebrow and cross my arms. Waiting for more. For better. Sometimes it's best to say nothing at all when dealing with someone who actually has enough of a conscious to actually feel guilty. Excruciating silence fills the air, and she begins to squirm with remorse as time ticks by. Her rigid stance slackens with shame.

"Fine!" Her little exasperated sigh is cute. "What?"

"Tell me what you think about when you're touching yourself?"

My voice sounds hoarser than I expect. But damn. Imagining her playing with herself drives me to the edge. Her head tilts. Mulling over something. I'm guessing whether to answer or not. Mute as she moves to the wet bar tucked in the corner of the room and opens a bottle of sparkling water. Surprising me when she takes a long sip. Staring at the white and red label instead of me.

"I imagine I'm on my hands and knees. He's behind

me, his body curled over mine so heavy and punishing that I can't barely hold myself up. But I do. I force myself not to crumple because I want him—I want it—so bad."

Fucking amazing how she can get me rock hard with just a few words. My own breath labors picturing her in that position on my bed. Naked and dripping and anxious for me.

"He whispers in my ear that he likes me that way so he can play with my nipples and tease my clit while he fucks me." Beautiful eyes drift shut as if she actually envisions the scene in her mind. "And he does. His hands are everywhere and I can't think straight. I can't even talk. I'm just over-whelmed with pleasure. I'm…"

As if she remembers herself, her voice fades away, and she looks up. Sadness I don't expect to see reflects back at me. Unlike the pure lust I'm sure flames in my eyes. Fire blazes in my entire fucking body. "Who is he?"

Need throbs in my tone as hard as my dick. But she shakes her head. "No one. He's faceless."

I don't think she's lying from the detachment in her expression. From the misery thudding in her inflection. "You've never had anyone fuck you properly then."

She spins back to face the counter and fiddles with her drink. Hoping to end the conversation. More accurately dis-agreeing with my assessment even though we both know it's true. But there's something else. Something more. Something telling. "You've never had anyone love you either."

Silence. The epiphany of her behavior. Of our entire re-lationship. "You've never loved anyone."

The accuracy angers her. Stiffness jerking her move-ments as she twists off the cap again. Self-conscious as she gulps down half the liquid and smooths her wrinkled tee with her free hand. Erratic movements to downplay her embarrassment. All of her willingness to open up slipping away with each smooth swallow of her delicate throat.

She tosses the bottle onto the silver tray. A clatter of plastic against the textured metal. Neither material yielding to the other. Kind of like the two of us.

"I'm taking a shower." She shoots me a defiant look. Challenging me to deny her. *"Because I want to. Not because you told me to."*

I let her go. Tired of fighting. With her. With my cock. With my usually dead conscience. Because I realize now that we're more alike than I ever expected. And I want her even more because of it.

I shut the door softly. Not bothering to turn the lock because he'll just break it down if he wants inside. For some reason though, I don't think he does. I don't think he will. And I'm not sure if I'm happy or sad about it.

I'm even less sure how I feel about myself after what I just admitted to him. I can't believe I told him something so personal. Kicking myself for revealing something so intimate. Hating myself for sounding so pathetic and pitiful. No one's ever asked me before what I like and somehow the truth just eked out.

Which isn't unexpected I guess. Men pay me for sex. Buying the ecstasy they've imagined. Purchasing the pleasure they've dreamed about. I mean sure they've probably liked me. At least enough to tolerate me fucking them or sucking their dick or playing their games. The focus always on them rather than me. The way it should be. The way I wanted it to be.

But to finally have someone who's genuinely interested in my desires feels different. Nice. Vulnerable. Flattering and terrifying that he knows me so well in such a short amount of time. To realize the embarrassing truth.

I've never loved anyone.

No one has ever loved me.

I've fucked and been fucked but never made love to anyone.

I despise the glistening in my eyes and whirl away from the mirror. Yanking off my shirt. The moist fabric under my fingertips reminds me of how gross I really am. Poor Nonna had to endure my funk while I enjoyed her generosity. Such a kind lady. I owe her an apology for more than just my disheveled appearance.

I pile the damp clothes in the corner and step onto the sloped tile designating the open shower. Welcoming the hot water streaming over me.

Masculine products line the shelves. Leaving me with no other option than to use his shampoo and body wash.

His.

Julius.

My mind still blown that I'm taking a shower in Julius Sabatini's house, and now I'm going to smell like him. Confused as hell by the fact that I like the idea. That I enjoy the familiarity of his scent on my skin.

Because no one has ever made me feel so comfortable. He's certifiable that's for absolute certain. I guess I am too. For accepting this so easily. Somehow he makes it impossible to resist. Not just from his force. But from his generosity. I now have more money than I ever thought possible. I never have to work again. With nothing to do but let him spoil me. Crazy how this is even real. Crazier that I'm not freaking out.

Yet, there is one thing missing. Which I'm going to demand as soon as I finish. I lather my hair and scrub my body. Grateful for my waxing session a few days ago since I don't have a razor.

A new toothbrush sits on the navy checked vanity next to an unopened box of toothpaste. My heart flip flops in my chest. Julius was in here while I was naked. And he didn't accost me. Proving he's not a complete asshole. Just an insane one.

Without access to any other clean clothes, my only option is to grab one of the black tee shirts hanging on the hooks in the walk in closet. Obviously expensive suits line the rest of the racks. Only a single shelf stacked with jeans and henleys. I guess he works even while on vacation.

I push back my shoulders before shoving down the door handle. Butterflies swirling in my stomach to confront him wearing only this improvised dress. I refuse to back down despite the fact I have no clothes or power. "Julius, I want you to…"

I talk to myself. The room is empty, and I'm lost without him. Uncertain where he is or why he's gone. The instinct to run again pulses in my veins but reason cuts the thought short. Irrational to think I could make it very far barefoot and exhausted. But I'm sure as hell not going to sleep in his room, let alone his bed.

I tiptoe to the door and peek into the hallway. The corridor empty and silent. I can't go back to the room that I think is his sister's so I jog in the opposite direction to the next open door. Neat and orderly without any personal items, which I'm hoping—praying—also means unused. I climb into bed and pull the heavy blankets to my chin. Snuggling in like a child yet soothing nonetheless. The king size mattress is heaven, and I can't help but burrow deeper. We can talk later. I'll set the ground rules for the two of us going forward. If he wants my compliance with his grandmother, then there's something he must do for me.

CHAPTER 10

SCROLL THROUGH THE MESSAGES ON PHILLIP'S PHONE. MY OWN device featuring the pictures of Syd thinking I'm going to let her get away with sneaking out of my bedroom and hiding in one of the guest rooms. Not like I won't come and claim her again. After I tracked her sweet ass thousands of miles, I'm more than willing to walk a few feet.

But my captain's urgent request prevented me from joining her in the shower. He fucking knows how much I hate interruptions. This time is no different.

"He's freaking out."

Yeah, I get that from the stream of panic attack texts filling up the screen. The rising, young boxer suddenly deciding he doesn't want to lose the fight Saturday night. He can't take the pressure, he says. Except he can. He fucking will. My cash in his account and the receipts from my bookies say different. When shit like this goes down, nothing can be solved except by having a real discussion. Fuck all of this technology. "Did you call him?"

Looking kind of sheepish with his brows dipped low, Phillip shrugs. Feigning a casualness neither of us buy.

"Yeah, but he didn't answer."

That I believe. Kid's fucking crazed with fear to defy me and doesn't want to own up to being a coward.

What I don't like is that Phillip didn't try harder. He knows I'm fucking distracted right now with the angel upstairs. I need to be able to rely on him to fix the bullshit. "So that's it? You make one lame ass attempt to reach him and now it's my problem?"

I'm too damned tired to have to tell him how the fuck to resolve this issue. "Fucking call him again. If he doesn't answer, send someone over there. Remind him that he throws it or he dies. There's no going back now." I hold up the obvious evidence and shove the cell into Phillip's face. "The proof of his guilt is right here."

Not that I could really use the string of pleas and confessions without implicating myself. But Chance "Blonde Fury" Anderson doesn't know that. All he needs to know is he works for me and does what he's told. "Make him understand that this loss is only temporary. Just like we talked about. He's talented and popular. He'll train hard and have the comeback of his career. Losing this match will be the best thing he's ever done for himself."

"Yeah, I'll tell him." Phillip's furious head bob doesn't assuage me much. "I'll make him understand."

"You do that." I slowly rise, smoothing down my jacket. Dismissing him with a sharp tone. Almost. "And, if you don't, I will."

With another violent nod, it's clear Phillip understands the implication. If I have to do his job for him, then I don't need him.

I do need her though. Once he races back to the patio with his phone in hand, fingers pounding the keypad, I jog back to her improvised hiding spot. Not even bothering to knock before I shove open the door and get the breath knocked out of me once again.

She sleeps.

Heavy, deep, and so incredibly beautiful curled tight under the white blankets. Dark hair splayed across the silk pillow case. Her nude cheeks pink from her warm bath. Tiny and fragile huddled in the middle of the huge mattress. Only better if she was snuggled on mine.

I get it though. She thinks she needs to prove her independence. Convince me she's untamed and uncontrollable. Deep down we both know better. She'll be happier with me. Because I know for damn sure I'm happier with her.

I'm too much of a bastard to resist and grab the corner of the cover. Slowly sliding down the comforter to reveal her delicate form swimming in my black tee shirt. God fucking damn. It almost hurts to look at her. Yet I can't tear my eyes away. I've never enjoyed the image of a woman wearing my clothes more than this.

Her small body twitches. Probably chilled from the breeze on her bare arms and legs. I force myself to tug the quilt back up her stunning figure. Already missing the sight of her as each inch disappears under the fabric. Leaving me hard and wanting from the thought of how she'll look in my bed the next time. Sans clothes of course.

Warm again, she lets out a contented sigh and fuck me if she doesn't utter my name. A promise of more blowing across her plump lips. With no other choice, I have to nuzzle her smooth cheek. Reminding her I'm here. That she's mine. That she's home.

She quiets from my touch and every ounce of my diminishing restraint forces me to let her be. Yet not let her alone. I'm not that good.

I drop onto the square yellow rocker a few feet from the end of the bed and slide out my phone again. Most of the world's asleep back home except for my guys, so I check the receipts from my clubs. Nice take from the weekend. My shipments made it through customs without any issues. But the brightest spot is that Ethan finalized the contract for the new property. A nice legit project to keep some of my business on the up and up. All good news from the team's updates.

None of which couldn't wait until later. But on days like this I fucking hate lying down because I know the damn guilt that will flood my thoughts in the silence. The darkness engulfing me worse than the blackness behind my eyelids. Desperate for a release from the evil always lurking in my soul.

Just like Joslyn used to give me. Not that she gave a damn about my sins. Or anyone else's for that matter. Which is what ended up killing her. But she loved me almost as much as I loved her, and I can't be angry with her for leaving me. She always wanted to be involved with everything I did. She actually thought she might lead the family someday and tried to learn from our father right alongside me. Not letting her fragility stop her from trying to be tougher than her brother. Although she definitely was in resiliency if not physically.

Syd stirs from my chuckle. Damn. I've been trying to ignore my hunger for her too. Fuck it. I've never held back from doing what I want, and I'm sure as hell not going to start now.

I strip off my clothes and slide in behind her. Tugging her petite body against mine. My cock perfectly nestled between her ass checks with only a thin layer of fabric separating us. Fuck me if she doesn't snuggle in. Her small hand curling over my thick arm wrapped around her waist. Just like it should be. Her head tucked under my chin. Fitting together perfectly like I knew we would. Letting her natural scent mingled with my soap engulf us. God damn fucking amazing.

Unwilling to think about my sister with my girl in my arms, I let go of her memories and focus on the beautiful reality in front of me. Drifting off more easily than I ever thought possible with my balls so heavy and taut and the stress of my problems weighing on me. Somehow her presence cuts through all of that giving me a peace I haven't felt in too damn long. Which scares the hell out of me.

Proving that I really am truly and completely fucked.

It's official. I'm so absolutely fucked.

I can't see his face in the dim light. Just a soft golden glow burning behind the white sheer roman blinds with the rest of the small room steeped in darkness. Yet I know Julius sleeps behind me. And only a demented person like me would actually not hate his huge body wrapped around mine.

I'm not even sure how he managed to climb into bed and curl behind me without waking me up. Normally, I'm a light sleeper. Maybe it's the rich food and heavy coffee. Or the coolness of the stone house perfect to cuddle under the thick blanket. Or the warmth from Nonna's welcome. I don't think anyone has ever been so pleased to see me. Well, anyone who didn't want to fuck me. Although, I guess she does want me to fuck her grandson. I giggle like the idiot I've turned into but catch myself. I do *not* want to wake him up.

Of course, I'm lying to myself. It's him. I slept well because he made me feel safe and protected and—dumb, dumb, dumb—wanted.

I lie still. Listening to his breathing. Soft and even. I count to twenty before I slowly lift his giant hand from my stomach and slide his arm behind me onto the cotton sheet as I scoot sideways. Rolling onto my belly and inching off the mattress until I can touch the floor with my toes. I carefully maneuver the rest of the way to the freezing tile. Ending up on my knees. Just like he probably expects me to be all the time.

Luckily he doesn't stir except for his fingers twitching twice. Almost as if searching for something. Or someone. I glide the quilt over him and tuck the edges around his body without actually touching him.

I glance around the elegant room. No idea of the time without my phone so I tap on his lying on the recliner. I guess he doesn't have to worry about security because the black screen dissolves from my touch without requiring a code or a print. That was easy. Except my heart races anyway from the image that fills the glass.

Me—running down the hall to this room. Damn. I should have known better. He has cameras everywhere. Even inside his own home. I swipe a few more times. All of my antics shot by shot. No wonder his goon caught up to me so easily when I tried to escape. The head start I thought I had was only an illusion. He'd been watching me the entire time. Another reminder of what a fool I am.

I pad down the corridor and peer over the railing. The bodyguard from the plane paces back and forth across the living room rug with his phone jammed against his ear. His voice rising and falling. Alternating between cajoling and threatening and back again. Definitely no escape in that direction.

My check for an alternate route from the balcony in his sister's room proves the same barrier. Four men block the access to the beach. I know just as many guards man the front gates from our earlier arrival. So that option is unavailable too.

I'm trapped.

And, I don't want to be anywhere near him when he wakes up.

I'm more careful this time when I search for clothes in her drawers. Now that I know who they belong to and how much they mean to him. How much she means to him. Without any siblings of my own, I can only imagine how much it must hurt to lose one. The pain very obvious for him and his grandmother.

My bare feet are silent on the stairs but the man in the foyer still turns around, and I give him a small smile and half wave like a moron. Uncertain if I should explain or ask or wait. Suspicion lines his forehead but he doesn't speak or stop me. So I keep moving. Searching for the place I know can ease some of my stress.

Both Nonna and Giada are gone from the kitchen. No evidence remains from our delicious breakfast. The table and counters clear with just the faint hum of the dishwasher running. The sun porch is devoid of people too but not equipment. The late day sun glints off the shiny metal rows of free weights while outside the opened doors a treadmill and stationary bike sit under a gorgeous pergola shielded from the sun with rich gold fabric draped between the thick white beams. An expansive oceanfront gym with the most beautiful views ensuring it's no hardship to work out here.

I lift my leg backward and grab by ankle, pushing the sole of my foot against my butt. Stretching out the tight muscles after being immobile for hours. Never expecting to sleep that long. Or that deeply. Which is crazy. I should've been too terrified to sleep after all I've been through. Fearful of what's to come. What else I'll endure from Julius. If finding him in my bed uninvited is any indication of what I can expect tonight.

Although I don't think he'll push too hard for what he wants with his grandmother here. Especially after her severe reprimand earlier, he'll treat me right. Which so far… he has. As much as I hate to admit it, he has been nothing but charming and generous. *If* I do what he wants. Which is where our problem lies. Neither of us willing to give into the other. Both of us deeming ourselves too dominant and independent. Each of us refusing to lose.

I extend my other leg and close my eyes. Giving into a few weak moments fantasizing about Julius and I living here. Running together on the beach. Sipping scotch on the balcony. Maybe even buying a boat to explore up and down the coast line and travel over to the mainland.

My eyes pop open. Cruel reality invading my imagination. I'm not that kind of woman, and he's definitely not that kind of man. We fuck hard and work harder. Too much and too often for any kind of domestic bliss.

I load on the weights heavier than normal. I need to build myself up if I'm going to escape from him. If I'm going to get away from who and what I can't have.

CHAPTER 11

TRAPPED.

My arm's pinned against my stomach, and I can't rear my leg back to kick out. I push up and swing my fist before I open my eyes. My other hand reaching for my gun only to rub across slick fabric under the pillow rather than cold metal. Fuck!

Shaking loose from the nightmare engulfing me, I shove against what confines me. A blanket. She covered me with a goddamn fucking blanket. Tucking me in like a fucking baby.

Once the adrenaline pumping through me slows, I smile. She takes care of me. As much as she wants to pretend she hates me and probably wishes I was dead, she still swaddles me to make sure I'm warm. Which I am. And, not just because of the comforter.

I grab my phone. Now lying on the nightstand rather than the glider where I left it. My piccolo leone doesn't cover her tracks well. That's all right though. I don't have anything to hide from her just like she can't conceal herself from me. Swiping across the screen, past a message from Giada that Nonna is resting too, until I get to the cameras, I find her working out. Sexy as fuck squatting with a fierce expression on her face. No wonder she has such a fantastic ass with the heavy weight load and flurry of reps she knocks out. My girl really is tough.

After a quick detour to the bathroom to piss and brush my teeth, I pull on some running shorts. Might as well get in a quick workout too. Both kinds, since she's here now.

Her pace has slowed once I reach the doorway, and I lean against the frame enjoying her smooth descent, hips parallel to the floor, and then a rapid push upward. The muscles in her thighs and glutes squeezing taut under her skimpy shorts. After about ten times, she pauses, blowing out a long breath, and attempts to lift the bar spanning her narrow shoulders off her back. Fatigued, her biceps shake and she struggles and fails to get an upward motion. Trapped with fifty pounds under her palms. I fucking hate the panic blooming on her face. This is why you never exercise alone.

"I'll help you if you'll allow me to."

Her eyes fly to the mirror and meet mine. So engrossed in maintaining her form she never realized she was being watched. Suspicious from my chivalrous offer, indecision frowns her face. She'd probably rather be hit than be helped. Although she's smart enough to know she can't be stubborn now. After a beat, she nods. Swift and terse, but still in agreement.

"Good." I step forward but instead of curling my hands around the bar, I run a finger down her spine. Feather light and leisurely from the base of her graceful neck to the waistband of her shorts. Despising the sports bra that keeps inches of her smooth skin from under my fingertip. "You're beautiful tiny lion."

"You're an asshole." Rage floods her voice. Her gaze locked with mine in a battle she won't win. "I thought you were going to help me?"

"I am." I can't stop from licking my lips from the magnificent feast standing in front of me. Under my absolute mercy. Bound to my control from her own self-created restraints. "I want to help you know how good I can make you feel."

I stroke down her slender thighs. Loving the sharp gasp between her parted lips and the buck of her hips under my palms. I rub my thumbs over the protruding bones on each side, and uncontrollable shock waves roll through her. "You're very sensitive here aren't you?"

"Julius…"

She feigns anger. A warning in her tone without any power behind her threat. Yet lust bubbles under the surface too.

"What other secrets does your lovely body hold?" I frame the cradle of her pelvis where my son will soon grow, and she leans into my hands. Delicate fingers grip the metal bar across her back even tighter. Damn thing interfering my complete domination of her. Yet also preventing her from fighting against something I know she wants. "I'm going to fucking love finding all of them."

Incapable of controlling myself, I glide my hands around her waist and trail up the faint indent on her stomach separating her toned abs. A fierce groan erupts in my throat from her body trembling under my touch. The budded nipples straining against the thick purple fabric covering her luscious tits. The scent of her desire mingling with the citrus infused breeze blowing across us. A perfect sweet and tart combination just like us. I growl in her small ear. "Tell me to stop. Tell me you don't want this."

Her eyes squeeze shut, and she shakes her head. Her ponytail swinging furiously across the silver rod from her force. "I shouldn't want you."

I take her indignant breathless whisper as approval to proceed and welcome the sharp intake of breath when I fist the hem of her black nylon shorts and yank down the slick fabric. Surprised and silent, she remains mute as they plunge down her shaking legs to puddle at her bare feet. Her gaze stares at me in the mirror while my focus remains on her gorgeous pussy. All my self-restraint vanishes from the proof of her desire glistening on the shiny rosy lips.

Only a fucking nuclear bomb could keep me from dragging my fingertip along the smooth skin, flooding my palm with her juices when I cup her mound. I promised myself the first time I fuck her I'd be slow and gentle but fuck if I can't keep that promise. Separating her labia, it's my turn to be shocked. The treasure of her pussy is literally fucking real—a tiny diamond encrusted on a small gold hoop dangles from her engorged clit. Fucking hell. I can hardly suck oxygen into my lungs with all the blood in my body racing to my greedy cock. "Damn angel you make me crazy."

"You make me weak."

Poised as a question rather than an accusation, uncertainty wobbles in her soft voice while I stroke her. Doubt swirls in her exquisite emerald eyes as I caress her. Seeking reassurance. Desperate for the security and protection I promised her. And, I'm more than happy to give her.

I circle my thumb around the lustrous metal. Relishing her pussy contracting from the attention. "Believe me tiny lion, there is *nothing* weak about asking for what you want. Whether it's given to you willingly, or if you have to take it."

My encouragement seems to bolster her confidence and her shoulders lift in spite of the burden weighing on them.

"I want to see Mack. I need proof that he's really okay."

I'm getting ready to fuck her and she's talking about another man? What in the fucking hell? She's damn brave, I'll give her that. Well aware of the response she'll receive by intentionally erecting this barrier between us. Proving she's not ready. Not by a long shot if any of her thoughts are about anyone but me or anything but my cock buried balls deep inside her pussy. Ruining my plans for both of us. "Fine. We'll finish up here and I'll prove to you yet again that I'm a man of my word."

I can't hide the irritation in my voice or my touch that we're having this same damn argument again.

"Yeah, I'm sure you're always honest. A real saint who never, ever lies."

"Exactly."

She laughs until she remembers that she's mad at me.

"So are you going to help me or not?"

"You're sexy when you beg."

Just as her mouth parts to protest, I finger her slick folds. Quieting all thoughts of protest as I pleasure her. Demanding her full attention on me and what I'm doing to her. Curling my fingertip to hook the bone beneath her clit while my other hand sneaks under the elastic hem of her sports bra and pinches her hardening nub. Her exquisite breasts heave despite her resistance to enjoying me teasing her and a heady glaze dulls her usually bright eyes.

I need her to come. I need her to come so damn bad from my hand and not hers. More than willing to work the hardest I ever have for a woman's release. For *her* release. I press my thumb in circles around her nipple, and she mews. But it's the long stroke of my index finger that makes her shudder. Over and over as she rides my hand. My wrist keeping her in place with unrelenting pressure on her pulsing clit as I massage deep within her. "Don't fight it Sydney. Let me make you happy."

She nods furiously. Burning friction against the scruff on my cheek. Yet her body stays coiled tight. Fighting the bar. Fighting me. Fighting herself. Unwilling to give in completely. "Let me give you what you like."

"I'm going to drop it Julius. I'm going to lose it!"

The only thing she's going to lose is herself from the orgasm unfurling inside her. I pull my hands away long enough to lift the bar from her quivering shoulders and bend slightly to toss it to the tile. The metal clangs against the unforgiving porcelain, bouncing twice before rolling into the curio cabinet. Shaking the water pitcher and stack of towels almost as viciously as her little body swaying in front of me.

Vulnerable. Terrified. Exposed. Both physically and mentally. Her shivering lips gap open to sputter some bullshit neither of us wants to hear. Fuck that shit. I sweep her up and quell her contentions by shoving my tongue in her mouth. Moaning from her arms curling around my neck and her hungry body rubbing up and down mine. Seeking to re-ignite the flames I created earlier. To burn us both with the inferno already blazing between us.

Proving she wants me.

And, I have to have her.

Cupping the back of her head, I refuse to break our kiss while I walk us to the chaise lounge. The heavy blue fabric still warm from the fading sun as I lay her down and cover her body with mine. Framing her face with my hands while she rasps underneath me. "Ti ho piccolo leone. Non ti lascerò mai andare. Non ti lascerò mai cadere."

I have you little lion. I will never let you go. I will never let you fall.

A foreign yet easy intimacy between us as she studies my expression. Stares into my eyes with burgeoning hope. Accepts the promises I swear to her despite having no idea what I say.

Unable to wait to for a response, I make my way down her body. Kissing every inch of her hot silky skin. Nuzzling her tits through the mesh fabric restraining them. Relishing her yelp when I bite one nipple and then the other. Ignoring her fists lacking any real force pounding on my back in retribution. Licking the trail down her belly and around her thighs, teasing her by avoiding the area she wants my mouth on the most.

"Julius?"

A frail, confused voice rattles from deep in the house.

Fuck! We're busted.

I scrape her clit with my teeth and let her groan burn into my memory because a memory is all I'm going to have to keep me going for a while. That and the taste of her from swiping my finger through her dripping pussy one last time. Gripping her chin to force her eyes on me as I suck her juices from my skin and let my own eyes roll up into my head from the sweetness.

Unsteady footsteps clicking on the travertine check my desire and I swivel to sit on my ass. Perching on the edge of the cushion with her legs on either side of me, her tits crushed into my back. Protecting both her and Nonna from the embarrassment of her nudity.

"There you are!"

Grandmother finally shuffles in. The huge smile on her wrinkled face even bigger than this morning if that's possible.

"I thought maybe you left already."

"We'd never leave without you."

My girl pipes in with a squeaky voice before I can answer. All earnest and sincere. Which I fucking love. Almost as much as her arms around my chest and her chin on my shoulder.

"Good! I'll find my purse and we'll get going. Now hurry up you two!"

Instructions aimed toward us as she plods away. Sydney sags against me. Heavy breaths of relief blowing on my bare skin once Nonna crosses the threshold back into the kitchen, sliding the door shut behind her. I lift Sydney's small hands from my stomach. Kissing her palms and each fingertip while her forehead rests against my back. Reassuring her everything's fine and we'll pick up where we left off tonight.

"That was too close."

I hop up and pull her with me. Loving how my restrained strength still smashes her into my chest. "From now on I'll fuck you upstairs. She'll never hear your screams or how much your pussy loves my cock."

"You are such a–"

One last hard kiss before I release her and swipe her shorts off the floor. Kneeling down like the gentleman I am, I help her step her feet into each side. Hating sliding them up rather than ripping them off. "Fino a stasera."

Until tonight. I love the confusion on her face and the lust in her eyes. She'll know soon enough.

CHAPTER 12

TEARS BURN MY EYES WHEN MACK FLICKERS ONTO THE SCREEN. I'm not usually so damn emotional, but it's been a hell of a few days, and I've missed my friend. Even more than that, I needed this reassurance that he's all right and Julius isn't a liar. At least not to me. I guess Mack's shocked too because he just stares at me for several long seconds before letting out a long sigh.

"He hit you?"

Disgust drips from his hard voice. My hand flies to my damp cheek. With all of the insanity swirling around me, I'd actually forgotten about my injuries. Another reminder of Julius' steadfast protection that I'm not sure I'll be able to convince myself of, let alone Mack.

I shake my head and force a smile. Reassuring him I'm okay. "No, it wasn't Julius. It was Sergei. He attacked me."

Fury snarls his lips as he swears. "That motherfucker."

I actually laugh from his comment. The levity breaking the tension a little bit. "You sound like Julius."

"I don't consider that a compliment." He leans closer to his camera. His wide frame bulging well outside the frame of Julius's laptop. Impatience lining his face as he scans mine. For more of everything, more of anything he can see to understand better. "What the hell is really going on?"

I flinch under his inspection and slide further back into Julius's huge leather chair. So large my feet dangle inches above the carpet. *"I don't know."*

Of course that's a lie. I know exactly what's going on. I just don't know how to explain the truth to him. Or I guess more accurately I don't know how to explain how I feel about Julius to him since I don't really understand my emotions myself. I just know I'm very, very sick in the head to like it. To like Julius so much.

"Syd?"

He knows me too well for me to fib. Easy for him to tell that I'm hiding something from him. That I don't want to admit what I know he won't like. I start with the easier confession first. *"He wants me to quit. He's paid me…"* I point to myself and then him with a shaking finger before laying my hands back on the cool smooth surface of the desk to hide my trembling. *"He's paid both of us so I don't have to work anymore."*

"Yeah, I about freaked out when that deposit dinged on my phone for an account I didn't know I had. I thought it was some kind of 'Nigerian prince' scam until I figured out where it came from."

I grin again from the image. He's always so meticulous about everything, especially money, I bet he was hilarious going crazy with his detective work. *"It's real and it's yours. You deserve it Mack. Don't be afraid to use it. To really enjoy it."*

He shakes his head. Denying the sincerity of my plea. Disgust drawing down his expression. *"I can't. I never will if you're suffering for me to have it."*

Damn. *"I'm not…It's not…"* I don't know what the hell to say. To admit that how Julius treats me is the exact opposite of suffering.

But he pushes on despite my stammering. "I've been racking my brain trying to figure out how to get you away from him. I don't have anything yet. Bastard's too damn rich and powerful. But I won't give up Syd. I promise I'll figure something out."

"It's okay. I–"

"It's not okay. He's fucking crazy. When they attacked Sergei's compound, his guys were giving me some bullshit lines about how 'Mr. Sabatini was going to take care of you and that Mr. Sabatini would make sure you'll always be safe.' Well fuck Mr. Sabatini. That's my fucking job. *I* keep you safe. *I* protect you."

Needless guilt flushes his ruddy face. I hate how he beats himself up over unwarranted shame. I stupidly reach for him and can only stroke the slick glass. Wishing he could absolve himself of the doubt he feels. "I know! I know you did and you do. He told me how hard you fought for me. How impressed he was by you!"

"Not that I give a damn what he thinks about me, but hell yes I did. You think I was just going to stand by and let them waltz out of there with you?" He sighs again, his head dropping low. I can't see his eyes or his expression, and the loss of both hurts me. "But they did anyway."

"You couldn't have stopped them. You're just one man against an army." Against another man more stubborn and crazier than you could ever imagine. "Don't blame yourself. I'm fine."

That assertion makes his head fly up. "Really? Are you really okay? Because being his prisoner doesn't seem fine at all."

"He's…" Why the hell can't I form words? Because none of them make any sense. That he's actually nice? Generous?

Seductive? Now I'm the one who sounds crazy. I attempt to divert his attention from the truth. *"His grandmother's here too. She's very sweet and kind."*

"She can't be that sweet and kind if she approves of him kidnapping you!"

Damn. His anger is killing me. The truth is going to be even worse. *"She doesn't know."*

That admission lights a fire in him, and he shoves against the screen again. Filling the laptop with his glowing brown eyes. *"Tell her then! Tell her that her grandson is a fucking psychopath and maybe she'll help you escape."*

So much sense and reason and logic. I should feel the exact same way. I should do what he says. Yet somehow I can't. So I do what I have to do to appease him. *"Okay, I'll try. I promise."*

"Are you sure you're okay? Your hair is wet and you look…dazed."

I tuck a damp strand behind my ear. Self-conscious that he's mentioned dazed, which is code for stressed, which really means he's too nice to say I look like shit. My fingers roam to my lips. Still swollen and sensitive from Julius's earlier assault that I welcomed like a starved woman. Not realizing how ravenous I was for honest affection. Or that I would give in so easily to his attention. *"Yes, I swear. I just took a shower. We—I—worked out, and we're going shopping for clothes for me and then probably dinner."*

"God, he really is a damn whack job. Who the hell holds a woman against her will and then treats her like she's on some kind of fancy vacation or something?"

Julius.

Julius Sabatini does.

"Where is he? I want to talk to him too."

Not a good idea. "I'm not sure. He set up our call in his office so we could talk alone."

"At least he gave you some privacy."

I nod. Deciding against mentioning the cameras he has everywhere and that he's probably watching us right now. Because defending Julius to Mack feels wrong—*is* wrong. But I know I would do it anyway. I'm not sure how or why my loyalty has shifted but I'd be a liar if I said it didn't.

"What about you? Are you okay? Julius said they didn't hurt you when they captured you and flew you home. Is that true?"

"Yeah, I'm fine. But I think I broke a few noses and got in a few black eyes before they took me down."

My smile is genuine this time. Proud and grateful for his friendship and loyalty. "I love you for that. More than you know."

"Yeah, yeah. I love you too." He feigns embarrassment and annoyance but I know the sentiment is sincere. The smile slides away and his gaze bores into mine again. Rare fear fills his expression. "Come home Syd. Do whatever you have to do to come home okay? I miss you. You don't belong with a man like him."

Funny how I used to think that too. "I miss you too. Just let…" I hope I'm making a promise I can keep. "Just let everything settle down and then I'll be back. I'll find a way for him to bring me back."

"Don't let that asshole–"

The screen freezes. Mack's fury seething for a second before pixelating to tiny blue dots. Julius really was listening and Mack's really gone. At least for now.

Her laugh is glorious. Sexy. Feminine. Real. I fucking love it. I'll be damned if I don't I fucking love her.

What I don't fucking love is the two men at the table next to ours enjoying her magnificence as much as I do. My tiny lion is too gorgeous not to attract attention. I'm going to have to do a better job of shielding her from assholes who think they have the right to ogle what belongs to me.

I nod toward Benton and then toss my chin toward the bastards. That's why I like this guy—he's quick on the up-take and strides toward them. With his low, deep voice I hear very few of his measured words beyond my name and the threat of torture which they respond to with the speed I deserve.

The taller one scrambles to grab his jacket off the curved back of his white wooden chair while the stockier guy stuffs his tablet into the red leather messenger bag at his feet. My reputation preceding me even when it's been too long since I've been here. I cause enough damage during my visits that no one soon forgets who I am or what I'll do if crossed.

Benton tosses a few bills on their table. In apprecia-tion for their swift departure they get their meal paid for. You're welcome motherfuckers. Unfortunately, they aren't as discreet as my guard in their noisy, nervous retreat, and Sydney's wine softened gaze flits over to them before return-ing to me. Disapproval curling her lips down despite the mis-chief still sparkling in her eyes.

"Oh, let me guess. The saint saves the world again."

She's kidding but I'm not. Serious as fuck with my re-sponse. "No, just you. I don't give a damn about protecting anyone else but my lion."

For a woman who thinks she's a badass, she sure blushes easily from my compliments and attention. The irony isn't lost on me either. Easy to spoil an angel who doesn't expect anything compared to the ones who demanded everything. And, of course, never received jack shit from me.

"Thank you for dinner. It was delicious."

"You're welcome." I wink at her. Checking to see if I'll get a rise out of her with the alcohol flowing through her. Making sure the waiter kept topping off her glass so she couldn't easily monitor her intake. "I'm assuming you're grateful for the clothes too."

"You know you wouldn't need to buy them for me if you weren't holding me hostage since I have a closet full at home."

More playfulness in her tone than I expect. I'm pleased that she seems to have finally relaxed. Accepting what I offer as real. Realizing that what we have is genuine. "Touché."

"Wow! It's a miracle! Julius Sabatini finally admits I'm right. Too bad you're not filming us now."

I was wondering when she was going to sneak that little acknowledgment of my unrelenting vigilance into the conversation. "No, I'm saving that for tonight in my bed."

Another flush creeps up her lifted cheeks. Unable to keep from giggling at me even if she's aggravated. "Pervert."

"Beauty."

She takes a long sip of her chardonnay. Admitting defeat without any words.

"Glad we got that all worked out." I tip my head to her out of respect for our new accord and allow the good humor to linger while we enjoy our drinks. Before I see if I can make her even happier with me. After a long minute, I transition into work mode and slide out my phone so I can show her the project I have in mind. "I have a business proposal for you."

Her answer is another carefree laugh. She thinks she knows me and what I'm implying but I'm about to prove her wrong. Very and happily wrong.

"A *serious* business proposal for you." I angle the screen so she can see the images I've pulled up. "We just closed on this abandoned Victorian that I'm going to turn into the first of many in a chain of luxury B & Bs. Both the interior and exterior are trashed but the bones are good. I'd like you to be the project manager in charge of the interior design and ensuring we meet all the historic codes for the neighborhood. I don't want any hassles with the preservation committee."

Despite the booze flushing her cheeks, pure shock radiates from her face. "Me?"

I love her little squeaky voice when I've surprised her in a good way. "Yes, you. That's what you earned your degree in, isn't it? I've reviewed your portfolio and your designs were raw but really good. Your grades were excellent until right before you graduated."

All the pleasure on her face evaporates from my last comment. One of the many things I'm curious to discover about her are the C's and D's on her transcript after the straight A's she earned until her final year. Her head falls forward. Ensuring her ebony hair shields her expression from me. A trick I've quickly learned she likes to use to hide from the truth she wants to avoid. "What happened?"

"Nothing."

An automatic response that rolls off her luscious lips too quickly and easily. "Bullshit."

She flinches from my response and smooths down the unwrinkled tablecloth with jerky movements. Flustered from a very simple question.

"Too much partying I guess. Senioritis you know." Scooting back her chair, she thinks she's dismissed and this conversation is over. Not by a long shot. "Anyway, I'm ready to go and–."

"Sit." That direct order gets her to finally look at me. With complete and utter disgust. Her glossy lips pursing in preparation of tearing into me. I can't let her secrets ruin our discussion, so I let her lie be for now. We have plenty of time, our whole lives actually, for me to discover the truth. "It'll be ready to kick off in about two weeks. We should be home by then and I can walk you through the house."

Anticipation forces her to obey me, and she sinks back into her seat. Wide eyes searching mine. Checking for any signs of deception. Any indication of duplicity. "You're taking me home?"

I tap the screen again and shove my cell back into my pocket. "As long as you behave…"

"You just can't stop being an asshole can you?"

This time I laugh. She knows me already. "So, do you want the job or not?"

"You really want me to do this?"

Doubt pulses in her tone and her expression. That I hate. She should be as confident in her design skills as she was in her escort business. Because although her books and records were shit, her strategy and profit were top notch. I smooth away any signs of my prior smirk. I want her to know, to understand, to fucking believe how damn serious I am about her and her talents. "If I didn't want you to do it, I wouldn't offer it to you. I'd be satisfied with just fucking you if I didn't think you weren't capable of doing the job."

Crude, I know. But it's the truth. The damn proof is sitting right in front of me from her and Nonna's shopping trip this afternoon. The sheer black tuxedo jacket paired with hot pink skinny jeans that would look idiotic on anyone else looks absolutely fucking stunning on her. "You have a good eye. A gift for putting together what works. That's what first caught my attention the night we met."

A blush as bright as her pants beams on her face from my compliment. "Thank you…for believing in me." Her soft voice falls even lower. "No one ever has before."

I push a little bit now that a crack weakens the shield she uses to protect herself with. "They should have. Then you wouldn't have ended up working for Belle's."

She doesn't seem surprised that I know the name of the agency that hired her before she graduated. Only nods.

"Didn't your parents protest? Surely they tried to stop you."

"They didn't know. We had…" She shakes her head. Keeping her gaze averted. So much she attempts to hide. "We had a falling out when I was in school and we didn't— we don't speak anymore."

"Idiots to let you go. Nothing's more important than family."

No response. Only another long drink with her eyes closed. Shutting down on me and our conversation. Which isn't what I wanted. I give her an out for now and signal the waiter. The older gentleman offers a quick dip at the waist before turning back to hustle inside the interior of the restaurant. He'll return in a few seconds, accompanied by the chef with a tray of desserts that she probably won't eat. At least we can take them home to Nonna.

A small smile eases some of the tension in her face when they return. Delighting in the quaint custom of presenting a variety of sweetened fruits and tiny desserts before coffee is served. Despite her own internal conflicts, she praises the gesture, oohing and aahing over the presentation and indulging in a miniature hazelnut cookie lined in chocolate. Confirming to the eager men the deliciousness of her treat and offering her gratitude.

I relax myself from her pleasure and savor the last of my espresso. Anxious to finish the meal and enjoy my version of dessert back at home now that we have all of our other business taken care of. Even Mack's disparaging comments about me during their video chat earlier couldn't ruin our evening. Especially when she defended me. At least with regard to Sergei. Me stealing her away and keeping her permanently still gets her a little riled. But she nor her friend nor anyone else will ever change my intentions toward her or my plans for us.

"Tell me about your sister."

The twitching of my cock from imagining those plans instantly ends from her unexpected request. I gingerly set the small cup down onto the matching saucer and reach for the bill. Ignoring her and the ache throbbing in my gut. I fucked up telling her about Joslyn. I should have just let her think they were an old girlfriend's clothes. Not like she wouldn't be any less furious with me.

"You've had the audacity to peruse my private files and learn about me so I have the right to ask about you."

Her voice is inquisitive rather than accusing. Which I haven't earned but appreciate just the same. Although I can't bring myself to answer.

"I deserve to know more about you. You owe me after what–"

"I don't owe anyone anything!"

Got to love my tiny lion. She doesn't flinch from my

harsh tone or my fist slamming down on the table. Rattling our plates as much as she rattles me with her directness.

We sit in silence. Neither of us willing to give in. She wraps the new black pashmina that Nonna picked out for her tighter around her slender shoulders as the night air grows cooler. While I welcome the relief from the fire she ignites in me.

"At least tell me her name."

She thinks I'm going to fall for her charms with her simple inquiry. That a gently posed request will make me spill my guts. She underestimates me. No one should ever fucking underestimate me. Including her.

"I thought I heard your grandmother call her Joslyn."

God damn it. I jerk up from my seat. The chair tipping over and slamming into the railing behind me. I only look at Benton because I don't want to fucking see the emotion on her face. "Take her home!"

He doesn't even nod before he's next to her, offering his arm to assist her up. A gentleman to her when I can't be.

"So I guess we're heading to the airport then if I'm going 'home'."

Not the time to antagonize me with her condescending tone and hostile attitude. I finally meet her gaze. Disappointment seeping through her ire. "Your 'home' is wherever I am, regardless of how much you fucking push me. So you better get used to it."

"I'm already used to the fact that you're a crazy asshole so no big surprise there."

Pure venom hisses through her tone and Benton practically has to jog to keep up with her as she twists and marches toward the gate at the edge of the patio. Unable to get away from me and into the Land Rover fast enough.

Once the other bodyguard climbs in, and the leading and trailing vehicles filled with the rest of my men pull out too, I know she's safe to travel back to the house. Regaining my composure, I blow out a long breath while I quietly pick up my chair and motion again to the distraught waiter whose gaze swivels from me to the receding vehicle with the lovely lion, and back to me again. Now I'm the one who needs to drink without worrying about how drunk I get.

CHAPTER 13

CLICK ON ANOTHER ICON AND RISK A QUICK GLANCE AT THE
doorway again. Julius still isn't home but that doesn't
mean I won't get caught. I'm surprised I've gotten this
far. With him watching me every second since we've arrived,
I'm sure he knows what I'm doing. Which means I need to
hurry up. Since I don't speak or read Italian, my search is
slow going trying to figure out which app is intended for
video conferencing. Even if Mack can't save me physically,
he can save me mentally at least. I don't want to be alone. I
don't want to be here. I don't want to be with Julius. I can't
believe I was stupid enough to ever think I did.

A spreadsheet pops up with wide columns filled with
huge numbers that surely can't be dollars. Well, as wealthy
as he is, maybe they are. Anyway, I don't care about him or
his money. I just want to talk to my friend. I close out of
the financial page and tap a tiny brown square inside a black
rectangle that kind of looks like a screen.

Yes! A white box with Mack's number pops up. I move
the cursor to the green telephone with a shaking hand. I
can't believe I actually found the software.

"What the fuck are you doing in my office?"

Damn.

He's drunk.

And, beyond furious.

Stalking to me while I'm trapped like the prisoner I truly am in his chair with nowhere to escape. No place to hide. No words to explain. So I don't. Instead I try to run.

Hopping up, I sidestep him. Or at least I think I do. His grasp on my waist lugs me backward and he forces me to sit on the smooth black leather again. Fuck him. I refuse to give him the satisfaction of thinking I'm scared of him. I lift my head to meet his gaze. Not backing down at all. "This is my house now too, and I was calling Mack. Because *he* isn't a dick and will answer me when I ask him questions."

"What's so important you need to talk to him about?"

The scent of his expensive scotch floats on his fingertips as he strokes my cheek. The intimate touch conflicting with his livid expression. I can't weaken from the agony pulsing in his body. From the pain cutting through his expression. Reminding myself his gentleness is only temporary. The real Julius showed himself at the restaurant. "I want to tell him how much I hate being here with you."

His long fingers linger on my heated skin before falling away. Curling into a fist that he slowly taps on his thigh. I hurt him with my cruel words, and shame warms my chest. I don't enjoy wounding him the way I thought I would. Vindictiveness is never as good as you expect when it's directed toward someone you realize you've grown to care about. He drops back onto the desk. A defeated slump of his shoulders as he shakes his head. "She hated it here too."

My heart pounds from his admission. Unsure if I should ask who he's referring to, even though I somehow already know. Like a coward, I take the easy way out and remain quiet. Sitting perfectly still as not to spook him or discourage the confession I hope he shares.

"Joslyn wanted me to fly Mom back to the US and have the doctors keep trying, but Mom knew it was too late. All she asked was for us to stay here with her until the end. So of course my sister was furious at her for giving up and me for letting her. But we both knew the truth."

All of my fury from his earlier behavior dissolves from his anguish. Offering such intimate details I never expected. Making me wonder if he's ever told the story of his family to anyone. Or worse, if he's ever even had anyone to share his grief with.

"Mom and Joslyn had the same heart condition so I think it scared her for herself as well as for Mom."

He takes a deep breath almost as if buoying himself to keep going, but it's me who feels like I can't breathe. All of the oxygen always instantly evaporates from the room when he's in it. Especially more suffocating tonight when his sorrow fills the air.

"When Mom became unresponsive that night Joslyn chased after me. But they weren't expecting her, and the stupid fucking guard gunned her down when she stepped out of the car. Damn motherfucker didn't even wait to see what she wanted. A twenty-year-old girl who could barely walk let alone handle a weapon shot point blank in cold blood just for trying to find her brother to tell him their mother was dying."

I don't even realize he's yelling until he's suddenly quiet. Silent rage engulfing him and sucking me into the darkness with him. My own heart breaks from the horror. The waste. The misery. Despite the ambiguity between us, I can't stop the pity flooding my soul and slowly stand. Watching him watch me with confusion as I wrap my arms around him. Resting my head on his chest. The racing heart under my cheek proving he's still in mourning regardless of how much time has passed.

Words seem inadequate. Insufficient to convey how sorry I am for her loss. For his. For all of theirs. So I don't offer any. I just hold his broad body to mine until his massive arms coil around me. Comforting me in return. Hopefully, consoling himself too in the process.

I broach the other mystery I wonder about him. "What about your father? How did he handle the loss?"

His grip tightens, pinning me tight against him almost to the point of pain. Unrelenting when I squirm in his grasp while he strokes my hair. Soothing and haunting in his repetitive movements.

"I killed that lousy bastard a long time ago. He never knew anything except that I would take care of the women he wouldn't. Until I fucked up. But I fixed that too."

Killed. His. Father.

Oh fuck.

He finally breaks his hold when I shudder, and I step back from his embrace. Jolting from the malevolence filling his eyes. Unequivocal malice staring back at me with more ferocity than I've ever seen in anyone before. "You fixed it?"

A deep frown narrows his dark, bloodshot eyes while he meets my gaze. Defiant and brazen as ever despite the careening of my voice.

"That bastard destroyed my family. He needed to feel the same loss. He deserved to know what it feels like to lose everyone you love."

I don't fight the shivering overtaking my body from the realization of the evil he implies. I only whisper in fear of his response. Not sure if I can handle what he admits but I have to know. "What did you do?"

"I strung him up by his balls. Literally." I don't bother to hide the bitterness in my tone or the satisfaction in my chuckle. "Amazing what you can do with the right tensile of wire. His brothers too. His boss. All of his boss's associates. Anyone and everyone who played a part in murdering my sister. They all paid. Long, slow glorious torture until their deaths."

I terrify her. From my face. My laugh. My words. All of it. Which I hate. But my future wife has no reason to fear. I won't make the same mistake with her that I made with my sister. "Don't worry piccolo leone. I'll never let that happen to you. My enemies will never touch you."

Panic pulses in her slender body. Uncertain if she be-lieves me. But very clear she realizes the danger. Also obvi-ous that she doesn't want to hear anymore, pushing away my hand caressing her face. My mouth near her lips. My body boxing in hers.

"Is that why?"

I must be drunker than I realize because I can't compre-hend anything beyond her apprehension. That I must elimi-nate at any cost. "Is what why?'

"Those men at the restaurant. And this fortress. And the guards. Everyone knows…" She swallows hard. Trying to keep going with her trembling lips. "They all know who you are and what you did. That's why everyone is so scared of you?"

I don't answer. I don't have to. She already knows the answer. I've never tried to hide who I am or what I do. "I loved my mother and my sister. I avenged Joslyn's death be-cause I had to."

My head shakes. Actually, that's a lie. "I wanted to. I reminded everyone that the Sabatini's won't be fucked with. That *I* will not be fucked with."

"Revenge…" Trembling hands touch her mouth. Almost as if attempting to stop the words from falling out. To realize the truth that she can't seem to bear. "Your world is violence and revenge and retaliation. You are that world."

"I fucked up not having Joslyn watched better. She should never have been allowed to go out on her own. She never would've been killed if I had her guarded every second."

I've never admitted the truth with anyone before. I've never shown any vulnerability before. I almost hate to look at her again. A few minutes ago I saw sympathy. Her small arms around me. Holding me with all her might to give me comfort. Except for my grandmother, no one has hugged me in years without wanting anything in return. Honest. Sincere. Amazing. I don't ever want to let her go. I *won't* ever let her go.

Now all I see is doubt. Tiny lion thinks she has reason to fear. I'm happy to prove she has nothing to be frightened of. My hand waves through the air. Reminding her of where we are. Of who I am. What I built. "I have Nonna here like this and you'll be protected the same way at home. Both of you will always be safe."

She slowly nods. Accepting—agreeing—with my assertion. Yet hesitation clouds her beautiful face when I hold out my hand to her. Always with the independence this one. Won't even let me be chivalrous to my fiancée. I let it slide for now since she's had an emotional night. Plus, I have a call to make. More bullshit to deal with back in the States although I'd much rather be exerting my dominance over her in my bed than my territory to some dumb ass. I kiss her warm cheek, breathing in her sensual new perfume, and step back to let her stand up. Gallant enough not to smack her cute ass as she scurries past. "Go ahead upstairs. I'll be there in a few minutes and we can finish our discussion."

The speed in which she runs proves she wants more than conversation too.

CHAPTER 14

KEEP SMILING.

I don't know what I'm doing anymore. This is wrong. He is wrong. I'm so very wrong for calmly sitting here and participating in this late lunch meeting with him and one of his business partners. Acting like this is normal. That we're normal. When neither of us is.

I pretend like I'm not panicking. A long sip of cool water. An understanding nod and bright smile when Julius looks up and gives me a playful wink from the paperwork taking longer to review then he thought. A robust thank you to the waiter for the trio of decadent cannolis bursting with thick cream. One each sprinkled with chopped pistachios, orange candies, or chocolate chips. The entire plate dusted with a heavy layer of powdered sugar. All to celebrate the purchase of the Victorian and me being the project manager. That I accepted before I knew how truly deadly psychotic he really is.

He thinks he loves me.

He thinks we're engaged.

He thinks we're going to live happily ever after.

But I *know* that's never going to happen. I can't let it happen. None of his delusions are possible. Regardless of how hard he works to make me delusional too.

Somehow I was lucky enough to evade sleeping with him last night. Easy to accomplish since neither one of us slept. I spent the night freaking out, while he worked well into the morning. Until we left the mansion for this meal. But I know my luck's running out.

And I've decided that so am I.

While he's distracted, I slowly scoot back my chair from the table. Forcing my hands not to shake as I rise and point to the restaurant door. Murmuring my 'excuse me' and that I'll be right back. Praying he'll think I'm going to the ladies' room rather than seeking an escape route. Hopefully I'll buy at least five minutes of a head start by cutting through the building rather than just bolting off down the sidewalk, despite how much I want to.

He's not quite as distracted as I thought. He jerks his head at one of the numerous men lining the railing. The guard quickly straightens tall and races to catch up with me. Damn. Even polite enough to open the door for me as I sweep inside and he gestures toward the back where a sign hangs that I think signifies the restrooms. Damn. Damn. Damn.

The biggest smile I can muster covers my face, and I nod my appreciation. Scurrying toward the restricted hallway, I manage a quick glance back to make sure he doesn't plan to follow me inside the bathroom. Although I've squeezed through tiny windows before, and I'll do it again if I have to.

Luckily, he sets up post between the open dining area and the end of the corridor glancing in both directions. With that bit of freedom, I scope out the doors. Beautifully intricate hand-painted figures of a woman and man grace two of them but the third includes another word I don't know. Praying I'm correct, I slowly turn the knob and almost cry out from the discovery of stacked boxes lining the left wall with a cut out to the right side leading to the bustling kitchen. But it's the exit ten feet in front of me that makes my heart soar.

My heels tap on the tile as I run. Blending in with the clinking of silverware against china as steaming pasta is drained and plated. Drowned in heavy red sauce from enormous ladles and loaded on trays for waiting servers. Too focused on my goal to check if any of them notice me, I shove against the cold gray metal bar and welcome the sunshine streaming across my already blazing face. Beckoning me outside. Enticing me with the opportunity for freedom. Only a gray dumpster and red scooter fill the small concrete pad. No one and nothing to stop me from running. So I do.

Across the narrow alley. Around the side of a red brick building. Toward the rows of compact cars parked nose to tail on the narrow street. Blaring horns and festive music and boisterous voices waft from the sidewalk cafes. The perfect symbol of my own celebration to be free.

Until everything goes silent. Everything goes black. Everything goes down as I'm sucked back into hell as pain explodes through my skull.

"She'll be all right. Groggy and maybe confused at first but that should clear quickly."

I tremble from the unfamiliar voice. The cold fingers on my wrist. The swimming of my head.

"Wait downstairs in case I need you when she wakes up."

Julius?

His voice seems so close I feel like I can grab it. Grab him. But grogginess keeps pulling me away. I think it's him. I want it to be him so I can have something to hold onto in my terror. Yet I touch nothing when I lift my hand.

"Leone."

A shiver vibrates through me when he breathes my nickname close to my ear. I know for sure this time. It's him. I have to find him. Reaching out again, I brush his shirt and clutch the fabric with what little strength I have.

He's here.

Really here.

Thank god.

I welcome his lips on my forehead. His palms on my cheeks. His heat on my shuddering body. Murmuring beautiful yet unknown Italian words against my skin. Although I understand the meaning infused in his tone. Relief. Regret. Rejoicing.

I blink again and again. Forcing my blurry eyes open. Bringing him into view. Discovering the worry lining his face as strong fingertips brush my temples. Gentle yet possessive as he frames my face with his huge hands.

"You scared the hell out of me lion."

So damn ironic. Now he knows how I've felt the past forty-eight hours. "What happened?"

"You ran."

Nausea swirls in my stomach. Not just from my pounding headache. Two simple words that sound like an accusation. That reverberate with a threat I never expected. Making me question that the only belief I trusted in him could be a lie. "You hit me?"

The concern pinching his flushed face explodes from rage. The tightening grasp tangles his long fingers in my hair. Constricting my movements as well as my heart with the force.

"I would never hit you Sydney. I would never put my hands on you in that way."

Low and fierce, his tone leaves no ambiguity. Offers no uncertainty. Ensures no doubt. "Do you understand me?"

I slowly nod in agreement to all three of him floating in front of me. Unable to focus on anything except his intensity regardless of how hard I try. "Yes."

Despite my agreement, the anger flooding his face grows fiercer. "My bodyguard fucked up in restraining you. But he learned very quickly and painfully the consequences for touching you. Now all my men know what will happen if they ever touch you."

Presented as confirmation. As reassurance. Yet now he's the one scaring the hell out of me. His thick, black hair tickles my freezing skin as he leans closer. His mouth warm on my ear. "Besides, the only person who gets to punish you for trying to leave me, is me."

Impossible to keep up with his tornado of fluctuating emotions from protective to brutal to carnal in only a few seconds. Right now, I only have one feeling. "Try it, and you'll be sorry you ever kidnapped me."

Laughter shakes his broad body hovering over mine. "You never stop impressing me, lion. Broken and trapped, yet you still don't give up."

I hate the pride pumping through me from his approval. I shouldn't give a damn what he thinks. Somehow I do. "I will never give up."

"That's why I want you."

I can't control the fire overtaking me. My own emotions of fear and fury fluctuating with my traitorous body responding to the huskiness of his voice. The need rasping in his tone. "That Julius. *That's* why I ran."

"What?" Confusion softens his expression but not his grip. "You know I want to fuck you. I've never kept that a secret."

Reminding me as if I'm the one who's obtuse. As if a man's transgression makes death acceptable. As if him wanting to discipline me and then fuck me is normal. "It's just too much. You're too much. All this killing and fighting. I can't live like this."

"You don't have a choice." An indifferent shrug dismissing my complaints. End of discussion, at least in his damaged mind. Final and closed to argument. "Fighting with you is fun, and, who I kill doesn't concern you."

"It concerns me if I'm with you!"

My eyes squeeze shut. Agony shooting through my skull from yelling and struggling and panicking. His grasp finally loosens from my pitiful whimper, and he gingerly strokes down my tangled strands. Offering more soothing words in his native tongue as his lips brush against mine in the softest caress. As if my distress upsets him too much to speak in English.

I lean into his hands. Finding strange comfort in the calming repetitive motion.

"Yeah, you're with me."

Again. How does he do this? Making me love the happiness in his tenor. "That's not what I meant and you know it."

Too much temptation from his silence. Wondering why he quit arguing. I can't resist opening my eyes only to see the disappointment pooling in his.

"I thought we were past this."

Frustration saturates his words, but the truth darkens his expression. I've hurt him. Disappointed him. Wounded him. Unfortunately, I have to keep doing it. "You were wrong thinking that. I don't want to be with you."

Pain flashes in his face. Disappearing so quickly I almost wonder if I imagined it in my groggy condition. But I know I didn't. Although the exasperation replacing the sentiment is very clear.

"You can and you will." His hold on me intensifies, squeezing me until my scalp tingles from the twist of my hair around his fist. "You have no other choice, and it's not like you have a better option to go home to. No family or friends and a job spent on your back making everyone else happy but yourself is not the life for you."

Cruel to me for the first time in his irritation. Or maybe it's the reality of my situation that's actually cruel. I don't know how he's figured me out so fast. I guess I'm more transparent than I realize. Which doesn't make his accurate assessment sting any less. "I have Mack."

His head shakes while he sneers from my assertion. "An employee doesn't count."

"He's more than just an employee."

I try to sound indignant yet fail. Mack's so much more than that, which probably isn't saying much since we only spend time together when we're working. Uncertain if we would still be close without our jobs bringing us together. Damn Julius for making me realize how tenuous that relationship is too.

"You've built this fortress around yourself and refuse to let anyone inside. But I don't care the reason why or that you don't want me. I'm coming in whether you like it or not."

Lying here in his huge bed, I feel as vulnerable as if I was naked while he stares down at me. Raw and exposed

141

despite being fully clothed with the heavy blankets pulled up to my ribcage. His gaze sweeping across my face, studying the resistance I attempt to mount. "That's ridiculous. I'm not keeping anyone out. I just like being alone. I'm independent. I'm…I'm free."

"You're hiding and you're lonely and you're miserable."

True and true and even more true. "No."

"Yes."

A sad smile confirms his assertion. His rough knuckles caress down my cheek yet he remains silent. At least not gloating. Which I'm not sure if his gentleness is any better. Kindness more than I can take in my embarrassed state.

"We're here for another two weeks. Once you recover, you can spend it locked down in this house…"

Such a controlling, crazy bastard. "You can't–"

"Or you can relax and enjoy the life I'm giving you. Your choice." His annoying pompous ass smirk returns. "If you choose wisely, then I'll hire Mack as one of your guards when we get back."

My heart slams against my chest from his offer. "Really?"

Pitiful that I sound this damn hopeful. Giddy to have some sense of normalcy in this dumpster fire of a relationship. Stupidly grateful to him for letting me see my friend. But I want to. So, so badly.

"Yes, and you know I don't lie."

"Oh, I remember Saint. Just maiming and murdering, but no lying."

"Exactly." He pretends to ignore my sarcasm but humor flames in eyes. Enjoying me teasing him. Although it's actually the truth. "Now get some rest. Dr. De La Rosa said to stay in bed. Too bad he's restricted everything else too while you're in it."

Pervert. I ignore his innuendo. My muddled thoughts churn from his irrationality. Mine too. Incapable of accepting his brutality. Unable to tolerate his easy dismissal of my disgust regarding the death of a man who's probably not that innocent yet dead just the same at his hands. The same hands touching me so gently and with such concern.

Dark spots swim in my vision when I shake my head. I can't think straight. Unable to understand the conflict of my head and heart any more in my mangled state. I need a break.

I push his forearm caged against my waist and blocking my way. Which of course he fights me trying to sit up with his hands and his snarl.

"What the fuck are you doing? I just told you to stay in bed."

"First, I don't take orders from you, and second, I have to go to the bathroom."

Worry, that never ceases to surprise me he's capable of feeling lines his forehead, and he slides next to me, drawing down the covers.

"I don't need your help. I'm not a child." I only sound like one.

"No, but you do have a concussion, which means you could get dizzy and fall. I won't let that happen."

Bossy but kind of sweet, I guess. Before I can tell him I'll accept his help, his strong arm curls around my shoulders and he guides me up to lean on him. Which feels so nice. Nicer than I want to admit.

We sit for a moment while he rests me against his chest. "Ready?"

I expect him to pull me to my feet but I should've known better. Julius Sabatini does everything over the top and full steam. Instead, he picks me up as if I weigh nothing and carries me into his enormous bathroom. *"I'm fine. You really don't have to do this."*

Like I'm not even talking. With a determined expression, he grabs a towel off the bar and spreads the fluffy white fabric across the turquoise counter. My heart spins almost as much as my head from his thoughtfulness as she slowly sits me on the heavy terrycloth.

Confident hands slide my dress up my body and over my head. Which I don't need to be naked to pee. *"What the hell are you doing?"*

The only change in his demeanor from my outburst is a stuttered breath and a word that I think means fuck in Italian when he glances down at my bra and panties. Almost as if he's trying to control himself, his gaze returns to meet mine. Focused on caring for me rather than wanting to fuck me. *"You really want to sleep in a dress?"*

I guess not.

He cradles me again and takes me to the toilet. Yanking down my thong before he sets me carefully on the surprisingly warm seat. Okay, this is taking it way too far. I shove against him. Without any impact or response but that doesn't keep me from protesting. *"I don't need an audience."*

His head shakes. Ignoring my argument. *"Very soon my son will be coming out of that same area so it's not like a little urine is going to freak me out."*

Now I'm the one freaking out. What the hell? He thinks we're going to have a baby together? That's even crazier than him playing nurse. I open my mouth to dispute that notion immediately and vehemently. But he's already striding back to the bedroom. Unconcerned with any dissent I might voice. Holy shit.

I know she's resilient but god damn I do not like her being tested to see how much. Flames of pure rage blaze through me again from seeing the sickening scrapes marring her slender back reflected in the mirror. The traces of blood streaked in her long hair. The bobbing of her injured head struggling to keep steady with her injury.

I'll never understand what that stupid fuck was thinking body checking her when all I ordered him to do was to stop her. I'll never know either since his head—well I guess his brains—are sprayed all over the alley. Damn stupid for me to make such a mess in public. I'm usually better at keeping my business private. But seeing him lying on top of my unconscious lion obliterated every shred of reason from my normally sane mind.

All I could think about was killing him for hurting her. For touching her. For scaring her. He deserved to die, and I'm damn sure not going to feel guilty about it. Besides, the cobblestones stained with crimson will generate rumors of the slaughter. Reminding everyone of my presence for years to come long after the blood fades away.

I grab one of my clean tee shirts because fuck me if I don't love seeing her wear my clothes since I can't have her naked right now. Not until she's a little bit better and a whole lot more submissive. Which won't come fast enough now that I've figured out she's a runner. So lock down it is. Can't feel guilty about that either. She brought it on herself. No hardship keeping her here with me twenty-four seven. Surprisingly, I actually like her company. Which is refreshing in and of itself since most women get on my nerves. Guess that's why I never kept any around. Or worried about them.

Or played fucking nurse maid to them. She makes me break all my rules without even trying.

My chuckle stalls when I hear a thud. And her whimper. Fuck! I shoot like a damn torpedo back to the bathroom. A rare ache stirs in my chest from her puddled on the floor. Her sweet head resting against the plaster as if she slid down the wall. So fucking fragile. "God damn it. I was coming right back. Why the hell didn't you stay where I put you?"

For once, no resistance from me scooping her up. Or from me bitching at her.

"Because I don't like you taking care of me."

Muffled from being crushed into my shoulder, her defeated tone almost guts me. "Why?"

"It makes me weak."

I kiss her forehead. The smooth skin freezing under my lips from her being half naked sprawled on the tile. I'm not sure if I'll ever be able to convince her of my sincerity but I'm damn sure going to try. "It doesn't mean you're weak. It means you're loved."

Another first for us. No back talk from my declaration. I force myself not to say more. Not to push. Not to demand her obedience like I normally would.

Maybe I can fucking learn to change too. At least with her.

She only flinches a little when I lower her to the mattress. Mute while I flick the lacy clasp between her breasts and guide the straps down her arms. Jesus. She's fucking gorgeous. Fighting all my instincts, I toss the bra onto the chair and glide my shirt over her head and down her swaying body. Appreciating her compliance because if she fought me with those magnificent tits jiggling in front of my mouth I'd have no choice but to fuck her.

Laying her down, I tuck the blankets around her shivering body and fold her tiny hand in mine. Doc said she needs to be monitored for the next twelve hours so that's what I'm going to do. *"Feel good?"*

"Yes." Finally, her body relaxes. Softening against the navy pillowcase with a slight nod. *"Thank you."*

My cock stirs again from her in my bed. Whispering and clutching me. She needs to get well damn fast. Unwilling to release her, I lean to flip off the lamp. Letting the long orange and yellow rays of the fading day wash over us.

"I don't believe in love at first sight and all that. It's unrealistic. It's only lust."

An unexpected admission in the dim light. Easy to confess behind closed eyes. Truth finally spoken with her defenses down. I'm just as candid. *"It's both. Just because it's fast doesn't mean it isn't real."*

"I'm not that lucky."

I brush down her silky hair. *"You are now. We both are."*

Silence. Either mulling over my proclamation or mounting a protest. Damn hope it's the former.

"I'm so tired."

Neither. I guess it's falling asleep. *"I know lion. Go to sleep. I'll be here."*

"I'm glad."

Fucking hell. She genuinely shocks me with two simple words. This time I don't resist my urge and kiss her slightly parted lips. *"Me too."*

CHAPTER 15

"I'M BORED. IF YOU'RE GOING TO FORCE ME TO STAY HERE Saint, you at least have to give me something to do."

She sashays her sweet ass into my office without knocking. Blatantly obnoxious to get a rise out of me. Which definitely happens with my dick. I push back from my desk and point toward my lap. Nervous laughter ruins her cocky demeanor, and she quickly shakes her head. Realizing her error.

"Not that."

I've been waiting for this tantrum so she's lucky I like her. Doc said to keep her on bed rest for three days but I made it six just in case. So I know she's going stir crazy. Antsy for a taste of freedom. "You need to be more clear."

"I'll remember that the next time." She shoves the keyboard out of reach and stands a few inches from my spread legs. Too many inches from where she should really be. "I've been a good patient. Resting, drinking herbal tea, reading books, watching movies." She juts out a curvy hip in exasperation and ticks the list off on her red-tipped fingers before curling them into air quotes. "All the things you 'allowed' me to do. But I'm done. Let's do something or go somewhere. Or I'll just go without you."

Breathless from her defiant spiel, I get a kick out of

her chest heaving up and down. Waiting to see what I'll do in response to her attempt at intimidation. So damn sexy with her antagonistic tone and attitude. She doesn't have to worry. I'll answer her sass with my own onslaught of menacing words.

I lean back against the cushion, tapping my fingertips on the arm rests. Relaxed and dispassionate. For now. I might be a gentleman but I'm definitely not going to be gentle. "First of all, you've been a fucking nightmare patient." An adorable yet feigned expression of shock fills her adorable face, but we both know she's full of shit. "You refused to wear the clothes I gave you to sleep in, you bit me when I was trying to help you brush your teeth, and you complained to Nonna that I'm a bed hog when in fact it was you who burrowed in next to me every night."

A magnificent blush creeps up her pale throat and across her too hollow cheeks. Now that she's well again I need to get her better fed and healthy. She's going to need her strength and stamina to keep up with me in bed. I stand up, eliminating the space she mistakenly thought she could put between us, and welcome her small but plump tits pushed against my chest as I glare down at her. Cupping her warm cheek with one hand and cradling the back of her head with the other. "And, second, if you ever fucking threaten to leave me again, you won't have to worry about arguing over clothes because you'll be naked and chained to the bed with *my* bite marks all over your sweet body."

Wide eyes flash in fear but I know she's faking. She likes egging me on. As much as I like fucking with her too. Trapped between me and the desk, all she can do is nod. Or lay back so I can really fuck her. But even I know that's not happening yet. "You forget that even the most ferocious lion can be tamed. It's you who decides if that's through punishment or pleasure."

I trace down the side of her heated face with the fingertip still bearing her teeth marks and twirl a wavy strand of hair around my finger. Giving a slight tug to demonstrate I'm not mad before I sit down. Nice enough not to pull her down with me. "Besides, Nonna's still anxious to teach you how to cook for me. That can keep you busy for a while."

She blows out a deep breath and swallows hard. The tip of her pink tongue darting over her lower lip. Finding her voice after I startled her. "Yeah, I love Nonna but we both have to admit that's a lost cause."

The toe of her new shoe nudges the edge of my seat dangerously close to my willing cock. Another three grand well spent on her wardrobe. Her rebellious smirk even sexier than what the black lace stilettos do for her toned legs.

"What else you got?"

Damn if I don't love it when her confidence returns. "You'll have to lose the heels."

An enormous yet fully dubious smile lights up her bright face as she kicks the pumps off to each side of my chair. Bringing her back down to almost my eye level without the six extra inches boosting her up. Dainty feet curling and flexing against the carpet in her excitement. Almost as eager as I am because I know she'll love it too. "And the dress."

Her succulent mouth opens to tell me to fuck off but I interrupt before she gets the chance. "Put on pants because it'll be easier."

"*What* will be easier?"

So damn suspicious. "You'll have to trust me."

My tone is playful but we both realize the deeper meaning behind my comment. That my request implies more than an enjoyable surprise. That I'm asking her to have faith in me to give her what she needs.

"Okay." Soft yet agreeable her voice holds no malice. More curious than frightened. *"I'll be right back."*

"I'll be right here."

She scurries away, giving me another opportunity to enjoy her perfect ass and lithe legs. Glancing back over her narrow shoulder, just like at the hotel, she gives me a shy smile. Checking that I'm still watching. That I'm still interested. That I'm still in love. Now and always, lion.

Yet this time she doesn't stumble from my scrutiny. The exact opposite actually. Seeming to thrive under my gaze. Confirming that she loves me too.

His huge hand engulfs mine as he helps me into the backseat of his crazy expensive SUV. Even crazier with the abundance of security modifications. I try to pretend the thick, black windows that I assume to be bullet proof and the gigantic weapons strapped on the ceiling and hanging on the barrier between us and the driver don't bother me. Obviously I fail when he shakes his head and whispers in my ear. *"No worries leone. They're just a precaution."*

I'm even more surprised by his obvious affection in front of his men. Seemingly indifferent with showing emotion or concern for me. Their expressions remain stoic with their eyes scanning all around us. While my gaze can't stop from lingering on him. Surprising me yet again with his tender side in the midst of a guarded compound and convoy of armed protection ready to escort us to his mystery destination.

My heart swirls in my chest for the second time when he slides inside next to me. Never releasing our entwined hands. Which somehow feels even more intimate than sleeping together. Since that time is spent primarily with me avoiding sex. Although he hasn't tried anything under doctor's orders. Obviously his unrelenting erection hasn't gone unnoticed, tucked against my ass as he holds me every night. I never argued against cuddling because he wouldn't have let me. Nor did I really want him to stop as much as I hate to admit the truth to myself.

Now, with my thigh crushed against his, our fingers tangled together, he's almost sweet. It's almost sweet. And, so very strange for both of us. I'm not sure if I can handle our growing connection. So like a coward, I ignore it. "Do my jeans meet your expectations?"

An exaggerated squint to signal his disapproval but the twerk of his cheek gives away his amusement. "Naked would be better, but they'll do."

Refusing to give him the satisfaction of earning a combative reaction, I simply nod. Even if he's not happy, I adore the outfit. Running my hand down the crystals embellishing the fabric all the way to my knees, I smile. Not used to being dressed so casually with a thin red tee and cute tennis shoes embroidered with red and blue flowers, I don't think I've ever been so comfortable. Physically or mentally.

I catch him watching me again. He pretends to be unaffected. Yet his eyes never leave my hand stroking my leg. Proving he does enjoy a little bit of kink. Relishing the idea of me touching myself. Maybe even pleasuring myself. I need to remember that.

Fuck! I mean I don't give a damn what he likes.

"You're gorgeous no matter what you wear."

Okay, maybe I give a little bit of a damn. *"Thank you."*

The thick black leather bracelet he always wears peeks out from under his sleeve. Compared to his luxurious clothes and affluent demeanor, the style is casual. Almost rugged. Surprising me with the contrast, I wonder about the meaning behind the jewelry. I tentatively stroke the smooth material. His expression remains neutral. Until he frowns. Slowly drawing down his cuff to block my touch. Sending a clear message that my interest is off limits. At least for now.

Tension I don't like burgeons between us again. Not that I really care if he's irritated or not. I just don't want his bad mood ruining the fun I hope I'm going to have since this is my first time leaving the mansion all week after he kept me bed ridden probably longer than necessary. I reveal to him what I realized cuddled on the sofa after about two days of him worrying and hovering over me. Even worse than Nonna. He feels guilty. *"I accept your apology."*

His body stiffens from my grateful words. His hand tightening around mine. *"What apology?"*

"The way you took care of me. I know it's not in you to admit you're wrong or say 'I'm sorry' but I know that you are for what happened."

An impassive expression fills his face. Unable or unwilling to accept that he's actually as transparent as I am. Faking bored while he taps on his leg with his free hand and turns his attention to his window. Scanning the fields lining the landscape. Impatient with the drive. Maybe with me. *"I fixed you so I could fuck you."*

Damn stubborn. I laugh and lay back against my seat. All of my anxiety evaporating from his act. He doesn't fool me. Or let go of me. Instead he lifts our entwined fingers and kisses them. Goose bumps sprinkle across my arms from the gentle touch. A wordless acceptance of my forgiveness.

My butt bounces against the cushion after we turn off the main highway onto an unpaved road. The rocky path thrusting me up and down just like the butterflies lifting in my stomach with anticipation as we follow the curving path through the dense trees. A perfect place to dump my body if he really is mad at me. "Is this it?"

I know she means if we've arrived at our destination, but damn if she doesn't sound slightly frightened. Reminding me again how insecure she really is about me. About us if she thinks she has anything to fear. "Yeah, lion this is it."

Her exquisite neck strains around the seatbelt to catch another glimpse outside. Her bright eyes searching the driveway for answers. I fucking love seeing her curiosity. And hope to hell she likes my surprise as much as I think she will.

I guess she does. With a sexy little gasp and her slender fingers pressed against the darkened glass as if trying to touch the gift I offer to her. Shiny metal glinting in the sun from the row of twelve vehicles parked side by side in front of my garage.

"Are those your cars?"

She looks over her slight shoulder at me. Waiting for my response. Making my dick stir imagining the same expectant image of her when she's on her elbows and knees in my bed. "If you mean did I pay for them, then technically no. I won them."

Bex opens the door and I slide out, turning back to

offer her my hand. Too late. She's already scampered out. Vibrating next to me with excitement as we walk the line. Inspecting the luxurious automobiles.

"See over there?" Her gaze follows my finger pointing to the entrance of the trail cut through the wilderness. "It's a three-mile track. Losers turn over their titles and try to win them back. Until then, they're mine to do with as I please."

"We're racing?"

Another squeak of astonishment. And glorious pleasure. She's fucking luminous when she's excited. "Soon. Right now we'll go together until you get the hang of it. Then I'll let you drive on your own."

"You trust me to drive one?"

I look her up and down just to prolong her agony. Pretending to question her abilities when I actually have zero doubt about everything and anything she's capable of. "Can you drive a stick?"

Teasing fingertips trace a feather light trail up my hardening dick. Her challenging gaze boring into mine. "What do you think?"

Fuck me if she's not flirting with me. Which I fucking love. Both her touching me as well as shocking the hell out of me. "That I'm about two seconds from shoving you to your knees and letting you prove you can."

Which I wouldn't hesitate to do. Except that I don't want my men to see or hear her screams after I fuck her mouth and then bend her over the hood to remind her exactly who the boss is. Her full lips squeeze closed and all her haughtiness fades away while she jerks her hand back. Not wanting to lose her opportunity to race. Another reminder of how smart she really is. "Now pick out which one you want and I'll take you for a ride."

Hennessey. Porsche. Bugatti. SCC. Ferrari. Tesla. Lamborghini.

One by one she peruses the selection. Lingering on the sleek cobalt blue 911 before finally smiling and giving me a huge nod in front of the tangerine Venom F5. Ugly color but damn great race car. I love that she can see past the familiar to select the best option for the purpose. Another reason she's going to kick ass on the Victorian.

"Very nice." She surprises me again blushing under my praise. "Let's go."

Not waiting for me to escort her, she strides around alone and yanks open the passenger side door. Independence that I appreciate but need to rein in just the same. Can't have my lion thinking she can do whatever she wants.

Her sunglasses are already moved from the top of her head to cover her sparkling eyes when I slide in. Slight hands running forward and backward parallel to her thighs on the black leather and diamond pattern seat in anticipation of taking off.

"How fast can we go?"

I thought I was too damn jaded for anything to excite me anymore, but I can't lie that her enthusiasm isn't contagious. Bored from racing the same old bastards again and again, it's actually enjoyable to introduce her to the sport. "The car's capable of going over three hundred miles an hour. However, with your fragile state we're going to keep it down to a reasonable speed until you're ready for more."

She shakes her head furiously at me. Disobedient as ever. "I'm fine, and I'm ready."

The interior's tight but she's small, and it doesn't take much effort for me to turn and haul her out of her seat and lay her across my lap. Cradling her sweet head in the crook of my arm so it doesn't slam against the window. I just got her better, I'm not damaging her again.

So damn stunning as she stares up at me after I slide off her shades. Ebony hair splayed across my bicep and plump lips parted in surprise stained with dark red lipstick I can't wait to see smeared all over my cock. I cup her flushed cheek. *"I will never take chances with your health or safety. If I don't think you're ready, then you're not ready."*

I infuse steel in my voice as hard as my dick with her trapped in my grip, ensuring my message is clearly received. *"Do you think I'd ever hurt you or let anything happen to you?"*

I see her mouth move more than I hear her breathless 'no.' Which is fine. I'm understood and that's all I need. I also understand what she needs when she strains upward. Her body raising slightly toward me. Seeking my touch to match my words. That I'm more than willing to give her.

Awkward with her jammed between the steering wheel and my chest, I cup my hands behind her delicate head. Bearing all of the weight in my palms as I lift her up and breach her parted lips. Soft and sweet and supple. Just like I knew she would be.

Never kissing a woman this gently before, I don't even know how I'm holding back. Doing every damn thing I can think of to restrain myself from fucking ravishing her. But when her hand finds my hair, tugging the short strands, attempting to keep me right where she wants me, I about fucking lose it. Delving deeper to own her and her luscious mouth completely. Savoring the taste of her essence on my tongue. Relishing the moan bubbling in her willowy throat. Matching the growl vibrating in my chest from her at my mercy. From her welcoming my affection. From her enjoying me claiming her.

Until I feel her tense. Damn. I reluctantly force myself to pull back but fuck me if she's not smiling when I meet her hazy gaze. Drunk with lust. Sated with pleasure. Glowing with delight. Hesitant fingers brush my lips. Tracing the skin and stoking the fire I can feel all the way to my throbbing balls. I kiss her fingertip. "You're gorgeous lion."

The grin brightens from my compliment. "You're not too bad yourself saint. Hopefully you drive as well as you kiss."

Fucking magnificent. "I do."

She's still laughing at my cockiness as I begrudgingly boost her up and shift her back to her own seat. Refraining from making a sarcastic comment as she exaggerates her movements yanking her seatbelt slowly across her perfect body and clicking the metal clip into the buckle. A show for my benefit but really all for hers. Can't have fun if my woman isn't protected despite all her efforts to thwart me controlling her.

Well maybe I won't keep my irritation to myself. "You're lucky I don't shove a helmet on that beautiful, damn stubborn head of yours. Which I'm about this close to doing if you don't fucking check the attitude."

Another giggle. Uncertain if she thinks I'm kidding. Or just doesn't fear my threats. Both options are shitty annoying.

"Come on! Hurry up! Let's go!"

As always her spirit drags me out of my surly disposition. Now I'm the one chuckling as she wiggles in her seat. Genuinely excited and free of the distrust usually holding her back from enjoying herself. *"Okay, okay. Don't say I didn't warn you."*

"Warn me about wh–"

Until you experience zero to over two hundred in less than ten seconds you have no idea the impact to your body. Pinning you back against the seat. Stealing your breath, your words, your vision until your brain adjusts to the force. Which hers does beautifully. Following the exquisite lines of the car as we bank to the right after the straightaway curves around the swaying willows populating my property. She doesn't say a word. Just smiles in awe as we blow past pines and firs in an evergreen blur. I'm just as taken. Not with the stupid car. But with her. My lion. My almost painfully exquisite lion who has become my damn world in less than a fucking week. Using the excuse of her needing me to keep me here days longer than I intended. When it was really me, fucking needing her, that kept my ass from returning home.

I fucking love watching her. Stealing glances at her for as long as I can without fucking killing us. Relishing her huge eyes. Sexy pink tinge of her ivory skin. Tiny fingers clutching the seat. Until her graceful hand curls around my forearm. Wanting to share the experience together as her gaze shifts to me. Full of joyful appreciation. For the experience. For me giving it to her. For us being together.

I'm beyond fucked.

My grip tightens on the wheel. I need to get just as tight of a grip on my fucking sanity. I don't think I've ever wanted a woman more than I want her. Fuck it. It's not "think" at all. I damn well *know* I haven't. *"Do you like it?"*

"I love it."

Reverence pulses in her voice to the same furious beat of my pulse. Both of us consumed with pleasure. And we're not even fucking naked. I can't help but laugh. Another first that I know to be true—I'm actually having fun.

We're just about to hit another straightaway so I need to show her what the car can really do. "Hold on Syd."

Punching the accelerator, we top out at three hundred and two for about three fourths of a mile until I slow us back under two hundred for the approaching curve. Loving her squeal as we skid on the left to shoot around the arc. Literally on our sides, asses off the seats, held in place only by our restraints.

Way too damn fast after I swore I wouldn't. But fuck if I could keep my word. Not with her exhilaration too damn intoxicating to resist taking her higher.

I get my own ass in check for five more laps. Keeping us well below two hundred the rest of the time. She doesn't seem to mind. The humongous grin on her radiant face and tight grasp on my arm never waver. Just like my contentment.

As much as I hate putting an end to her fun, I think she's had enough for the first time and pull into the first bay. Almost all of the others filled with the returned cars. Now that I have Syd I'll have to save a couple of spots for her. Damn certain she can beat several of the pussies who try to compete against me. So she'll need her own baby to race.

This time she remembers to let me take care of her. Waiting for me to come around and open her door. An elated shriek greets me as I take her small hand and draw her out of the car and up to me. But she wants a whole hell of a lot more than my assistance. Slender arms shoot around my neck as she engulfs me. Fucking easy to slide my hands across her back to return the embrace.

"Oh my god that was so fun. Thank you. Thank you. Thank you."

"You're welcome."

I should put her down. But fuck that shit. In the battle of what is right versus what feels right, I always do what my instinct tells me, and I'm never wrong. I raise her all the way up and wrap her legs around my waist. Feeling her heart pound against my chest. Smelling her flowery perfume. Enjoying her relaxed body melting into mine.

Only for a few glorious seconds until she lifts up. Uncertainty shrinking her shoulders. I cup her face. Reassuring her that allowing the walls she's built around herself to crumble won't ever cause her any misery. "I had a blast too."

So fucking stunning with her wild tangled hair and glowing expression. The real Sydney sits before me. Not the polished perfect persona she normally presents to the world. But the young woman with the free spirit and gentle heart who seems to have been hiding behind the façade. "I love that smile, lion."

She squirms as if trying to slide down. Hell no. I push us up against the door frame. Protecting her back with my forearms but jostling her enough that her gorgeous round tits bounce under her tee shirt. Smashing her pert nipples into my ribcage when I crook my head closer to find her ear. Relishing her shiver when I skim my lips across her skin. "Worth taking off your dress earlier?"

"Yes."

Fuck if she doesn't squeeze me tighter with those magnificent toned thighs, and my cock answers with a twitch of its own. Rising in unison with her heavy breaths. "I think so too."

I love her close. But I need her closer. So damn much closer. I tug her shirt tucked neatly into her jeans until I can feel the slight bones of her back under my fingers. I don't think I've ever touched skin so soft. I swear she fucking purrs when I rub my palms up her spine.

"Everything is taken care of..."

My head jerks up from her shoulder at the sound of Paolo's voice. Fucking really? Twice I'm about to fuck her, and twice I'm fucking interrupted. I'm going to have to fucking barricade her in my damn bedroom.

"I am sorry Mr. Sabatini. I did not mean to barge in...I am not used to a young lady..."

His words fade away but I know what he implies. Yeah, I'm not fucking used to it either, never having brought a woman here before. But I sure as hell like it. I wink at her as she smirks and slides down. She'll pay for her amusement later. Nothing funny at all about her thinking I'm never going to have the opportunity to fuck her.

Contrite and embarrassed, Paolo bows his head in apology. Still deadly in his actions when warranted despite his age yet also respectful in his deference to me. Especially when he's at fault.

I keep her slightly tucked behind me so he can't reach out to her. Refusing to allow even a handshake. Fucking irrational for me to doubt a man I trust implicitly enough to manage my home and provide security for my grandmother but I really don't give a damn. No one touches my lion except for me. "Paolo, this is my fiancée Sydney Martin."

"The pleasure is all mine signorina."

I shove down her arm when she offers him her hand. She jerks away from my touch but doesn't fight me in any other way. Which is good because she will quickly learn I won't tolerate her insubordination in front of my employees.

"I'm not his fiancée. But the Sydney part is accurate. It's a pleasure to meet you too."

I should fucking kill him where he stands for the smile he's trying to stop twitching on his lips. But then Nonna would cry and carry on, and I don't have time for her to be on my ass any more than she already is.

Instead, I grasp Sydney's fingers and lead her outside and into the waiting vehicle. I've got a few things to take care of before the fight, and then I'm finally going to fuck her whether she's ready for me or not.

CHAPTER 16

CAN'T SLEEP.

Not without him. Uncertain as to when I got comfortable in his bed. Or, even worse, how I've gotten used to having him in here with me. No sense in lying to myself. I don't want to drift off alone. I don't want to be alone.

The clock reads only eight minutes since I last checked. Might as well give up and go find him. Going downstairs by myself in the middle of the night feels weird. I grab my robe. Tying the black silk belt tight around my waist lest I run into Nonna. Or even worse one of his men. None of them would dare touch me but I hate feeling like some kind of prize or prisoner. Even though I guess I technically am.

Peaceful silence greets me on the steps and in the foyer. Only moonlight flooding the empty rooms except for the small den next to Julius's office. I guess he's finished working and watching the boxing match he seemed so interested in earlier. I pad quietly in my sock feet not wanting to disturb anyone. Or more accurately not call attention to myself. I stifle a giggle. I'm probably kidding myself with that thought too. He's probably following my trail on his phone and already waiting for me.

I peek in the open door. My heart flip flops. He's so damn handsome. And so fucking dominant. His thick arms draped across the back of the couch, pulling his shirt taut across his delicious bulging muscles. His long legs sprawled out in front of him. Owning the sofa. Owning the room. Owning me.

Dark eyes meet mine when he looks away from the TV. His quick gaze skimming down my bare legs before returning to my face. Pleasure and desire searing me from the same emotions flaming in his expression. He wants me as much as I hate to admit I want him.

"Come here."

More of a growl than actual words. My head says fuck you. My heart says hurry the hell up. I hate the turmoil. The doubt. The fear.

Apparently, he does too from the displeasure lining his forehead. Impatient with me for disobeying him. For denying myself. So I stop fighting what I feel. For the first time in six years, I follow my heart instead of my head. Swallowing my stubborn pride, and allowing myself go to him.

I can't give in too much though. Refusing to run or show how much I want him. I edge the perimeter, trying to discretely scooch onto the cushion next to him. Asserting my independence and claiming my side of the furniture. Of course, that's not good enough, and he yanks me next to him. Tucking me against his rigid body. Forcing me to curl myself around him with my head on his shoulder. Which feels weird and warm and wonderful.

I guess not to Phillip who hops up and strides out of the study without a glance back. If what Julius says is true, and he's never brought a woman here before, then the bodyguard probably feels just as awkward. Nothing personal toward him at all, but I'm glad he's gone. Already self-conscious enough without an audience, I don't need him watching Julius manhandle me.

Julius's lips on my forehead ease some of my discomfort. Whereas I don't think he had any embarrassment to begin with. He never does. Making me wish I could be as confident as him. Especially when his hand roams over my hip. His chuckle from my involuntary twitch heating my face. I need to get back in control. Of myself and of him. "When does this thing start?"

I ignore his huge hand caressing my leg. Fingertips brushing the hem that he could easily peel away to reveal my panties underneath. Yet surprisingly he doesn't broach beyond the edge. Keeping his touch mostly pg-13.

"This *thing* starts in about two minutes. You're just in time."

Humor floods his voice but he doesn't stop stroking my thigh. Almost comforting to him as stimulating as his touch is to me.

"Do you really like boxing this much? To stay up past two am to watch it?"

"I'm about to win a lot of money."

Julius is utterly gorgeous. No doubt about it. But when he's cocky, he's absolutely breathtaking. Lighting my already wired body on fire with his self-assurance. "Don't be so smug. Your guy might lose."

"I hope so."

That makes absolutely zero sense. He'll win if his guy loses? That's only possible if…Fuck! "It's rigged? You rigged it?"

I try to twist away. Disgusted by him yet again. My efforts yield no real effect with his enormous arm holding me down. Trapping me against his broad body while I struggle.

"You should be happy. No maiming or murdering this time."

The bastard's teasing me. Throwing my own words back at me when he's guilty of crimes almost as bad as those. Strong fingers nudge my chin up to face him. A mischievous twinkle in his eyes while he gloats.

"Players, coaches, officials…it happens all the time. Everyone can be bought. I'm just the guy with the balls and money to do it this time."

Terrible. "Don't you get tired of being dirty?"

He leans in. So close his full lips singe my skin when they brush against mine. The same raging inferno inside me blazes in his chocolate eyes. "The dirtier, the better."

I can't seem to catch my breath. I know it's wrong. I know I should tell him off. I know I've never had a man look at me the way he's looking at me. I know I don't want him to stop. I'm already going to hell so I might as well go with him. I might as well give in. I might as well kiss him.

So, I do.

Tasting the decadent scotch on his tongue. Loving his tightening grip encircling my back. Grinding against his erection bulging through his pants.

"Boss, I–"

All of his weight and warmth are suddenly gone as Julius raises to his knee and lunges for his gun on the coffee table. Roaring at Phillip to get the fuck out of here. Firing off a shot that explodes through the air, shattering the quiet and ripping through the drywall. Shards of plaster blowing through the room like confetti.

Oh shit! Julius's free hand curls around my neck when I attempt to roll away. Pinning me to the sofa. With force and fright. My words gurgle in my throat from his grip. "Julius please."

He slides the weapon back on the glass and smiles down

at me as I beg him to let me go. Actually smiles like the lunatic he is. Calm and composed, he brushes back a strand of hair tucking the wavy lock behind my ear. "I missed on purpose. He's fine."

Adrenaline kicks in, and my body trembles beneath his. My ears ringing from the proximity of the explosion. My head swimming from the insanity. He thinks it's fine to shoot at a man for walking into a room. He thinks I'll be fine after threatening him with death for interrupting us. When I'm not fine at all. "This isn't–"

"Don't you get it?"

No I don't. Not him. Not this life. Not any of it. "Get what?"

My exasperation doesn't seem to daunt him. "I will kill him or any other man if they ever see you naked." Crazy, evil Julius returns along with the hardness glinting in his expression. A possessive tone and touch that's so frightening and foreign to me I'm not sure if I can fully comprehend them. "You are never to be treated like anything but my wife. Which means always respected, worshiped, and protected."

Now I'm the one who's losing my mind. I close my eyes trying to make sense of what he's saying to me. Or more accurately the impact his vow has on me. Something in his words, his ferocity, his reverence floods the hollowness in my chest. Filling my heart with the love I've never experienced. The emotion I've never felt. The sincerity I've never known. Everything I didn't know I wanted that now seems like only Julius can give to me.

"Look at me lion."

I don't want to. Afraid of what I'll see staring back at me. But when I blink my eyes open all I see is…love. Insane, impossible, incredible love.

"There's my good girl."

I laugh. Slightly hysterical from the emotional upheaval raging inside me. "I'm nobody's good girl. I'm nobody's good *anything*."

The authentic smile evaporates. Replaced with rage. Directed at me and my assertion by the harsh shake he manages lying on top of me. My head bobs from the intensity as he hisses.

"Don't you ever fucking disparage yourself Sydney. I will not have it."

I keep pushing when I shouldn't. When what I should do is what a normal woman would probably do in this jacked up situation. Just accept his ridiculous declarations of love, let him spoil me like a mad man, and live happily ever after. Or least as long as it lasts until he tires of me.

But I can't.

Not when I'm terrified that everything will all come crashing down around me. That I'll fall, and he won't always catch me. That someone will remind him of who I am, what I do, how I was, and he'll be too disgusted to remember that he thinks he loves me. "I'm an escort, Julius. A hooker. I fuck men for money. I–"

Tears prick my eyes from his hand smacking down over my mouth. Not just from the force of his palm slapping against my flushed skin although it does sting a little bit. But from the pain of reality settling in too.

"I don't give a damn about what you *were* and what you *used* to do. I fucking hate it but it doesn't change how I feel about you. When I'm old and looking at my legacy, there's no one else I want by my side except you. I don't need some fragile wallflower. I need a real woman who can battle next to me just as much as with me." A glimmer of hope flickers in my battered soul from his disregard of the past. His vehemence to focus on the future. "And any man who ever says a word about you will be dead."

His fingers lift from cupping over my lips and stroke through the watery trails on my cheeks. Tender and soft. "Because I love you piccolo leone, and you are mine."

His.

Not disposable. Not temporary. Not only good for one thing. But the tiny fierce lion of one of the most powerful, most dangerous men in the entire world who will do anything to protect me. Who loves me. I shiver from the thought. "Julius please?"

This time begging for him to never let me go. I think he knows it too when his fingertip brushes against my tongue from my deep breath.

"Please what?"

I shudder again from his hoarse whisper. "Fuck me."

Fuck. Me.

She fucking means it. Dilated eyes and panting chest and licked lips. Glorious.

Even when she's at her most vulnerable her resiliency still shows through. This woman could never be weak regardless of how much she fears giving in. I don't think I've ever known anyone with as much tenacity as her, and I'm more than happy to give her exactly what she requests. Give her what she needs. To believe, understand, accept that I want her. Hell that I loved her even before I fucked her.

I flip us over. Groaning from her thighs straddling my legs. Pussy against cock. Chest to chest. Fist in hair. Tongue on neck. Leaving the first of many marks on her silky ivory skin.

She responds just as eagerly. Desperate fingers clutching my shirt. Holding on tight. Bracing for whatever I'm going to do to her. Unaware of what I'm going to do for her.

Which is slow my ass down and take her upstairs so I can ravish her properly. Slender arms coil tight around my neck as I stand. As if I'd ever fucking drop her.

I ignore the damage I caused as we step into the hallway. But of course she doesn't. Her gorgeous head lifting from my shoulder. A little gasp sounds in my ear as if she realizes something.

"What about Nonna? Do you think she's frightened?"

My sweet lion. So protective of the ones she cares about. "Her room is soundproof. She didn't hear a thing. The guys will clean up the mess, and she'll never know the difference."

Her small body relaxes against mine. So I tell her more, that I think she'll like, as I carry her up the steps. To eliminate all her little worries so we can concentrate on just us. "I have a call button in there in case she needs help, and her room is impenetrable if the house goes on lock down. She can survive any level of attack. Just like I'm having done to our bedroom at home now that I have you."

Petite fingers cup my cheeks. An intense gaze studying my face. Almost making me stumble from the astonishment, from the gratitude, from the joy filling her expression. "For me?"

"Yeah, of course for you."

Any motherfucker that makes it far enough to get to me inside my own damn house takes his chances with survival. But I'll never risk her safety because of my enemies.

She seems to understand the shift I make for her. Happiness turns to hunger, and her legs squeeze around my waist. Her tits grinding into my chest as she lifts to kiss me. Urgent and greedy with her tongue tangling with mine. Tempting me to go ahead and shove her against the wall and fuck her right on the landing.

But I force my legs to keep walking. Down the hall and into my—our—bedroom, kicking the door shut behind me. No more fucking interruptions. This place would have to burn to damn the ground before I'd stop this time.

She clings to me so tightly as I easily yank the tie loose around her stomach and slide her robe down her slim shoulders. Helping her with a slow strip tease while we slip the sleeves down one arm and then the other. Stealing the damn air from my lungs from her nervous little laugh.

I lay her down. Slow and easy so she isn't spooked. I want her docile and relaxed. At least for the first time I fuck her. Positioning her the way I want her, I pose her arms perpendicular to her body and push her legs slightly open after I tug off her tiny panties. Plenty of time to spread them wide open when I'm ready.

"You're so damn beautiful."

I only stare at her eyes. The rest of her is fucking magnificent too. She works hard to stay in shape which is great. I'm not going to lie—her body is fucking amazing. But it's her soul, her spirit, her spunk that I'm really in love with.

She reaches for me but I shake my head and motion to the original locations. "Back where I put them leone."

"Why?"

Fear throbs in her voice from my harsh tone. Reminding me I need to be more gentle with her. Which is definitely not natural. And definitely not easy with her bared to me.

"Because this is about you and for you. What I'm giving to you tonight."

Seeming to understand my meaning, she drops her arms back to the sides. As much as I hate thinking about all of the motherfuckers who've had her before me, I use the reminder to check myself and my eager cock. I know she did all the work. She fucked them instead of the other way around. Giving them everything while she received nothing in return. Because I've been that guy. The asshole who just takes. Or only doing enough to make sure the chick got off. Not because I cared but to keep my reputation intact.

It was all about me.

Now, it's all about her.

I want her to know the ecstasy. To be the first one being fucked. To be the first man to show her she's loved. To prove I'm the only one who can.

I'm still a selfish bastard though. The first caress is for me. My fingertips ache with the need, and I'm too damn greedy to deny myself. Two long strokes grazing down her torso to press hard against her hipbones. Making her jerk off the bed. Imagining them flexing against mine as I bury myself in her. Jesus. I can't fucking get enough of that. Loving how responsive she is when I'm near her glorious pussy. When she trembles in anticipation of where I'm going to touch her next.

Of course I can't hold back and go in for more. Trailing the curve of her tits, the rock hard nipples, the swell of her hips. Strumming the pink folds already glistening with proof of her desire for me. Which I can't lie is fucking incredible to see.

I separate the lips. Opening her for my fingers and my tongue and my cock. Flicking the jewel in her clit with my thumb. Enjoying the gasps and mewls bubbling in her parted mouth. Her body arching up, seeking more. But I'm in no hurry. I sweep through her sweetness and bring the essence to my tongue. I don't think I've tasted anything as decadent. I leisurely swipe again and bring my drenched fingers to her mouth. "Taste yourself lion. See why I want you so damn bad."

She hesitates. Never having been pleasured in this way. Which I feel all the way to my impatient dick. I'll be the only man to give her this gift. To see how fucking stunning she is when I shove my tongue deep and long inside her.

"I'm…"

Fucking adorable. She's actually shy. Selfless I suppose. Not used to accepting such lavish attention. I glide back and forth across the bare pink skin before dipping inside her folds and mouth simultaneously. Which makes her moan the most fucking beautiful moan I've ever heard.

When her desperate fists ball the bed sheet, I'm fucking done. Too difficult to resist. Too much to stand. Too exquisite to stop. I have to have her pussy in my mouth. Not allowing her any time to recover before I shove her thighs up and apart, planting her feet on the mattress on each side of my shoulders. Lifting her hips to meet my tongue. I lick a few leisurely laps before I graze her swollen nub with my teeth. Sucking in the slick petals while I slide my fingers deeper inside.

She shrieks from my invasion, and her hands drive through my hair. Trying to control me. Uh un leone. "Put your hands back on the bed lion, or I'll tie them up."

"Why?"

Anger sparks in her tone, and she stiffens in my hands. Attempting to pull away from me which is never fucking happening. Ready to battle but she has no fucking clue the long, drawn out fight we're going to enjoy tonight. I lift my head from her heaven, her arousal still on my lips, and meet her riled gaze. "Because I don't need your help. The only person getting you off tonight is me. The only person who gets to touch you is me."

Defiance conflicts with appreciation in her exquisite face. Still unable to let go completely and submit to me. Well, then I'm going to have to force her. I wipe her juices off my chin with the back of my hand and wink at her. Thriving on the fear blooming in her pensive eyes. I yank off my belt and grab her ankle as she tries to twist away. Too late for that.

She kicks and snarls as I easily manhandle her small frame. Wrapping the taut leather around her wrists and then around the white wooden plank spanning the headboard. Twisting her onto her knees, she is totally and completely trapped. And going to be totally and completely fucked.

"Damn it Julius! Let me go."

"Never. Not now. Not ever."

Long hair sways across her smooth back as she struggles. Stilling when she realizes I've won once again. That I'll always fucking win. So fucking spectacular just like I imagined with her looking back at me over her shoulder. "Fuck you!"

I chuckle as I shed my clothes. Calm and unhurried. Well at least I pretend to be. My balls are so damn heavy and aching I can barely stand. Smirking when she watches me stroke my cock a few times before I climb back onto the mattress.

A shudder rolls through her as I smack her ass a few times and then soothe the sting with my fingers returning to stroke her between her thighs. Curling to reach the spot I discovered before that makes her mewl. Her head drops down to rest on her crisscrossed arms, and she stops fighing against her restraints. Welcoming me ravishing her as her pussy contracts around my hand and her body leans into my touch. "I've tasted you and fingered you and now I'm going to fuck you, piccolo leone."

A whimper gurgles in her throat when I move from her dripping pussy to straddle her hips. Total backfire when she stiffens underneath me. Her head flying up to crash into mine. She tries to scramble away, jerking to the side attempting to break my hold on her. Not fucking happening. I force her back under me. Curling over her trembling body, I position her perfectly so I can coat my cock with her arousal and push inside her.

"This isn't about me. It's about you." She seethes with some kind of fucked up misguided anger as I drive deeper. "You're just trying to be the star of my fantasy."

Still needing to bust my balls even while they're slapping against her perfect ass. I kiss her graceful ear. Making my intentions crystal clear. "No lion, *you* are the star of *mine*."

The fury seeps away as the words sink in, and finally delicate hands grasp the bonds securing her. Bracing herself. Allowing me to pound into her. Which I fucking do. So hard and furious we're both gasping for air. Because I'm a fucking mad man when it comes to her with only one mission. To get her there. To get her off. To get her convinced. "You are the only woman I've ever dreamed about fucking."

I have one hand on her perfect tit and the other on her throbbing clit. Tugging and twisting in unison while I suck the fragrant skin in the crook of her neck. My own body shaking from her arching into me. Meeting my thrusts and answering my demand to fucking own her as I murmur in her ear. *You never have to doubt me. You never have to question my love or my loyalty.*

"Wh-what? What are you saying?"

She's breathless and convulsing and so close to flying, I have to give her what she needs to come while I'm already planning how I'm going to fuck her next. I pull almost all the way out before slamming home again. Over and over, until I'm seated so deep I can feel her cervix resisting the intrusion from the head of my cock and her body almost buckles beneath me. Just like I knew she wanted. Now I'm taking it one step further. *"I'm saying I love you."*

The declaration pushes her over the edge, and she screams out for me. So I give her more. I give her everything I've got. Biting her shoulder and cupping her pussy to pinch her inflamed clit between my palm and my dick, mixing the pain and pleasure I know my dirty lion likes. My own release unrelenting as I keep pumping. Filling her with my seed while I hold up her limp body. Allowing her to rest for only a few seconds before I flip her over and fuck her again.

CHAPTER 17

I WAKE UP ALONE.

But reminders of him are everywhere.

Around me. His clothes in messy chaos across the floor from his urgency to strip last night. The gouges in the drywall from the headboard slamming into the plaster from his force. Rips in the sheets from me holding on tight from his affection.

On me. Teeth and tongue marks peppering my skin. Bruises on my hips and legs and wrists. Hair tangled in knots and his spicy cologne seeped into my pores mingling with our sweat.

In me. My throat raw and scratchy from screaming. My nether regions sore with every movement climbing out of bed, with every step across the room. My thighs streaked and sticky from his release.

I've never been more disgusting.

Or beautiful.

Or happy.

My giddy smile only increases from my phone sitting on the nightstand rather than his. He must have had it all along after he rescued me from Sergei. I should be pissed as hell he kept my cell from me but I'm too deliriously drunk on lust to be mad. I snatch it up, and my heart flip flops from a text from *Saint* on the screen.

Call Mack or anyone you want.

A little bit of my exhilaration dissipates from reading my friend's name. I want to talk to him because I miss him. But I also dread the lecture. The interrogation. The disappointment. I know he won't be thrilled for me despite me being beyond ecstatic for myself.

I'll worry about that later. Right now I need a shower desperately. I type a quick *thank you* to him, and then swipe for my favorite playlist as I walk. The lights in the bathroom flicker before I even step inside, and the shower kicks on. Steam circling quickly from the hot water hitting the cold tile. That has never happened before.

"You're welcome lion."

Julius's rich voice surrounds me, echoing off the hard surfaces in the massive space. Pervert's spying again. "Stop watching me, you creeper!"

I fail at sounding genuinely angry. Difficult to be sincerely upset at someone spoiling me. He must agree because I hear his laughter until it fades away. My body tingling from his contented chuckle. From his happiness. From the happiness he gives me.

The bag I thought I'd lost forever in the explosion sits on the counter. I dig through and grab out my shampoo and body wash although it wasn't a hardship using his products. Tapping on the screen again a few times to pump up the volume, I slide my phone next to my make-up kit and step under the waterfall. Warm and soothing on my battered yet satisfied body.

I realize I'm still smiling when I wash my face. Surprising me since I rarely smiled before. Not genuinely anyway. Now I can't seem to stop.

My favorite song greets me when I shut off the

abundant spray. Now I'm really, really lame with my giddiness and catch the beat while I dry off and then brush my teeth. Wondering if I remember the routine from the pole dance class Val and I took with that wild instructor. So damn raunchy but fun. I drop low to see if I can still hit the mark with her voice in my ear encouraging us to pretend like we're sliding down onto a dick. Bobbing up and down for his pleasure as well as our own. Or, if we were hating on men, then imagine our favorite vibrator. Shaped like a cucumber I mumble to myself as she used to shout. That girl was a hot mess. But damn her moves kept us in good shape.

Let that booty hit the floor. Swing that ass around and strip it to the core. Make him chase for you. Make his heart race for you.

I laugh at the dork I am, dancing and singing alone. Until I realize I'm not. Twisting toward the door with my fingertips gliding up my thighs, I startle from Julius stalking toward me. A blur of untamed darkness. Almost feral before he pounces. Jerking me around to sheath his chest.

His hands cover mine, and we roam my body together. Mimicking my earlier move and sliding our coupled fingers over my legs and pussy and stomach. Lingering on my breasts to thumb my nipples. Agony and ecstasy swirled together from the tenderness lingering from last night. An erotic display in the mirror of me writhing under his touch and his primal, practically angry domination of my body.

"Did you ever dance like this for anyone else?"

His heartbeat pounds against my back while his fingers dip inside me. Stroking with an urgency that makes me moan. Riding his hand with a desperate need I didn't even realize I had.

"Did you?"

I can't form words from his furious tone and paralyzing

caresses, and shake my head. An approving growl rumbles against my throat.

"And you never fucking will."

Wetness glosses his fingers all over again when I see his hand move to his belt and hear his zipper. He's going to fuck me here. He's going to fuck me hard. He's going to fuck me. I can't wait.

Strong hands bend me forward and curl around my wrists forcing them against my lower back while he guides himself inside me with one long thrust. Pain mingling with pleasure from the force of my already tender body. "Julius I–"

"No."

My palm shoves her satin cheek, caging her head against the mirror. I don't want to hear a damn fucking thing about any other fucking men. She's mine, and she's going to take me. Fucking right here and now. "Whatever it is, I don't give a damn. All I want to hear is that you want me to fuck you."

I fucking love how utterly beautiful she looks at my mercy. Her gorgeous body displaying the proof of my love for her. Her inquisitive eyes never leaving mine. Her perfect tits smashed against the glass. Her succulent ass pushed into my stomach as I plunge into her.

"I want you to fuck me."

Jesus. Her music picks up again. A pounding beat that I can feel in my racing pulse. The only lyric I can make out are the words 'never mind.' Everything else slurred together. All the other verses intelligible like he's drunk. Kind of like I am over her. Flying high with her dainty wrists clamped under my fist and her legs spread wide to take me deep. Grunting and thrusting like a damn wild animal as I have her trapped with nowhere to go. Driving me to the edge with her moans and whimpers.

Yes. No. More. Stop. She has no idea what she wants with my demanding cock in her clenching pussy, my tongue sucking on her slender neck, my thumb plucking her engorged clit. I'm making her fucking crazy just like she is me. But I really fucking lose it when she cries out my name. Her release flooding my balls and thighs as she climaxes. Eyes squeezed shut. But I need her to watch when I come inside her.

They blink open when I abandon her throbbing nub and yank back her hair. Sliding her chin up the foggy mirror, steamy from her panting. "Look at me lion while I fuck you."

I don't even recognize my own voice. More than the normal dominance. Harsh and guttural. Demanding with a possessiveness she must understand too as her pussy clenches around me again. Her hips moving with me. Her entire body trembling. She needs to come. She needs me to make her come. "You are the one. The only one. Always the one."

A manic nod of agreement is all I need too, and my own body shakes with my release. Filling her up almost painfully as she collapses from the force. We slide down the mirror together. Always together.

CHAPTER 18

W E'RE GOING HOME.

Much to Nonna's disappointment after we stayed in Sicily much longer than Julius originally planned. I think she secretly hoped he was enjoying himself so much that he would simply forget about ever returning to the States. That we would remain there and live happily ever after with her and the beach and our new mutually shared racing hobby. But his world, his real life—gritty and dangerous—kept beckoning, and now we're on the way to his house.

My house now too I guess. Such a strange feeling to know I'm going to be staying in his mansion from now on instead of my apartment. Although, I have to admit, not a terrible sensation either. Oddly enough, the idea of living with him permanently makes me somehow feel free rather than tied down. A contentment that I never expected to find after being independent for so long. Too long, I guess, to realize what I'd been missing.

Which has only taken a month of him spoiling me with love and affection and almost constant sex to recognize how lonely I was. How lost. How lifeless.

Now my world is filled with him and his grandmother and maybe even a baby. Which is definitely his idea not mine. The thought simultaneously intriguing and terrifying. Believing I was destined to be permanently solo, I've never even considered having a boyfriend or a husband. Let alone becoming a parent, especially with an insane, ruthless mob boss. Yet another facet of our relationship where he offers me no choice.

Forcing both of us to eschew any birth control since he had himself checked right before he kidnapped me and then confirmed I was clean after perusing my records. Well that, and preventing me from fucking anyone else since the last time I completed the monthly tests I always take. Which I hated him for at first. For controlling me and claiming to know what was best for me. I guess now I realize he was correct, yet so utterly wrong about how he went about proving himself correct. I've finally accepted that I'll never change him but have learned to accept his obstinacy along with his other domineering and overprotective behavior.

I glance over at him. Still captivated from the thrill of him sitting next to me, from his possessive touch as he talks in his phone. His chiseled jaw made sexier with his evening scruff. His ebony hair messy from my fingers stroking the silky strands earlier on his jet. His talented hands squeezing his cell in irritation. Protecting me from the details of his criminal empire by conversing in Italian.

Despite any claims otherwise, he owns my destiny now. So I choose happiness within my circumstances rather than fighting him forever. Since he vows that's what we are. Somehow I'm finally starting to believe him.

He lifts his hand from caressing my thigh and swipes his screen again to stop the incessant buzzing after he just clicked off another call. Grumbling something that means he's frustrated.

"Damn." Sliding the cell back into his jacket pocket, he returns his attention to stroking my leg. "I need to stop by my club and take care of something. Then I'm going to take you home and fuck you until you can't walk."

I laugh and shake my head. Always matter of fact and straightforward with his intentions. Not wasting a second on any romantic preamble or attempt at seduction. I guess I'll have to accept too that he's not the sweet talking type. That's okay. I'm not really either. Maybe truly perfect for each other like he continuously assures me we are.

"You think I won't?"

Trying to pick a fight over my amused reaction, he challenges me. Which, if I dare to counter his assertion, will just end up with us fucking right here in the SUV. I definitely don't want to smell like sex when we're out in public, so I give in. A little. "I believe you Saint. I fully know what you're capable of."

That makes him smirk, damn cocky bastard. Too handsome and sexy for his own good. His fingers streak higher and lick at my already dampening panties. He growls in disapproval from finding my thong.

"I like it better when you're naked."

"Well, I like it better when you're a gentleman."

Now his laughter fills the backseat. Both of us well aware he's never gentle when it comes to taking me. The fading bruise on the inside of my wrist proof of his penchant for tying my hands to give him full and unadulterated access to my body. I wonder how he'd respond if I try that on him tonight when I pleasure him for the first time. I turn toward the window, hiding my smile. Not very likely. Well aware he'll never submit to me or anyone else. But hopefully he'll finally allow me to return the favor to him since he hasn't yet. So focused on pampering me, he's sacrificing his own needs and I don't like it.

I don't like it at all.

For the first time in life, I'm giving of myself because I want to. Not because anyone's paying me to. Or expecting me to. Or forcing me to.

Forcing.

Terror floods my body thinking of him. I haven't had any nightmares for weeks. Not since I've been with Julius. But the building we've pulled in front of brings everything back. All the disgusting memories flooding my mind. An involuntary shudder engulfs me, and I can't stop shaking. "This is your club?"

A slight shrug of indifference lifts his shoulders, if not his interest. His mind still deep in thought from whatever issue brings us here. Unaware of the panic rushing through mine.

"One of them. I've got several but I keep an office here."

The vehicle comes to a stop, and there's only a few minutes for the security sweep of the perimeter before his driver opens the door. To get out. To go inside. To be in there. I press back against the cushion. An involuntary response to my body's resistance to climbing out of the Infiniti. "I'll just wait here for you, okay?"

Damn. Not the way to negotiate with him. He appreciates confidence and directness. I force myself not to whisper. "I mean I–"

"No, leone. You go with me. You're always with me."

I want to find comfort in his affirmation. I can't. Not when I'm this freaked out. "I really don't mind. Take all the time you need."

He twists all the way around in the seat to face me. A

hardness in his expression that means I've pissed him off. I've insulted him in some way. "You think I would leave you out here alone? That I would risk your safety?"

"But your men…"

His head jerks with one curt shake. Discussion over. If I was in my right mind I would argue until I couldn't breathe. But as much as I don't want to be anywhere near where I was attacked, I don't want to be alone either. All I can do is nod and accept his hand after he slides out. Hoping he's strong enough for both us tonight.

Stay here alone.

What the fuck?

My lion really has a lot to learn if she thinks I'd leave her exposed with all the enemies who know my vehicle and would question—and likely seize the opportunity to at-tack—the SUV left running in front of my club. My men are the best but that's too much of a risk to take with her.

Her petite hand trembles in mine. Another reason to get her inside. Warm her up with a drink before I take her home and fuck the chill out of her. I tuck her small body against me as my guys clear a path for us through the crowd. Interrupting the dancers smashed together as the music pulses at deafening levels. Some of them too drunk or high to notice. While others gawk and nudge each other. My presence is a big enough deal alone to cause a stir. With her, they're going fucking crazy. Especially the women. Jealous of her beauty and her place beside me. A clear message to everyone I'm officially taken.

I bypass my booth to keep prying eyes off of her. I've

shown that she's mine and that's enough fucking visibility. Instead, I take her to the waiting area outside my office. Where she won't be fucked with and will be easy to claim her as soon as I'm ready for her. Hopefully less than five minutes since that's about all I'm giving Vladimir. Fucker will be sorry if he pushes my good will and my damn patience any farther. Any lenience he received from his father's service to me ends tonight.

"I—I need to go to the ladies' room."

Her breathless request pulls me down to look at her gorgeous face. Unusually pale and lined with uncertainty. I'm not sure what the fuck is going on with her but as soon as I settle this other bullshit, I'll find out. And fucking fix it.

I nod to Bex. "Straight there and back. No deviations."

The guard nods and steps closer to her. "Yes sir."

Almost as if hypnotized she follows his gesture to go first. Not arguing against my orders or accusing me of being an over-protective bastard. Something really is fucking wrong. Damn it. Now I'm even more pissed than I was before.

I shove open the door. Motherfucker leans against my desk with his ass on my papers. His arms crossed with a nonchalance neither of us believe. What he does believe is my fist connecting with his jaw. Stupid bastard slides across the smooth wood before landing on his stomach on the other side. Instantly rolling to his side and cupping his face like a pussy instead of a man. I don't have time for his shit.

I drop into my chair and click on the monitors, pulling up the hallway. Catching Bex on guard outside the restroom. I keep my gaze locked on the screen waiting for her to appear.

"What the fuck Sabatini?"

That's what I'd like to know. About her. Since I sure as hell don't give a damn about him. "You're a fucking idiot. I'm done talking to you. Get the fuck out of my office."

"Done? We haven't even started."

"Even better since absolutely nothing you say interests me."

The door finally swings open. and she just stands there. Rare timidity hunching her shoulders. Taking a deep breath, she presses her fingers against her chest as if attempting to slow her heartbeat. Flinching and shying back when two guys passing by slow down and glance her way. Then she does what I never fucking expected again. She runs. Son of a bitch!

I haul ass over Vladimir still sprawled on the floor and race into the corridor. Adrenaline flowing like lava through my veins making me fly past Bex already chasing after her. I catch sight of her a few yards ahead of me and easily close the distance between us. Ready to tear into her for her disobedience when I jerk her around to face me. Until she crushes her shuddering body against me. Clutching my jacket and burying her face in the fabric.

"I needed you."

Fuck me. She wasn't escaping. She was searching for me. "I'm here lion."

I engulf her. Trying not to smash her tiny frame in my arms with my own rage bellowing from my suspicions. "Did someone touch you or speak to you?"

"N-no."

Good because I didn't want to have to take the time to murder someone when I need to take care of her. Caressing her head and holding her tight, I give her all my heat, my strength, my love. Yet she still convulses against me. God damn it. I hate fucking seeing her like this. Genuinely frightened. Despite my protection and reassurances. I don't know what or why but I will end it now. I will give her whatever she requires to feel safe. "Let's go home."

"Thank you."

She's truly grateful. Which I'm glad but also fucking hate. As if she thought I wouldn't allow her to leave. That I would force her to stay when she's terrified. That I would let her to suffer for even a fucking second.

I nod to Bex over her head. More than ready to get out of here. Get *her* the fuck out of here. So she will understand that I mean what I say when I tell her I will always give her what she needs even if she doesn't know yet what that is.

CHAPTER 19

MY LION IS BACK.

Although definitely not in the way I like.

Silent the entire ride home I didn't push while she floated in her reverie. Allowing her to work through whatever is bothering her. Keeping my own mouth shut and my hand tight on her quivering shoulder as I kept her folded against me. We don't need words when we're together. As long as she remembers we are together.

But when she rips her fingers away from mine as I escort her into the house, she ends any tolerance and patience I reserve for her. "Remember yourself piccolo leone. I won't hesitate to spend the rest of the night taming you again if needed."

Actually not a bad way to spend the rest of the entire weekend. Can't let her know that though.

This time she tremors with rage. Looking me straight in the eye. Her harsh gaze flooded with pure loathing. "Fuck off Sabatini."

She stomps away. Obviously out of her god damn fucking mind to think she can get away with talking to me like I'm not the boss. Behaving like I will not punish her defiance. Acting as if she knows where she's going when she sure as hell doesn't with that mouthy attitude. I follow her into the study. Slamming the door behind me. No one leaving until I fuck the fight out of her, and she finally explains what the fuck is going on. "The only fucking I'm going to do is to you."

"Of course that's all you care about. Just like every other man I know."

My fury matches hers now. Uncertain as to what has triggered her doubt again. But I'm fucking done explaining myself. Finished proving myself. More than over her damn tantrum. "I can lock you up without fucking you if that's what you really want. Keep you prisoner in my room until you learn to fucking trust me."

"I don't trust anyone." She spins around without me having to force her. A recklessness in her eyes I fucking hate. "Especially you."

Especially me. A devastating accusation that hits me harder than I thought possible. Because I'm the only one who can hurt her. The only one whose opinion matters to her. Since she seems to think so low of herself for which I'll never fucking understand.

"Because you only think you know me. But you don't. No one does. They only know what I show them."

"Maybe." I step closer. So close I can feel her heart beating. Too close I guess when she stumbles backward. "Or maybe what really scares you is that I see the real you and you don't like it."

Absolute silence. I swear to God an entire minute passes before she moves. Or I fucking breathe. But I refuse to rush her because I want to finally find out what the hell is keeping her from giving herself to me.

Finally, she shakes her head. Slow and determined before a sneer twists her ruby lips. Then a smile. Then a full on laugh. Throwing her head back as she trembles. Cruel and vicious. Thick with a bitterness I've never heard from anyone before.

"The real me, huh? That's what you think? That you know the real me? You're a fool, Julius. A god damn fucking fool."

So many words fill my mind. My heart. My mouth. But never cross my lips. I can't console her. Can't argue or question. She needs to admit what's she's finally been hiding.

"I fucked him."

Animation drains from her face. Hollow as her tone. Strange how quickly she's disappeared inside herself. I speak just as quietly. Refusing to agitate her more. "Who?"

"The man who raped me."

Motherfucker.

"The man who held me against the wall in your club and squeezed my throat and forced his dick inside me as I begged and pleaded and cried for him to stop. But he didn't. He didn't listen. Or care. Or stop. So five years ago I offered myself to him. My very first fucking client—literally. And for ten grand I fucked him."

God damn. "Syd–"

"Shut up." She bellows at me. Her voice raspy and sharp and desperate. "Just shut the fuck up."

My voice pulls her from the memory. She's back. Wild. Furious. At him. At herself. And I'm going to let her take it out on me.

"I fucked him in that same hallway. And this time I didn't beg or plead or cry. I let him. So there's the real me. Your fucking tiny lion. The woman you think you love. That you think you fucking know. I'm nothing but a worthless whore who lets men pay her for sex so she's in control. So I'm in god damn fucking control."

She glares at me. Her small body convulsing. Delicate fingers balled into fists. Chest rising and falling with heaving breaths harder than running a marathon. Because finally stopping from running from the truth takes so much more than hiding.

"Good for you."

Her crazed eyes widen. Not at all expecting that response. A chink in her armor. "You made things on your terms—your way. That's exactly how to fucking handle things. You're in charge. You're the boss. Nobody fucks with you."

Chink. Chink. Chink. With every word I say she softens. Lowering the shield. Letting me see the vulnerability underneath.

"No." She slowly shakes her head. Almost dazed from the reprieve I give. "He can't fuck with me anymore."

No because I'll get his name, and he'll be dead by morning. "You fucking owned him."

She sways. Grasping at the sofa table for balance.

"You fucking own all of us."

One step. Small feet sliding over the carpet.

"Including me."

Another step. Sleek brown boots pushing into the plush strands. I hold out my hand. She makes the decision. She calls the shots. But I have to offer the absolution she so desperately needs.

"I do?"

"Yeah, piccolo leone, you do." Closer and closer until shaking fingers finally touch mine. "You always have and always will."

Fat tears stream down her flushed cheeks. The most emotion I've ever seen her allow. One shuddering breath and then another until a huge sob finally breaks free. I scoop her up. Coiling her slight body to my chest. She doesn't resist yet doesn't cuddle in either. My girl's too tough to permit herself that kind of weakness.

I carry her out of the room and up the stairs to our bedroom. Kissing her forehead before I lay her gently on the silk sheets in my massive bed. My body curving around the ball she's made herself into. Sheathing my chest to her shivering back. Nothing else I can say. Nothing else she wants to hear. So all I do is hold her as she cries.

Sunshine greets me when my eyes blink open. Unaware I'd fallen asleep after soothing her for hours. An even better surprise, she's tucked against me. Curled into the crook of my arm, with her hand wrapped around my waist and her leg draped over mine.

"Hi."

My usually damn jaded heart and always eager dick spring to life from her welcoming inflection. Confirming she cuddled with me of her own volition. She's finally letting me in. "Hi."

"Thank you."

Her gorgeous eyes filled with gratitude as she stares up at me. "For what?"

"For not being completely repulsed by me."

Never. "Like you are of yourself?"

A deep sigh blows across my chest as she nods. Her silky hair tickling my bicep. "Yes. I'm a horrible person."

I shrug against her assertion. Not bothered or believing her in the least. Especially compared to me. "So am I."

She doesn't argue. Unwilling to try and convince me otherwise. Which is what I fucking love about her. She accepts me for my faults and demons. Just like I do her. "No fucking judgment here lion. I love you exactly the way you are."

"I know, and I'm grateful."

I'm fucking grateful when her fingers slide over my bobbing cock desperate to be released from the confines of my pants. I can't remember the last time I slept in my clothes. Or with a woman still wearing hers.

Allowing me to roll her on her back, I prop up on my elbow and stare down at her mascara smeared cheeks and puffy eyes. Still so damn beautiful it hurts me not to be buried inside of her. Thankful she doesn't resist me wanting to fuck her face to face. A solemn tenderness between us that neither of us are used to. Proof once again that we're more than just fucking. Attestation that we're genuine and permanent and indestructible.

Her luscious mouth opens willingly when I dip down and kiss her. Slow and soft while her slender fingers cup my face. Ensuring the connection between us. And trying to control the pace. Ironic since she always accuses me of being stubborn and bossy. I smile against her lips, and she presses back against the pillow. Studying my face. Always damn skeptical too.

"What?"

"Just my lion being a lion."

She feigns irritation but her grin gives her away. "What that hell does that mean?"

"It means take off your fucking clothes so I can fuck you properly."

Her head falls back with laughter. Which I love but don't

have time for. I grab the purple vee neck dipping between her cute tits and rip the material down her body until she's bared to me with only lingerie and boots preventing me from seeing every glorious inch of her.

"Damn it Julius! I liked that dress!"

"I did too."

Her flimsy bra and panties shred just as easy, and my tongue sweeps across her throat before she can bitch anymore at me. Only an appreciative moan vibrating in my ear as I suck in the sensitive skin. The first of many marks she'll receive today from my affection. She returns the favor with urgent tugs of my hair. Yanking the strands with a sting all the way to my scalp. Proving I'm fucking her the way she likes to be fucked when her hands roam down to my belt.

I lift enough for her to release the buckle and drop the zipper. Groaning myself when she frees my cock and lavishes attention over the taut skin. Fuck her touch is incredible. Using the tiny sliver of remaining will power I barely possess, I pause to kick off my shoes and shove down my boxer briefs and pants. "Better get those boots off angel or I'm going to fuck you in them."

While she's sexy as shit in the thigh high leather, I don't want anything keeping her legs from wrapping tight around me. No hesitation at all as she scrambles to sit up and glide them down her calves and elegant feet. Still not fast enough though, and I palm her chest to force her back down on the mattress while I kick at the high heels to remove them from the space I need to fuck her thoroughly and completely.

Enormous eyes watch me with a tentative gaze. Nervous, as well she should be. Because she knows, as she's reminded me before, what I'm capable of. I push her thighs up and wide so I can plunge in hard. Fucking getting off from her lifting her hips to welcome me. Breaking any guise of gentleness I was under before she showed me her glistening pussy. Which she realizes her temptation of me if her scream is any indication when her body slides across the sheets and she slams into the headboard from the force. I cup my hands around the top of her head to protect her as I thrust into her. "Fuck leone you know you need to brace yourself for me."

She fists the damp fabric on my back in an attempt to slow me down, to gain control, to keep up with me. But I don't think it's possible with her pussy spasming so damn hard around me. Already this close to me getting her off.

I forget how petite she is. How the cradle of her hips isn't wide enough to accept me as deep as I want to go. I *need* to go. I flip us over and can't barely force air into my lungs with her looking down at me with such pure and utter desire. With her gorgeous tits bouncing from me gliding her back and forth on my cock. With her dainty fingers gripping my forearms flexing from the force of me gripping her hips to drive farther inside her. Again and again until her back arches away from me.

"Too much." She swallows hard and licks her lips. Struggling to catch her breath and steady herself on my stomach. Fucking incredible with damp strands of hair sticking to her cheeks and forehead. A hot beautiful mess. "I can feel you in my kidneys Saint."

Fuck! I'm hurting her. I need to fucking check myself so I don't break her. "Then fuck me how you want to lion."

I loosen my hold but can't let her go completely. Caressing down her slick arms, her drenched back, her soaked thighs while she resumes a slower pace. Sliding up and down my throbbing cock. Clenching tighter as she chases her release. Digging her short nails into my chest.

When she whispers my name, I can't hold back. I sit up and take over. She's going to watch while I come inside her. I tangle in her silky locks and yank back, forcing her eyes open. Using my free hand to push off the bed to ensure I pump my seed inside her as far as possible. *"I've tamed you."*

Her little body stiffens against me. Wanting to fight but knowing even more that it's true.

"I own you."

Ragged breaths blow on my cheeks. Her hips riding me as much as I'm rutting into her. Taking me like I knew she could.

"I love you."

Finally the crazed nod and cry of relief I've been waiting for. She jerks against me over and over as the orgasm rips through her. Pinching my biceps as she clutches me while she flies.

"I love you too."

Fuck me. I lose what's left of my mind and all of my restraint from her finally telling me. Shooting with so much intensity I buck into her like a damn animal unable to think of anything else but filling her up with my baby. Creating the family we're going to have. Ensuring she's connected to me forever through our children.

She collapses against me, and I nuzzle into her smooth shoulder. Feeling my own heavy breaths on my hand as I stroke her satin skin while I recover. "Sorry. That was supposed to be sweet love making."

"You're not capable."

Her contented laugh vibrates on my neck. "You're right. Not with you."

We float in our own bliss for a few more minutes, but I

can't fully relax until I know the rest of the story. "Don't get all riled up but I want to know what happened. Who is this motherfucker who hurt you?"

"Does it really matter now?"

She doesn't sound angry but I am. "Of course it fucking matters. Now stop fucking around and tell me."

I wait impatiently. Hugging her tighter against me so she remembers there's nothing to fear from me except me fucking her too hard. I keep rubbing her back while she snuggles into my chest.

"Ryan played baseball and everyone said he was good enough to go pro. Which he was I guess, because he got signed. We had a lot of mutual friends and when they went out to celebrate him making it, he asked me to go. I was excited. I really liked him and thought maybe we'd start dating."

With my free hand I wrap the comforter around her waist and across her legs although I know her trembling isn't because she's cold. Or maybe it's me who's shaking her that hard. Every detail raging inside me from this bastard.

"I only had one drink but he got pretty drunk and when he asked me to go outside with him to get some air I thought it was a good idea." Her voice falls so low but the anguish screams at me from what she's leading up to. "When we were in the hallway he pushed me inside the alcove by the restrooms and started kissing me. I was embarrassed because he was grinding into me right there where everyone walking by could see. But he was so strong. I couldn't stop him. I tried but I couldn't fight him off."

My damn club. Anything goes when people are paying. I don't give a damn how drunk or high they get. But not fucking that. Not fucking assault. If I'd only known I'd have beat him dead right then and there, and I could've protected her from the torment.

"It was like one of those weird out of body experiences. All I could think is that he's raping me with all these people around and no one has any idea."

Son of a bitch. Probably a shit load of people would have helped if they'd known. Including me.

"Anyway, my parents disowned me after they found out, and I had to find a way to pay for school. I was on scholarship but still had rent and my car payment and everything. My sorority sister worked for Belle's and made it sound so great. I could make minimum wage at the mall or thousands in one night. I didn't really have any choice. I couldn't stay in school and make it on my own."

"I don't like it but I get it." I kiss her temple as her head rests against me. "I understand now how desperate you were."

"After his friends found out they taunted him about being able to afford an elite escort so he hired me and I fucked him. I guess it's stupid but I felt like it would make everything okay because I made the decision. I made *him* do what *I* wanted. But it didn't make it okay. I still felt…" Her voice cracks, and she sighs a shuddering breath to calm her emotions. "I still hated myself."

Should be the exact fucking opposite. "Nothing to hate lion. You're a fucking bad ass."

I swear I feel her smile against my skin despite her agony. Hopefully reassured from a compliment which is a thousand percent true. No bullshit at all.

"I guess I have to be to have tamed you."

Now we both chuckle. Her because she thinks she's right, and me because she's fucking adorable. Crazy but cute to think that. But I'll let her believe it because I love her.

We cuddle for a few more minutes before she wiggles off my lap. My softened dick falling out of her, missing her already. Without much effort he could be ready and willing to fuck her again. But she's spent and only gives me a sleepy smile as she steps onto the carpet. Gathering up her ruined clothes but failing to chastise me for destroying her outfit, which is another surprise.

Oblivious to anything else from her exhaustion, I swipe my phone and text the details I've got to Phillip. Not much, but enough for Mitch to find him. Instructing that once he's found I'm going to personally be the one to deliver the punishment well overdo for this cocksucker.

"Are you coming?"

An involuntary smile curls my lips from her gorgeous face and small hand she holds out, enticing me to join her. I can already hear the difference in her voice and see the liberation in her relaxed body. That my feelings haven't change. That I'm proud of her. That I love her even more than I did before.

I gladly accept her invitation and her kiss on my cheek after I rise. We'll take this bath together and permanently wash away all the remaining reminders of him in her heart and her mind. Then once I'm finished with him, he'll vanish permanently from this world.

CHAPTER 20

DON'T KNOW WHY I'M NERVOUS.

It's Mack. My friend. My *best* friend. Who just wants me to be happy. My stomach twirls again. Or so I thought. When I called to tell him I'm home and I'm in love and I'm offering him another job working for Julius, he wasn't happy at all. About any of it. Hopefully, in person, I can explain things to him better and make him understand how much I miss him. How much I need him.

I sign the receipt and hand the clipboard back to the older woman. Still smiling as she hands me the duplicate copy from the enormous donation they're collecting since Julius won't allow anything from my old life to be brought into my new one with him. Of course I'm keeping my diploma, a few photos, and my grandmother's wedding china. Everything else is being hauled away. All the furniture, clothes, and non-perishables belong to the Sacred Heart Thrift Shop and Food Pantry.

Now I wait for Mack. Optimistic that meeting at my apartment to give him the few things I have of his will be easier than talking at Julius's house. Kind of neutral territory. Well, more emotional than neutral. After years of chats about the book he was enjoying or the girl he was flirting with at the coffee bar down the street or the battle his cousin was facing when the cancer returned. Everything we would share with each other during the time spent with him escorting me from the customer's door to my own.

"Hey."

I spin around from sliding a saucer into bubble wrap from his bleak voice behind me. "Hey! It's so good to see you."

Using my full hands as an excuse not to hug him. Out of respect for Julius who talks on his phone in the bedroom. Unreasonable for him to forbid me from touching another man but I've learned to accept his jealous streak along with his other flaws just as he's accepted all of mine. Both of us recognizing our imperfections and trying not to exacerbate them for each other. And, I don't want to argue in front of Mack.

Although I'm a little hurt Mack doesn't attempt to embrace me either. "How have you been?"

"Worried out of my mind."

Damn. I knew he wasn't going to make this easy but I never dreamed he'd be so upset. "I know. I'm sorry."

He nods and looks around. Confusion lining his face from only my boxes left in the empty space. Until the realization hits him, and he swears under his breath. "You're moving in with him?"

Now I'm the one to nod. The whirlwind romance too complicated to explain. I don't think he wants to hear the details anyway.

"That's just crazy, Syd. Fucking crazy."

This time I laugh. Trying to confirm I recognize the absurdity of the situation too. Yet he doesn't join the merriment. Instead he walks around the living room. His sneakers silent on the beige swirl carpet as if he's inspecting the place for the first time even though he's been here a hundred times.

"I had plans for us."

Not at all what I was expecting him to say. Now it's my turn to inspect him. Trying to garner clues from his face of what he implies. Although his slack expression is devoid of any emotion. "Plans?"

"Yeah." His head bobs a few times. Slow and deep with contemplation only he seems to understand. Yet he never meets my gaze. His focus drawn toward Julius's voice wafting from down the hall. "I was biding my time until it was my turn."

"Your turn?"

I sound like an imbecile. Parroting everything he says. Dumbfounded as hot fear flickers in my chest. Something's off with him. Something's really off.

"I knew you didn't care about any of them. You were just fucking them because you were hiding from something in your past. That you never admitted to me." His furious eyes catch mine. "But you probably did to him didn't you? You told Julius why you were hurting yourself?"

Sweat rolls down my back despite the chill engulfing me. Too frightened to answer because I know the answer will only infuriate him more.

"I knew you were this close…" He holds his thick finger and thumb apart a few inches, raising his hand to his eye, peering at me through the narrow width. "This fucking close to retirement, and I would have you all to myself. We could finally be together. Until that bastard ruined it."

Nodding toward the corridor, he unbuttons his jacket and pushes the gray fabric to the side. Revealing a thick black holster stuffed with a gun that I didn't even know he owned. Never aware he carried a weapon when he guarded me.

He slides the Glock out of the strap, training the barrel on the doorway leading to Julius. The delicate pink plate slips from my trembling hand. Bouncing and rolling off the stack of brown packing paper. Splintering from a crack I'm too terrified to be upset about. "Why do you have that?"

"I thought I was coming here to save you. That I needed to rescue you from him. I guess I don't."

"N-no." I take a calming breath. Praying the soothing motion will relax him too. "I'm okay. I'm not his prisoner anymore."

"That's so sick. You're fucking sick in the head that you'd rather be with a man who kidnapped you than one who loves you and takes care of you like I do."

"You motherfucker!"

Julius.

Oh shit. I put my hands up trying to stop him. Stop Mack. Stop everything. But it's useless. Too damn late as both of them aim their weapons at each other. I can't reason with Julius when he's like this so I try to reach my friend. "Please Mack. Don't do this. We can figure this out. I love you."

"No you don't. You love him."

I do. As much as I hate it I love Julius, and he doesn't deserve to die because of me. I force a smile on my face and an agreeable tone in a frantic attempt to sway him. "I'll give him up. I swear. It'll be you and me, okay? We'll be together just like we used to be. You'll take care of me just like you always did, and I'll–"

"I know we will."

Deadness takes over his expression and his body stiffens. The decision made in his mind.

Mine too.

I jump in front of Julius, but jerk backward when fire lights through me. Tumbling to the floor. My elbow scraping across the rough texture. But my arm doesn't hurt as much as my chest. Wet and hot and throbbing.

The ground feels really good though. I'm so very tired and want to lie down. I'm cold too. Shivering in the fading light. While people scream and argue. Mack falls down too. I guess he's sleepy like me.

Strong hands lift me.

Julius.

He's sad and mad and worried. Shaking me. Stroking my hair. Pressing his lips against my skin. Saying words I don't understand. He knows I don't speak Italian.

I try to tell him I love him and I'm sorry and I didn't mean to hurt him with what I said. But my mouth won't seem to work right. My tongue arguing with my chattering teeth as I grasp for his shirt. Although I can't seem to reach the fabric. Red now instead of white.

"Don't close your eyes lion. Don't you dare fucking close your eyes."

Silly Saint. Always yelling. Doesn't he remember I never obey? That I'm too damn stubborn for my own good? Like always, I ignore his demands and let the warm, sweet darkness swallow me.

If I wasn't holding my lion's tiny hand, I would punch this motherfucker in his god damn mouth. Spewing on and on about the shit they've done to try and help her when all of it means nothing with her still unconscious. Still trapped in this bed with too many wires going who knows where in her frail body. Still terrifying me that she'll never open those gorgeous jade eyes for me again.

"Mr. Sabatini please know we're doing everything we can for your fiancée."

Wife. She should be my wife. We should be on our honeymoon. I should be fucking her every second of every day to make her belly round from my baby growing within her.

Instead she doesn't even have a damn ring. Fuck. So much shit I was going to do. Say. Fix. Buy. Until that motherfucking cocksucking bastard tried to steal her from me.

"Sir?"

I cannot listen to his shit any more. "Get out."

"Excuse me."

Indignation sharpens the physician's voice that has nothing on the rage I feel for him. This asshole is going to die if I have to unwrap my fingers from hers. Without taking my focus off of her, I slide out my gun and point it at him. Not even bothering to use words to threaten him. Less than one second later the door swings open and bangs closed again. Good riddance.

I lay my Glock next to her leg as a warning to any other idiots who think they want to come in here and run their mouths at me. I lean forward and kiss her forehead, cool under my lips. "I know lion, I know. I overreacted but he had it coming."

The knob clicks again from Phillip stepping inside. Smart enough to remain silent about what just happened since I know he knows from the troubled look on his face.

"Your grandmother will be here in about an hour. Paolo is bringing her up."

Since Sydney won't wake up for me, hopefully she will

for Nonna. Who can stay with her while I take care of the other motherfucker who hurt her. "You have the other situation under control."

"Yes, he's ready and waiting for you as instructed."

Which means not even a hair on his stupid prick head has been ruffled. I get to have all the fun of making him suffer. I'm going to fucking love doing this for her. She'll know without a doubt how much I love her.

With nothing left to report, he heads back to his post in the hallway. Good. I like having her all to myself. I stroke Joslyn's bracelet on her narrow wrist. The jewelry would slide right off if she wasn't lying down. Jos always swore the leather wrap would keep me safe so I know Syd needs it more than me right now. She probably should've been fucking wearing the good luck charm all along. "Did I ever tell you the meaning behind it?"

I chuckle a bit from the memory of Jos's enthusiasm from presenting the heartfelt gift to me. The man who always wears custom ten thousand dollar suits pairing them with a ten-dollar trinket she bought at one of the granola, hipster music festivals she loved. "The thicker pieces on each side represent us as twins. The thin middle strand is our connection. If you pull hard enough the pieces will tear apart, but she said we would never let that happen."

Pain that always stabs my chest when I think of her radiates through my body. A throbbing cocktail of regret from the past and fear of losing this future pounds in my muscles. "She was a really good sister. You would've liked her. When you get better I'll tell you more stories. I'll tell you anything you want to know if you just open your eyes lion."

Nothing. Only the rise and fall of the damn ventilator forcing air into her lungs. I hate these fucking machines.

I run my fingertips down her pale cheek. Ignoring the stupid, ugly tube stuffed in her dainty mouth. Making my stomach turn from thinking about it being snaked down her throat. Wishing she would smile from my touch. Maybe she will from my confession. Women like being told they're right. At least that's what I've heard since I've never actually told any since I'm the one who's always right. Except this time. "You know every single thing you've accused me of is true. All of it. I'm crazy and stubborn and selfish. But with you I should have been different. I should've been better."

For the first time ever, I have to admit what I never thought I could. To say the words I never thought would cross my lips. "I'm sorry."

Fear steals my voice that she may never hear my apology but I keep going. "Of all people, I shouldn't have been an asshole to you. But I'm going to make it up to you. I will make the people pay who hurt you. I will always protect you even if it's from me. I will try my damnedest to ensure you're happy being with me."

I lay my head down on our coupled hands. Waiting, waiting, waiting for her to respond. Gutting me when she doesn't.

Orders bark from the hallway in a frail yet decisive voice. Never underestimate a worried grandmother. Phillip's head appears in the window before the door opens, and she shuffles in. Her wrinkled hands flying into the air in almost a touchdown pose from her distraught realization of how bad things really are. She hugs me from the side. Perfect so that I don't have to release Syd any sooner than I need to.

"Three days is too long for her to be asleep. I will make these doctors do more and take better care of her."

Oh shit. Now she's the one on the rampage. I grab my

gun and tuck it back into my waistband in case she gets any wild ideas of shooting up the place. *"You do that Nonna. You kick their asses."*

She nods. Definitive and done. Confirming I'm leaving my lion in good hands while I'm gone. *"I have to take care of something but I'll be back soon."*

"Yes, I will watch over her."

I kiss Syd and then Nonna before hustling out into the corridor. All gazes hit the floor as I stride down the hallway and wait for the elevator. Relieved that no one is going to say a fucking word to me unless it's to tell me she's okay. Otherwise, I don't want to hear it.

CHAPTER 21

I WATCH HIM FOR A LONG MINUTE.

He's been in there for hours. You'd think he'd be exhausted. Pacing back and forth in the small room. Running his hands over and over his buzz cut. Peering into the blackened window that reveals nothing of the dungeon on the other side. Must be running on adrenaline.

I tell myself to have patience. Use restraint. Maintain control. But Sydney's condition has released the beast within. Needing to unleash the monster craving damage and destruction and devastation. I rarely get to let him out with all the enforcers on my payroll. Sometimes you just have to do things yourself. Especially when you're going to fucking enjoy the hell out of it.

I grab one of the bats propped against the wall and shove open the door. His worried gaze meets mine and shock traps him in place while I stride toward him. Already winding up a huge swing as I walk. A glorious crack of wood against skull and then nose to concrete as he topples from the force. Seeping blood slowly dying his white blond hair to red.

He lays motionless on his side. But I'm not ready for him to be unconscious yet. I kick him hard enough to flip him onto his back but not enough to hurt him. That's what my slugger is for. A gurgling moan bubbles in his throat as he clutches his brutalized head.

Good. He's awake.

I get close enough for him to hear me but not soil my loafers. I don't want to have to take time to change into clean shoes before I get back to my lion. *"Game's over dumb ass. You lost."*

A garbled attempt at begging is the only answer I receive. Gesturing to Carlos and Zach, they hustle to do my bidding. Lifting the asshole onto the torture table that I hope is fucking freezing against his bare arms and mangled scalp. They don't even have to strap him down he's so damn out of it.

The metal vibrates like the chiming of bells from me tapping the tip of the bat on the beveled edge. Giving dumb pussy ass Ryan a little taste of what's to come. Of the pain he's going to endure. Of the suffering I'm going to love doling out to him. His mutilated head attempts to twist side to side. Which is kind of difficult with ripped skin and a few pieces of bone missing. Fuck if I'm not relishing his well-deserved agony.

His scream echoes across the concrete as I break his right hand first. No more pitching.

Then his left. No more catching.

Then each foot. No more running or sliding home.

Lifting my arms above my head, I use every ounce of strength to crash the sweet spot down onto his crotch. My hands ache from the reverberation of the impact, and his body flops in spasm a few times before white sticky vomit spews out of his mouth.

Well fucking look at that I gave him a seizure. He's out, and I'm gratified. Privileged to retaliate in Sydney's behalf.

Honored to beat the hell out of him when she couldn't. Now he can lay there and suffer until he dies. Just like he deserves.

Carlos gives me an approving nod. "Damn boss. That was quick and brutal."

The guys admire my work. Making sure to avoid the chunks and ooze while they circle around his limp body. Probably a little jealous they weren't the ones to inflict the abuse. Hell, the way I'm feeling I might kidnap some more of the men from her past life, and then I'll let them have their fun. "Call me if he comes to and I'll come back and finish the job. Otherwise, you know what to do."

I pause in my quick steps down the corridor when I catch sight of Ryan's league photo on the screen in the empty waiting room. The announcer conveying a troubled tone regarding the baseball star's sudden disappearance. Ensuring that viewers understand the gravity of the situation with his car inexplicably abandoned on a country road with his cell phone and wallet still inside. Obviously, not robbery. Detectives are thoroughly investigating every angle to determine how, why, and when he went missing. Yeah, good luck with that boys.

The satisfaction from ending Syd's tormentor evaporates instantly from Nonna shaking her head furiously at a confused man outside of the lion's room. I draw my weapon, and point it at his face until I'm up on him and press the barrel into his forehead. The black case in his shaking hands clatters to the floor, and his arms fly up in immediate surrender. Good. This motherfucker knows who the fuck I am and how quickly he's going to die if he doesn't explain himself very, very soon.

"Boss! It's the jeweler you wanted me to call."

Phillip's deep voice rises above all the gasps and shuffling of feet from the other people in the hallway retreating out of the line of fire. Well fuck. Why didn't someone say so? Damn tired of being the only fucking person protecting my woman, I shove my gun back into its spot again and swipe the metal box from the tile. Assuming the rings I want to inspect are inside. Old man's on our heels, all red faced and flustered, while I escort Nonna through the door. Not sure why he's still upset, everything's fine now.

"M-Mr. Sabatini, if you'll allow me please, I'll unlock the case and show you the selection you've requested."

He seems calm when I hand the thick container to him although it takes him three tries to type in the code and unlatch the clasp. Well worth tolerating his ineptitude once he reveals the sparkling rocks inside. They're all massive and luxurious and perfect for the woman amazing enough to be my wife. I tug a square diamond out of a slit in the black velvet and hold it up to the light. Spreading tiny rainbows across the white walls from the glistening stone.

"An excellent choice. It's an extremely rare colorless solitaire with almost flawless clarity. A little less than thirteen carats in a cushion cut flanked with two carats hugging each side."

Rare like my lion. "It's her size?"

"Yes sir. We matched the ring your assistant provided."

Perfect. I nod toward Phillip waiting in the doorway. "He'll pay you."

Relieved from my dismissal, the jeweler gathers up his stuff and eagerly follows my captain. While I'm eager too.

I slide the platinum band on lion's delicate finger and smile from her sheer beauty as well as Nonna's admiration of my choice. Of my woman and of her new ring. My grandmother's brown eyes shiny with happy tears. Murmuring as she pats my back and praises me over what a good boy I am. Although I'm neither good nor a boy, I appreciate her approval just the same. Comforted when she sits next to me so we can keep vigil together.

Yet now I'm fucking aggravated again. Her pale lips look dry. Chapped from the damn plastic hose constantly forcing them apart. Her skin too cold to the touch. A tinge of blue in her fingertips. Her long hair tangled around one of the wires leading to her heart monitor. Fucking hell. No one allows my lion to suffer. Including me. I yank out my phone and pound the keyboard to order Phillip to get someone the fuck in here for her.

I lift the cover to tuck her arm underneath and slide the hem up to her throat. Plenty of time for someone to get their ass in here.

"Yes, Mr. Sabatini."

I'd shoot a man for talking to me with that condescending tone. She's damn lucky Nonna is here or she would expand her vocabulary of swear words from my usual tirade. Instead I slowly rise up to my full height—all six, six of me—and turn with my gaze already burning into her. Now my lion would stand her ground but this rude chick stumbles backward with every stride I make toward her. Closing the space between Syd's bed and the door, now glued shut with the woman's back pressed against the wood. I stare down at her. Relishing her fidgeting in terror. "I need blankets and some chap stick for my fiancée. Do you think you could manage to get me some?"

"Of course. Not a problem."

Yeah, I didn't think it would be.

After she hightails her patronizing ass out of here, Nonna tsks in disapproval. "I do not like her. She does not take care of Sydney the way she should."

"I know but we don't have to worry. I think she'll be better in the future."

Or she won't be back at all if Phillip walking in with a stack of white quilts and a tiny yellow tube of lip balm is any indication. Nonna takes both out of his hands, busying herself with tending to Syd while my captain casually tosses his head. Trying not to alert my grandmother that he needs to talk to me. That's something's really fucking wrong for him to have to give me an update that will take me out of this room.

"This better be fucking important."

He blows out a deep breath. Not sure if he's preparing me or himself. I open my mouth to tell him to hurry the fuck up. But he jumps in before I can admonish him.

"You're going to have to calm down. The hospital administrator is on his way up here to talk to you because you've fired three doctors, scared the shit out of the nurses with all your yelling, and pulled your gun twice in front of witnesses."

Damn. I do know better than to leave witnesses. "I give zero fucks about any of this."

"I know you don't care but they're talking about banning you from the property if it doesn't stop. Then you won't be able to see her."

This will be a god damn war zone if anyone thinks they can keep me from her. I will kill every motherfucker who tries to stop me from being with my lion. I don't give a fuck who they are. "Okay."

"Boss?"

His blue eyes blink several times in astonishment. I'm not usually so agreeable. Especially to unsolicited advice. Probably the first, only, and last time I've ever heeded his warning.

I snarl through clenched teeth. He should be happy I haven't punched him in his. "I said okay. But don't ever nag me again or I'll fucking end you."

Ignoring the threat, he glances around again to ensure no one's nearby. "We've located her friend. We should have her in a few hours. Do you want me to bring her up?"

Thank fuck. "Yeah, get Nonna out of here first." I glance at my watch. Already past seven. I'm losing fucking hours up here. "Take her home for dinner. Lydia can put her to bed. Then have Bex bring Val up."

The second person they've kidnapped today. Hopefully this discussion will be just as rewarding.

CHAPTER 22

I LIFT MY FOREHEAD FROM THE MATTRESS, AND MY GAZE SHOOTS straight to lion's face. I must have drifted off for a second and wish I could kick my own ass for being a weak bastard. I can't miss her waking up. I can't miss those fierce eyes opening for me. I can't miss her slim fingers reaching for me. I scrub down the scruff on my face. I didn't miss a damn thing. She remains silent and still. Both qualities I fucking hate in her and for her because they definitely aren't her.

My back and neck throb from being hunched over for so long. I massage my shoulder before checking my buzzing phone. Better be good news.

The End.

It's better than good. Fucking fantastic. Baseball bastard's dead. I twist the cell around and show her the text. "Look angel. You never have to worry about Ryan again. So wake up, and we'll celebrate."

I guess she's not in the mood. I kiss her anyway. Warm and soft just like she should be. "If only I'd gotten to punish Mack the same way. That's a regret I'll always have. I'm sorry I let you down."

She doesn't seem mad. "Is there anyone else you want me to take care of? Any other men who hurt you? Say the word and I'll kill them. I'll be damn thrilled to kill anyone else you want. All you have to do is ask. Or even if you don't, I'll do it anyway."

The god's truth although my offer doesn't faze her. She keeps snoozing. Making me wonder if she hears me. Thinks of me. Dreams of me. Damn. I just want to be in there with her. To heal her broken body and bring her back to me.

Voices argue in the hallway. Hushed and stilted but still upset. That shit better stop before they upset my lion. Suddenly the corridor is quiet except for the squeak of the door. Phillip half leads, half drags a shaking woman into the room.

"I told you we're not going to hurt you."

The lady ignores Phillip's assertion and exasperation. I'm sure he's reiterated that to her several times already but I legit understand why she doesn't believe him. Hell I wouldn't either if I was in her situation. Her brown wide eyes meet mine and trembling hands fly to the basketball size bump under her dress. God damn we've kidnapped a pregnant woman. Shit.

Since she's almost as petite as lion, I remain seated. Attempting not to scare her any more than we already have with another big man hulking over her. I flip my palms up to confirm I mean her no harm. "He's telling you the truth Mrs. Vernon. I just want you to talk to Sydney. Then you can go."

Her gaze jerks to her friend laid out on the bed like a damn science experiment with all the shit in her and on her. Her shoulders droop, upset by Sydney's condition.

"Oh no."

Treating her with the respect she deserves, like Syd would want, I keep my voice soft and slowly motion for her to come closer. "Please just talk to her. You might help her wake up."

Rare for me to be this polite and earnest. Must be lion rubbing off on me. My girl's a good influence.

A cautious step forward, and she glances at me. Double checking my reaction or lack thereof. I keep my ass pinned to the seat, and she seems to trust that I'm not going to attack her. Walking forward until she's near enough to pat Syd's calf. As close as she'll dare with me sitting a foot away.

"What happened to her?"

"She was shot. Took a bullet meant for me."

I hate saying the fucking words. Loathe to admit the disgusting truth. Livid at Syd for doing it and myself for allowing it.

Val's hand flies to her mouth unable to conceal her gasp or horror. Neither of us have to pretend I'm not who I am nor deny the criminal aspect of my reputation. That's not what this is about. "I need her to be okay."

Kind of declaring the obvious since Syd's recovery is the only reason she's here. But I need her to understand my desperation. My fear. My weakness.

Luckily, it's also obvious that she understands them completely and nods. Her eyes full of sympathy I don't deserve as she stares at my huge hand coupled with her friend's.

"Okay, I'll try."

That's all I can ask.

Taking a deep breath, she keeps her focus on my woman. "I've missed you. I'm sorry this happened to you. But when you get better we can catch up." She looks at me. Uncertainty pinching her face. Seeking my approval. When I nod, she offers a tentative smile and sits down in the chair beside mine. Encouraged enough to go all in.

Grateful, I keep my mouth shut. Listening to her tell

lion about her pregnancy, the names she and her husband, who's an accountant by the way, are considering, that Kristi is going to be the godmother but they haven't picked a god-father yet since her brother-in-law is a jack wagon.

A slight blush warms her cheeks from my chuckle. No wonder Syd likes this lady. I don't comment beyond my laugh, unwilling to stifle her, and she keeps going. Filling her in on her job that she loves as a creative director for a small public relations firm but might quit after the baby is born. Detailing some of the campaigns she's worked on. Did Syd see the billboards for the new organic supermarket? Maybe she could work part-time. But she's worried then she'll fail at both.

After twenty minutes she finally peters out. As disappointed as I am that Sydney hasn't responded to any of her stories.

"I'm sorry."

Me too. "I appreciate you trying. Thank you."

This time she directs her comments to me. "She's still so beautiful. I really have missed her."

"What happened between the two of you?"

"I don't really know. We didn't have a fight or anything like that. Our weekends were busy with clients. I…" Some realization seems to hit her and her face pales. "My husband…he doesn't know I worked for Belle's."

While blackmail and coercion are my specialties, I'd never use the tactics on her. Lion would never forgive me. I shake my head with an absolute conviction. "I will never tell him. You have my word."

"Okay. Thank you." She does that weird nervous thing girls with long hair do where they shake the hair over their scalp and then flip the strands to the other side. Looking exactly the same as they did before. "We still hung out through the week but it just seemed like she drifted away. I don't think she ever really recovered from what happened with her Dad."

She sighs with regret that I don't understand and begins to stand. I wrap my free hand around her wrist. Preventing her from moving. Scaring her as bad as when she first got here. Being a fucking bastard but I have to know. "Please. Tell me about her parents."

I let go. Well aware if she tries to run Phillip will stop her. But I don't want to chase her down. I just want her to explain to me why Sydney doesn't speak to her family since she never would.

I allow her to stand this time. Aware she needs to feel free. To reassure herself she's safe. Her hand returns to her belly, and she strokes absentmindedly. Grounding herself before she speaks. "She told them what happened…that she was raped." Her voice cracks along with my knuckles. An involuntary habit that makes her startle. "He blamed her. He said she must have done something that made him do it. He called her a whore and told her he never wanted to see her again."

Son of a fucking bitch. What a god damn asshole.

"I never understood why he treated her like that. My father would never do that no matter what."

Mine would but that's to be expected in my world. These girls should be treated like princesses. Undeserving of that bullshit. "I don't understand either."

She sighs and glances down at the slim silver watch on her wrist. "It's getting late and I need to go. But I can come back tomorrow after work, if that's okay. I want to help her if I can."

"Thank you."

I should say more. Display more gratitude and appreciation. But my mind's already moved on to what I need to do to keep my earlier promise to lion. Another man who hurt her is going to die.

With an awkward wave, she scurries back to the hallway, and I pick up Sydney's hand again. Entwining her fingers in mine while we wait for Phillip to check in. Anxious to give him his next assignment.

CHAPTER 23

"**H**E'S DEAD."

Son of a bitch. Phillip's finally grown a pair of balls that I'm unfortunately going to have to slice off slowly and painfully for defying me. No one dies until I order it or I kill them my damn self. Which is exactly what I wanted to do with Sydney's bastard father. I guess Phillip can infer the irritation on my face because he jumps in with more details before I can even respond.

"Brain tumor. From the records Mitch accessed, it looks like the cancer was diagnosed in July before Sydney's senior year and then he died in October." He scrolls down the screen reading more while I try to calculate the timing from what limited information Syd shared with me. "Aggressive and un-treatable. He suffered from headaches, dizziness, confusion, memory loss, and personality changes, so they ran a bunch of tests and found it. Really bad off at the end with paranoia, hallucinations, seizures, and physical attacks against his wife and the hospital staff."

Fuck. He's been gone all this time, and she had no idea. God damn. I fall back against the cushion. She's been berating herself because of someone who literally wasn't in his right mind. Ruining her life because she thought he didn't want to talk to her. Destroying herself because she believed he never wanted to see her again.

All of which crushes me because she's been suffering for no reason. I lean forward again and cup her silky cheek. Comforting her from grief she doesn't even know about yet. "What about her Mom?"

He taps a few more times. "After he died, she moved to Arizona and lives with her cousin. Works as an aide at the elementary school. Not much else. Doesn't look like she dates anyone or goes out much. Doesn't even own a car. Takes the bus to work. Keeps to herself."

Probably suffering from fucking guilt as well she should be. She may not have been able to keep her husband from breaking Syd's heart, but she sure as hell could have reached out to her daughter on her own.

"Do you want the guys to go and get her?"

"No. Not yet."

"Okay. Whatever you want boss."

His tone isn't as confident as his words. He's questioning me. Hell I'm questioning myself. I haven't really slept in almost five days. I'm fucking exhausted. My damn head is pounding, and sometimes I literally can't see straight. Wavy lines rolling in front of my eyes marring my view of my lion. But I'm not sure if I can sleep even if I tried.

"One more thing. Detective Clark is on his way up for you to sign your statement."

Fucking great. Dumb ass is just trying to annoy me because he can't pin anything on me. Ironic that I'm actually innocent this time. Except for failing my lion. It should fucking be me in that bed instead of her. "I don't want him in here with her. Find a place for us to meet so I can get it over with."

"Will do."

The quiet, red-haired nurse sweeps in with her cart of supplies as my captain leaves. Her gaze locked on her towels refusing to look at or address me. I know she's terrified, but I think she's naturally timid too. Which is fine. I'm not in the mood to talk either. She can bathe lion while I take care of this prick. Relieved she won't be alone while I'm gone.

Motherfucker stalls for as long as he can. Making a lot of lame insinuations and daring me to challenge him with a bunch of bullshit insults. I let all of his antics roll off me until he finally gives up and shoves the tablet across the desk to sign. Not that I can claim to be that tolerant but despite how spent I am I have enough wits about me not to get my ass hauled downtown. Don't want to waste a fucking second waiting for my lawyer and the cops on my payroll to garner my release when I should be with Syd.

I toss the stylus toward his disappointed face and stride away. Missing her so much my body actually hurts. Fire hotter than hell blazes through my muscles as I sprint closer to her room. The door is open. The door is never fucking open. Privacy. Noise. Germs. I'm not sure why but the damn door is never open. And her bed is never empty.

She's gone.

The woman I love is gone.

Just crumpled sheets and quiet machines remain behind.

Hell the fuck no.

I spin back around. Scanning both directions of the hallway. Nothing and no one. Pain radiates out from my chest, and I can't catch my breath but I keep moving. I keep running to find my lion. My shoes pounding on the white tile. My pulse pounding in my ears. My heart pounding against my rib cage.

Around the corner, the first doctor I fired stares at a tablet. His thick black glasses perch on the edge of his nose before they smash to the floor when I grab him. Shoving him against the wall with my forearm jammed in his throat. I push and push until his eyes bulge from the force. Clawing at my skin and kicking at my legs. "Where the fuck is she? Where the fuck is Sydney?"

He tries to shake his head. A slight movement fighting against my weight crushing his windpipe. He's out of his god damn fucking mind to think I'm going to accept he doesn't know. Or that he's not going to help me find her.

Hands grip my shoulders. My arms. My waist. Pulling me off of him. My damn men have the fucking audacity to try and stop me from fucking killing him. Fucking killing anyone who keeps her from me.

I swing out. Clipping Bex in the jaw and then Tobias in the gut. Before Phillip's voice booms through the chaos. "She started coming to and freaked out. They're sedating her and repairing the damage to her wound from her fighting them."

Coming to.

Freaked out.

Fighting them.

Lion. My body sags as my weary mind races to catch up. To understand the meaning of his explanation. To revel in the relief of his description.

I find him in the crowd of faces. Swimming together as I fight the dizziness trying to take me down. He better be telling the fucking truth. He better be telling me the straight up fucking honest truth, or I will murder him where he stands. "Take me to her."

He nods. He's calm. I'm calm. The doctor sprawled on

his ass trying to suck in oxygen isn't calm and I don't give a damn. He got what he deserved.

My guys part the way like I'm fucking Moses, and I follow Phillip down the hall. Ignoring the grumbles of shock and disgust and reprimand from the staff. Fuck them. Fuck all of them. They don't know jack shit, or they wouldn't have let this happen. They would've made sure she was fucking okay before they let her panic and hurt herself.

Phillip pauses, well aware he's in my damn way. I slam through the gray double doors marked *No Admittance*. Ready to scoop her up and take care of her. Never leave her again. Never fucking fail her again.

Garnering disapproving scowls from the staff as I hustle down the hall, I scan each surgical suite until I find her. A blue sheet draped over her frail body as a woman in green scrubs, her face obscured by a huge white mask, blots the blood on lion's chest. Syd doesn't move or speak or look. Just lies there mute and motionless. God damn it.

The quiet nurse from earlier stops talking with the doctor next to her and twists around. Giving me the first genuine smile I've received since we got here. No reason for her to be fucking happy when they've broken her again. When these incompetent assholes have made her unconscious again. "What the fuck did you do to her?"

All of her cheerfulness fades from my question. Actually everyone freaks the fuck out. Standing fucking still as statues while they gape at me. Like I'm the one with the fucking problem for screaming. Like I'm the one who's fucking crazy. Like I'm the one who shouldn't be losing his shit.

Only the man next to her is fucking brave enough to approach me. To finally speak up and tell me what the fuck is going on. "I'm Dr. Shelton, Mr. Sabatini. Sydney woke up much quicker than we expected and was in severe distress. We had to take her back under so she wouldn't hurt herself further. But we'll bring her back out. This is only temporary."

Thank fucking god. "You better not be lying to me."

Seemingly offended by my threat, his expression hardens yet his gaze fails to waver from mine. "I'm sorry you're upset, but this is what Sydney needs to recover from her trauma."

This son of a bitch has no idea what she needs. What I need. How much I need her.

"After she…"

He's interrupted by the ruckus in the corridor behind us. My name being taken in vain. Which isn't the first time and won't be the last.

"We need to speak to Mr. Sabatini."

The physician shakes his head at the furious man who steps inside, denying his request. "Let him stay. Deal with it later."

Outrage fills the guy's expression. Weighing the decision in his mind. Determining if he should do what's best for himself or for Sydney. No worries. I'll decide for him and reach for my gun. But before I slide out my weapon he nods. Finally conceding to the order and backtracking his stupid ass out of here.

Thank fuck because I didn't want to have to shoot him in front of Sydney. She'd bitch at me about that until I'm on my death bed.

I cut Dr. Shelton a little slack after his honesty and defense of me. Although he better not think I won't shoot his ass too if he fucks with me. "What do we do now?"

"We wait–" His palm flies up when I attempt to

interrupt. Probably already well aware of my lack of patience and resistance to waiting. Lucky he's helping Syd, or I'd slice off his hand for his disrespect. "We have to bring her out slowly over a few days. We'll decrease the sedatives until we can talk to her so we can remove her from the ventilator and check her capacities."

"She'll be okay then?"

I sound like a fucking pansy ass. Full of fear and worry. But fuck if I'm not both over her.

"There are no guarantees. But I believe so. And I promise this is the best way to give her every chance for a complete recovery."

He seems sincere. Not flinching under my scrutiny. None of the other motherfuckers watching us disagree with him or his assertion.

I nod and approve his request to proceed. I guess I have no damn choice but to wait some more for my lion.

CHAPTER 24

AFTER FOUR HELLISH LONG DAYS, HER GORGEOUS EMERALD eyes are finally open. Fucking open and locked with mine. Full of fear that fucking slays me. Giving me the strength not to drop to my knees and thank a god who would laugh his ass off to hear from me. I clutch her hand tighter as she watches me. Fighting against everything in me not to pull her into my arms and hold her with everything I'm worth to ease the trepidation flooding her exquisite face.

"I'm Dr. Shelton, Sydney. You've been injured but you're safe now. The tube in your throat is to help you breathe. Do you understand?"

The lion nods. A fucking beautiful glorious magnificent nod. Tears actually prick my eyes like a pussy but I don't give a damn. Only this woman has the power to make me cry.

The physician gives her an encouraging smile, matching her head bob with his own. "Good. Now I'm going to perform a few tests and ask you a few questions. Is that okay?"

She agrees with another nod. Never taking her eyes off of me. Glancing down at our entwined hands. Confusion flickering on her face from the ring on her dainty finger before bringing her gaze back to my face.

"Follow my finger Sydney."

He taps his shoulder, and she looks at the same spot.

But immediately returns to watch me. Testing all my restraint not to kick his ass out and engulf her. I have to make sure she's all right. I can't fuck up her recovery since we've made it this far.

He tugs his tie. She obeys. Tie, then me.

Wrist, then me.

Nose, then me.

Doc nods and smiles. All enthusiastic and encouraging. To me and to her. "You're doing great. Let's try a few more."

I smile too, reminding her I'm here. I love her. I'll protect her. She never has to worry about anything ever again.

"Is it sunny outside Sydney?"

She flicks her gaze to the bright window and nods. Then back to me. God I need her.

"Are you forty years old?"

A quick head shake before she stares at me again. Dumb ass should have given a lower number. Even I know women get wound up about their age. Easily pissed off if you imply they're older than they really are.

"Do you have blond hair?"

Another denial with her eyes never leaving mine.

"Good Sydney. You did very, very well." He nods to the nurse, waiting for his next direction. "Let's prep to extubate."

Returning to Sydney, he keeps the same calm and soothing tone. "This means we're going to remove the tube in your throat. We'll turn off the ventilator and place an oxygen mask over your mouth and nose to help you breathe during the transition. It might feel weird but shouldn't hurt. You'll probably feel like you need to cough and that's fine. Go right ahead."

He glances over at me. Straightforward yet cautious

because I know my reputation proceeds me. "You might want to step out for this part. Sometimes it's not easy to watch."

Fuck that shit. Lion needs me, and I'm never fucking leaving her. "No."

Only frowning not arguing. Good. Because I'll fire him too if he tries to kick me out.

Accepting the gloves offered to him by the nurse, he slides the latex over his wrists and grins at Sydney. "Ready?"

So damn brave. She doesn't even flinch or cringe when the doctor unhooks the coupler and grasps the edge of the thin plastic. Slowly leading the hosing out of her mouth. Weak fingers squeeze mine, and she arches off the bed following his movement while the nurse attempts to keep the mask over her nose. Taking everything I've got not to crush her hand as I suffer along with her. "You're doing great lion. Almost done."

Luckily I'm not a liar because the tip finally slides between her teeth. She sucks in a huge breath before releasing a shit storm of coughs. Giant tears rolling down her pink cheeks as they shove another fucking tool in her mouth that sounds like a damn vacuum cleaner.

Rage swells in me while panic blooms in her. Terror exploding in her wild eyes. Her free hand fighting the intrusion. Grasping at the wires and the doctor and the instrument. Trying to escape from the constraints trapping her.

Just when I'm about to start massacring people from them taking too damn long, they stop. Removing everything except the oxygen. I fucking hate this for her but so damn glad to see her breathing on her own and the color returning to her sallow skin. After a few more raspy barks, she swallows and sinks back against the pillow. The nurse attempts to attach the elastic cords behind her head to keep the mask in place but Syd's defiant as usual. Shoving the plastic away.

"You…"

Fighting against her ragged throat, she struggles to keep going with her hoarse whisper. I stroke across her damp forehead. Dappled with sweat beads from her earlier thrashing. *"What lion?"*

Agony worse than any torture I've endured churns through my taut muscles from her flinching from my touch. Recoiling from my palm on her cheek. Wincing from me comforting her.

"You shot me."

You shot me.

God damn son of a bitch.

You'd think she's the one I slammed in the head with a bat and lost her fucking mind with the adamancy of her accusation. Of the irrational anger in her tone. Of the fury in her relentless gaze. "I would never shoot you lion. Ever."

Her face pinches in confusion. Of which she really is damn disoriented if she thinks I'd ever hurt her.

"But you…Mack…had guns…"

Her allegation fades as another coughing fit overtakes her, and the nurse helps her with sips of water. The woman glances at the doctor looking for guidance. They both know what brought Sydney here but aren't aware of the details. They don't need to fucking know. I shove my thumb over my shoulder dismissing them. Neither argues, happy to leave if the speed of their steps is any indication.

She shakes her head as if trying to clear the fog. To

make sense of her memories that have somehow gotten fucking jumbled in her gorgeous mind. That I'm more than happy to clear up and correct. "That motherfucker tried to shoot me but you jumped in the damn way."

I've never been scared before. Until her. Until then. Until now. "So if anyone should be pissed, it's me. I don't know what the fuck you were thinking taking a bullet for me. You never sacrifice yourself for me."

I'm way louder than I should be. I mean fucking shit she just woke up from a god damn coma. But I can't be any angrier than I am now.

"You're mad at me?"

Incredulity rings through her voice despite how weak she is. "Fuck yes I'm mad as hell at you. You almost fucking died. I almost lost you."

Maybe she thinks I will still lose her when she turns her face away. Closing her eyes. Shutting me out. Disregarding my fury. But that's never fucking happening, and we both know it. "Go ahead and pretend like you're sleeping lion. This isn't over. Not by a long shot."

Despite my rage, I hold her hand softly between mine. Until she attempts to draw her fingers away. I grip her tighter. Locking her down. Locking her to me. Locking her to us. "Don't."

She softens from my snarl but doesn't speak or move. Ignoring me and the issue between us as always. That's fine angel. I'm not going anywhere. I'll be at your side forever whether you like it or not.

CHAPTER 25

"**N**OW, MISS MARTIN. WE HAVE A COUPLE OF OPTIONS after your release. If you have family or friends who can assist with your care, you could stay with them. Or, you could move into a rehab facility while you recuperate. We're lucky to have several excellent resources in this area. We just need to check into them to find which one has a bed available for you."

I open my mouth to let her know a rehab facility is the only choice in my situation, but Julius's voice bellows across the room instead.

"You stay with me lion."

The social worker jumps from his furious tone. But I just ignore him. I will not cower to his temper. Or follow his orders. Or allow him to control me. I've put up with his insanity for the last two weeks, and I'm not doing it anymore. I've made up my mind about what I need, and it isn't him.

He strides toward us as if he owns the damn place, which knowing him he probably does. Undoubtedly bribes doctors and nurses to care for the people he loves to assault. Peering closer at the yellow name tag on her chest, he yanks the brochures off the tray extended over my legs. "You can go Mrs. Washington. I'll be taking care of her. No need for any of these."

"Well...I...this is..."

The poor woman stutters and stumbles backward from my bedside. Hoping to escape from Julius's vicinity as well as his embarrassingly obnoxious behavior. Unfair to her to be trapped in our battle, I force an indulgent smile as if everything is fine and nod to her. "It's okay. We can go through this later."

"Yes. Sure. Of course." With a timid reach she grabs her file folder from the faux wooden top and the pamphlets from his hand. Grabbing the edges of the slick papers almost as if to ensure her fingers don't touch his. "I'll come back later."

We both steam in silence until the door closes behind her. "How dare you dismiss her?"

"What the fuck were you thinking?"

"I'm not living with you!"

"If you think you're going to get away from me, you're out of your fucking beautiful mind."

Yelling over each other isn't going to solve this problem. Or fix anything between us. Nothing can. I turn toward the window. The rain pounding on the glass as hard as the throbbing in my head. "Get out Julius. I don't want you here."

"I don't give a damn what you want."

Goosebumps lift on my neck from his warm minty breath in my ear. His scruff on my cheek. His hand around my throat. Hating my traitorous body coming to life from his heat and his scent and his touch. Gentle but insistent turning my face back to his. "Obviously. You never have, and I don't think you ever will."

Lust gleams in his eyes, and his fingers grip tighter. Restraining himself from fully manhandling me.

"You better be glad you're in that hospital bed lion, or I would fuck that damn mouth of yours into submission."

"I'd like to see you try."

A raging snarl thunders from deep in his chest. Echoing across the bare walls. Oh shit. I've pushed him too far. The rolling table slams into the opposite wall from the force of him shoving it out of the way. Not allowing anything between us.

"You think I won't fuck you here and now." He lifts me from the bed and cradles me to his chest. His touch gentle and careful in contrast with his vicious tone. Ensuring no harm to me or my wound despite the frustration thudding his voice. *"That I wouldn't love to make you scream loud enough for the nurses to come running."*

I hate him touching me. Cuddling me and coddling me. I hate myself even more for craving him. Snuggling in and letting him hold me. Comforting me when the only other person who ever did that is dead. And almost killed me.

Mack shot me.

My friend shot me.

I don't know how to be okay because my best friend shot me.

I shove against Julius. Twisting and fighting to get away until agony rips through my injury almost as bad as my heart.

"Damn it lion. Stop. You're going to hurt yourself."

His arm wraps around my torso trapping my arms in his hold. So damn strong I'm immobile. I pant from the exertion. Overwhelmed from the effort of fighting with him and trying to make sense of everything and drowning in this flood of emotions that I hate. Being numb is so much easier. I'd forgotten how much my heart can ache, and I don't think I can stand the pain.

Closing my eyes feels so nice. I just want to sleep. To feel safe. To feel loved. To feel whole. But every time I let myself feel that way, I get hurt. Julius is no different regardless of how much either of us pretends he is. "Please just let me go. Please leave me alone."

"No."

I give up and let him win again. Listening to his heartfelt murmurs despite having no idea what he's saying. Wishing things weren't so complicated, and I wasn't so fucked up in the head. Forcing myself not to cry because of him or Mack or anyone.

"Tell me why you won't let yourself love me."

My heart breaks from his raw plea. Almost as broken as I am. "Because the man who was supposed to love me from my first breath to his last, disowned me. The man who gave me butterflies and made me think maybe he could be the one, raped me. The man who claimed to be my only true friend in the entire world, shot me." I can barely breathe with him squeezing me against him. I can barely talk from my voice cracking. I can't stop though. He has to know. "So if you wonder why I can't believe in you, it's because I'm tired of discovering that what I believe about the men I trust isn't real."

"There's nothing more real than this Sydney."

I've never wanted to believe in anything more than that. More than him. More than us. Hating that I'm so confused, I beg him for patience. "I just need time. You're smothering me. You have to give me some space. Can't you understand that?"

"You can have all the damn time you need. But not space. You live with me, you sleep in my bed, until you realize I'm not going anywhere and neither are you."

I open my mouth to argue. But I'm exhausted and can't seem to form the words I want to say anymore. Floating too deep in this heady haze to articulate my reasoning. Drifting off to his whispers against my hair. I'll tell him later. He'll believe me then.

CHAPTER 26

SHE SWIRLS THE RUBY LIQUID IN HER GLASS AND TAKES A long sip. Emptying the tumbler. She shouldn't be drinking with pain killers but of course she disregards the doctor's orders as much as she does mine.

I finish my own scotch and pour a second. We've been home for a week, and the only thing we seem to agree on is our choice of alcohol. Worse than arguing, we don't even speak. I work. She sleeps. I chase. She runs. I hurt. She hurts worse. I try to comfort her. She resists me. Both of us fucking miserable, and neither of us can figure out how the hell to fix what's broken between us.

My damn phone buzzes for what seems like the fucking hundredth time since I walked in here and found her staring at a blank screen with her expression almost as vacant. She said she wanted to work on the Victorian, but never even clicked on the file. Guess I'll have to hire someone else.

I glance at my cell. Fuck! Val is checking on her since I'd forgotten to update her like I promised I would after she found out lion woke up. Maybe Syd should talk to her friend herself since she doesn't have any interest in conversing with me. "It's Val Vernon. She wants to see how you're doing."

The first spark of life I've seen in her all day—hell all

week—as her head flies up, and she gapes at me. "How does she even know?"

I guess I never told Syd with everything else such a fucked up mess. Not that I thought she would care with the depression she's mired in. "I brought her to the hospital. I thought maybe if she talked to you that you'd wake up."

"You did that…for me?"

Shock flushes her pale face. Her gaze boring into me, studying me, as if she's never seen me before. A frantic search for the meaning behind my proclamation.

"I did every single fucking thing I could think of so you'd be okay."

Realization of my intentions makes her succulent mouth fall open. "That's why Nonna is here too?"

"Of course."

A slow nod as she frowns, huddling into herself while she ponders my assertion. Yet, she doesn't ask for more, and I don't offer. Obviously she doesn't believe me. About this or anything else. I want to shake her. To scream and swear at her to make her understand that I would never do any of the things she fears. But if she doesn't accept how much I love her by now, then I don't think she ever will.

I leave her to her bottle. I have my own demons to nurse.

The door slowly opens, and beautiful lion peeks inside. As much as she claims she wants me to leave her alone, she always searches for me. Never wants to be too far away from where I am. Caught snooping when our eyes meet, she steps all the way into my office. Even from across the room I can feel the stress ravishing her little body. Coiled taut from her battle with me and herself.

Wrapping her robe tighter around herself and then crossing her slender arms, she watches for a moment. Silent yet intrigued. Until she gasps from the comprehension of the image he creates. Her sharp breath audible over the buzzing needle.

"Oh my God! What are you doing?"

I love the impact of my decision on her gorgeous face and in her stunned tone. "If I let you leave—which I'm never going to do, just to be absolutely clear—do you think I'd pick up with someone else? That I'd bring another woman here and fuck her and love her and make her my wife? That I'd fucking touch her with these hands covered with your marks?"

Even the artist is affected by my questions. Glancing between us with his own surprise before returning to his work.

"I don't know."

Frown lines mar her expression. Her plump lips part and then squeeze shut again. Reluctant to argue. Unwilling to concede. No worries. I don't mind doing all the talking. "You do know."

She shuffles closer. Taking her own sweet time. Never pulling her blazing eyes from the blood smeared on my knuckle. Never wavering from staring at her name wrapped around my ring finger. Not the wedding band I want, yet permanent just the same. "You've known all along."

She sits down on my left leg watching intently as the needle pierces my skin. I curl her closer, trying not to get blood on the white cashmere but she doesn't seem to notice or care. Hypnotized by the animal taking shape on my right palm. Hurts like a motherfucker but worth the pain to see the love in her eyes. The adoration in her face. The reverence in her fingertips as she brushes my wrist. As close as she dares to touch not to interfere with Darren's work. Awed by his unbelievable talent with the detail and color captured perfectly.

Her sweet head lays on my shoulder. *"I love it."*

"I love you."

That declaration makes her look up, and I have to kiss her smiling lips. Chaste and brief. For now. Once he's finished, I'll show her with more than just the symbols on my hands how much.

Her gaze, shiny with rare tears, locks with mine. Dainty fingers cup my face while I stare down at her as if making sure I see her. Hear her. Feel her. *"I'm sorry. I don't what's wrong with me, why I've been acting so crazy. I–"*

"Shh. We're both fucked up. No judgment here. You know that."

An enthusiastic nod. She knows and agrees. Thank fucking god. I take wild loose strands of her silky hair and tuck them behind her ear. Offering my understanding with my touch and my words. *"I mean you got fucking shot. That's not something you can easily overcome. But let me help you. Let me take care of you. That's all I want."*

"That's all I want too."

I kiss her again and she snuggles in. Her small body and troubled mind finally relax. Satisfied I accept more than her apology. I accept everything about her. Just like she does me.

"Thank you for Val and…just…everything."

Everything.

A single word that means so much. To her and to me. Heartfelt and sincere from her broken whisper. *"You're welcome."*

A little sigh blows on my throat before her soft lips brush my heated skin. "I want a matching tattoo."

I have to force myself to hold still when I laugh so I don't cause him to mess up. "Never fucking happening lion."

As expected, she opens her luscious mouth to argue with me, and I shut her down with my fist in her hair and my tongue in her throat. Ending any discussion of her doing anything that will cause her any more pain. Starting my dick twitching with her ravenous moan. I pull away for Darren's sake because I know he doesn't want to watch my girl ride my cock as he brands me. She's still grinning as she tucks her head back under my jaw while he finishes. Which is fine. We can fuck and fight later. Just like we always do.

EPILOGUE

"ARE YOU READY NONNA?"

I speak as loud as I can without waking Ava. Grandmother doesn't hear or see as well as she used to. Confined to bed most of the time now. But her frailty hasn't impacted her spirit. Unable to dampen her enthusiasm at all for this visit she's been waiting nine months for. I make sure her thin arm is fully supported by the pillows before I place her great-grand daughter in her embrace. "What do you think?"

"She is the most beautiful child I have ever seen."

Tears stream down her wrinkled lifted cheeks. Crying and laughing at the same time. Fuck me if I don't get a little emotional myself as Syd lays her head against my shoulder and wraps her hand around my bicep. My name circling her ring finger, the edges of the dark pink letters peeking out from under her huge rock. Just like hers is on mine, beneath my black band.

Exhausted from the trip but my lion's happy too. That her family is all together. Her Nonna is delighted, her daughter is safe, and her husband is concealing his neuroses better than normal. Both of us well aware they always linger just below the surface. Because if she thinks I won't flip the fuck out again if something ever happens to her or our child, she's the one who's fucked up in the head. But knowing that she'll love me anyway, in spite of my irrationality, keeps me pretty close to sane. At least most of the time.

I press my lips to the top of her beautiful head. Breathing in her intoxicating scent mixed with the salty sea air she'd been craving. Knowing how much this place relaxes us both. "I love you lion."

"I love you too saint."

Her gorgeous body melts into mine, and I absorb the peace she offers. All of my girls are finally content. Just like I always wanted.

The End

ACKNOWLEDGMENTS

I can't believe this is my tenth book! I definitely didn't make the journey alone, so I have several people to sincerely thank for all of their assistance and support. Thank you to Tracy C (aka Samantha K Bookey) for beta reading and for enlisting the help of her son Zacary C for his guidance on the medical aspects of the story. The two of them truly made the story better and more realistic. Even if suctioning phlegm isn't sexy! LOL!

Thank you to Anna Brooks who tells me what works and what doesn't. She's always right.

Extra special thanks to Lynn Kline Underwood, Joy Westerfield, Sarah DeLong, Katrina Haynes, Kristi Smith, Sheena Taylor, and Lori Amey. You ladies help me more than you'll ever know. I am forever grateful.

Check out the first chapter of *192 (one ninty-two)*

chapter
1

I fucking hate this bastard.

The way he shovels huge chunks of sausage into his mouth with his hands. Instead of using a fucking fork like a normal person. Wiping the grease from his stubby fingers after each bite on the crumpled napkin next to his plate. His lips smacking and spewing crumbs while he speaks with Dante, his brother and most trusted captain. Gloating from the expansion of his territory as his team—not his lazy ass—brings down another family encroaching on his domain. Reveling in his power and money and dominance. Unconcerned with everything and everyone else except himself.

Including her.

Especially her.

My pulse pounds in my head from her absence. Only one reason she's not here. No question that he hurt her. Just how bad are the injuries.

Finally, the arrogant prick shoves away from the black walnut table. The coffee mug bucking against his untouched bowl of strawberries from his gratuitous force. His barrel chest strains the buttons of his thick white dress shirt as he rises. Too big for a crisp look, he settles for comfort instead. Of which he deserves absolutely none. So fucking ironic he prevents pain and constraint for himself while doling out both to the person who deserves torture the least of all of us.

From the sound of his chair legs scraping across the tile, the housekeeper scurries in, offering him his gray cashmere coat with trembling fingers. Which he yanks out of her hand without bothering to look at her. Not a word of thanks or appreciation. At least better than the slew of profanities he usually berates her with. He nods toward me while he rams his huge arms into the gaping sleeves. Already huffing from the exertion.

"My stupid, clumsy wife fell again. Check and make sure she's okay." An irritated smirk lifts his ruddy right cheek. "If not, just take her out back and shoot her."

It takes everything I have to chuckle instead of drive my fist into his gut. Smile rather than punch his stomach so hard he chucks out bacon and blood and bile. "No problem."

Once he waddles past, I pull out my phone and scroll through my messages. Counting to twenty-five after the door slams shut behind him. Waiting for the rumble of one of the garage doors. I'll play the game. Act unconcerned. Pretend there's no rush. Feign oblivious to the truth of the situation. I'm just performing another monotonous duty assigned to me. Nothing else. Even though she's my only fucking reason for being here. My only fucking reason for enduring this shitty assignment.

I stride to the stairs and pause again, bending down to tie my shoe. Never letting him or anyone else see me hurry. Made that mistake once before, and ended up on driveway duty for a month before I got assigned to guard her again.

Once the ceiling camera pivots to scan the living room, I jog up the steps. No response when I knock on their bedroom door. Closing my eyes, I slow my breathing to focus on listening for a sound. Any fucking sound to prove he hasn't killed her yet.

Absolute silence.

Tapping again, I pray to a god I don't believe in that she's sitting on the bed. Waiting for approval to leave. Hoping for release from her cage. "Viviana?"

Nothing.

Fuck it. I shove down the handle, and an inferno roars through my throbbing chest from her curled into herself on the tan carpet. A protective mechanism that never saves her from his wrath.

She remains balled in agony when I drop next to her. "God damn him."

"I—I'm okay."

My fragile warrior. So broken yet still so surprisingly strong. "Yeah, laid out on the fucking floor isn't okay."

"Sometimes it's just easier to stay down."

Fucking bittersweet to touch her. Only permitted when he's attacked her, and I have to tend to her wounds. Silky strands slide under my fingertips as I brush the long, black hair off her exquisite face. Grateful no bruises or blood mar the flawless ivory skin this time. "Come on. Let's get you up."

A sharp shriek, she can't muffle as much as she tries to, oscillates across the huge room when I lift her to a sitting position. Reigniting my fury that he's put his hands on a woman. Especially one as delicate as her. Too petite to defend his blows. Too proud to protect herself from his torture. Too plagued by a misguided obligation she sure as hell doesn't owe him.

Short pants puff between her red puckered lips to ride through the pain. Probably bruised ribs again. I force myself not to rub across her torso and feel for broken bones. Uncertain if I could stop myself from caressing her more. When all I want to do is scoop her up and get her the fuck out of this hellhole. "What happened this time?"

Despite her agony, a deep blush spreads across her flushed cheeks. Too embarrassed to answer. Which means the worst possible transgression in that bastard's eyes. She started.

Fuck. The last fucking thing I want is her carrying his baby. But the possibility of her getting pregnant is the only thing keeping her alive right now. Although she doesn't realize the real reason behind his insane drive to impregnate her. "I'm sorry."

"Me too."

Only a whisper. From mental as well as physical anguish. "Maybe we should stay home today. Let you rest."

Her head flies up, and she finally meets my gaze. Tears shining in hers. Less from the pain and more from my suggestion. Imploring me with a pitiful plea I can't resist.

"Please Roan. Please take me. I can't miss."

Absolutely ridiculous this daily excursion provides her only opportunity to leave the house without him. Yet I can't blame her for wanting to escape. If only for two brief hours. "Okay."

Gratitude softens her begging grip on my forearm. A tentative smile actually lifts her gaunt cheeks. Impressing me once again with her resiliency. Astonishing me with her tenacity.

"Thank you."

As gentle as I can manage, I pull her up the rest of the

way and stand her on her dainty feet. She sways a bit. Her slender arm curling around her torso again while her gorgeous face blanches. But fuck me if she's not determined, and after a short minute, she rolls back her shoulders and steps toward the door. Clutching my bicep for balance.

For as horrific as the abuse is to her body and her mind, we manage to walk in amenable silence down the stairs, through the kitchen, and into the garage. Can't appear to be anything more than employee and employer's trophy wife. Even though she's so much more than that to me. Originally, because of my promise to her father. Now, because of her.

Adhering to the normal routine, she pauses at the SUV, waiting for me to open the door and offer my hand to assist her with the climb inside. Not because she's a bitch, but because that's what nine years of mafia wife training taught her. She's a princess and needs to behave as such.

"Thank you Roan."

"My pleasure Mrs. Moretti."

No, not my pleasure at all. So many other fucking things I'd like to do for her. To her. Pleasure her more than she could ever imagine. Revere her body with the absolute adoration and attention she's never known. But I can't. I remind myself for the millionth fucking time. She's not mine. This is just a job.

Once she's settled against the cushion, I yank the seat belt and carefully drape the heavy strap across her trembling body, continuing to recoil from the stinging ache she must feel in her side. Providing a small respite from the agony in her torso by keeping her from having to reach backward to grasp the harness herself. Another gorgeous flush pinks her cheeks. Both of us well aware I've crossed a line I shouldn't. But she doesn't reprimand me like she should. Admonish me like I deserve. Just lights up with a grateful smile that I think of as I jack off in the shower almost every morning. A budding connection between us that no one else knows about.

Or so I think. Caught in the gaze of Nobbie, Moretti's most trusted mechanic, when I step back from the vehicle. As nonchalant as I can manage, I offer him a courtesy nod and push the door shut. He gives a languid chin bob in return. Doesn't appear to give a damn about her, me, or our morning expedition. Just keeps the cars running and free of bombs and bugs. As long as Moretti stays off his ass and out of his face, he's happy. Like all the other hired help on the motherfucker's payroll. But I've still got to be more fucking careful. I cannot fuck this up again and be separated from her. Or put her in any more danger than she already is.

Funny how much more oxygen there seems to be in the car once we pass through the massive steel gates edging the property. Unable to stop myself, I glance in the rear view mirror, seeing rather than hearing her sigh of relief. Mimicking mine when we cross the line between charcoal travertine pavers to black asphalt. Breaching the boundary between hell and the pitiful version of the only heaven she knows. An inadequate freedom, yet all I can assume is the fleeting taste gives her the will to endure the other twenty-two hours of the day.

"Have you seen the new building going up on Wilford? The neo classical architecture is unusual for the neighborhood, but the design really looks gorgeous. I love how they're revitalizing that area."

Current events. Another staple of her breeding. To have genial conversation in all situations. Whether at dinner parties or fundraisers or meetings with her husband's associates. "No, I haven't."

I know she hasn't either. Just an article she read from the stack of newspapers waiting for her at breakfast every morning when she's allowed to eat. With censored and monitored access to the internet, she's primarily stuck with flipping pages old school style rather than scanning online. "Maybe we can swing by afterward and take a look."

Excitement explodes across her exquisite face before fear smothers the enthusiasm just as quickly from my suggestion for an impromptu field trip. "Thank you, but we'd probably better get back right after mass. I don't…"

Want to get the hell beat out of me for being late. She doesn't have to imply the threat we both know too well. Her worry the same as mine. Anything can set that asshole off, but staying out longer than allowed would be an egregious offense she would most definitely suffer for.

But I'm allotted about ten minutes leeway for traffic and construction once we leave St. Mark's before I get the inevitable status check. Just enough time for a fast drive by. "We should have a few minutes to spare for a quick peek."

"Really?"

Fucking sad how quickly her huge smile returns from my assertion. To give her a glimpse of something she usually only gets to read about. To see a brief view of the real world instead of the constraining walls of Arturo's mansion. "Yeah, really."

"Thank you Roan. Thank you so much."

A subtle shiver of excitement jerks her slight body as she clasps her small hands around her little black purse again. Fuck me for a being a pussy ass that I'm ecstatic too. A rare opportunity for me to give her a bright spot in her normally shit ass existence.

Her expression softens to a more solemn countenance

when I park in front of the entrance. Intricate designs, carved deep enough to drag your finger through the channels, embellish the burnished wood doors. Incapable of completely masking the rich baritone voices resonating from inside. The largest cathedral in the city, famous for having a glorious choir perform even during weekday masses. I can see why she loves coming here. Not just an escape from the monotony of her life, but because of the solace the ambiance inspires.

Unwilling to let her struggle for even a second to unbuckle her restraint, I hustle back to her and jerk the handle. Relief fills me from her relaxed demeanor and motionless hands. She waits for me. My fingers brush across her thigh as I reach for the black plastic button. Powerless to help myself from touching her again.

I'm a fucking selfish bastard for pushing the limits of her modesty yet I fucking swear I can feel the heat radiating from her slim leg even under the silky fabric of her gray skirt. Wide eyes meet mine as she swallows softly. I'm a fucking fool for thinking she could feel anything for me. Would ever break the sincere vow she made to accept Arturo for better or worse three years ago. To renege on her promise to accept the duty of producing an heir to strengthen the partnership between the two families. Or so her father let her think. *"Let me help you princess."*

Luscious lips part with a quick intake of breath, yet she only nods. Once I release the seat belt, I hold out both hands, slowly sliding her off the bench and balancing her once her silver heels reach the concrete. Never releasing her until the grimace frowning her normally docile face dissolves, and she stands up completely of her own volition. *"Okay?"*

"Yes, thank you."

The breathless whisper stirs my desperate cock, and I force myself to let her go before I jerk her against me and taste that sweet pink mouth. Instead, I tuck her to my side, my arm swallowing her tiny waist, to avoid the tenderness afflicting her rib cage, and stride evenly inside. Hoping hard as fuck that Arturo doesn't have men watching us anymore. Because that interaction was too fucking obvious. And I'm too fucking stupid. But I yearn for her touch as much as she yearns for freedom. And I'm scared as hell neither of us will ever fucking have either one if I don't pull off this mission.

Resonant voices fill the cavernous space while I guide her to the confessional. Fucking ironic she has no sins to seek forgiveness from, yet always remains the first person to engage in the sacrament every morning. That's an argument I lost a long time ago when I questioned her about her commitment to this ritual. Rather than reprimand me for my audacity, she just smiled that indulgent smile I like to believe is only for me, and reminded me we all have faults. No one is perfect.

Except for her.

A lime green light glows above the decorative frame, signaling the priest's presence as well as the unoccupied booth. She gives me a shy smile before she steps out of my protective grasp and into the closet size room. After a quick sweep of the interior to ensure the chamber really is empty, I nod and close the door behind her. Now it's my turn to wait. And try not to think how fucking pitiful she looked gingerly lowering herself onto the red leather kneeler. I deserve to burn in hell to plot a man's death while standing in the middle of fucking church. The only person I hate more than him right now is myself and my inability to do anything about Arturo's savage mistreatment of his wife. At least not yet anyway.

Working as a mercenary for the past eleven years, I've never minded solo missions. Get in. Get out. Get gone. No complications. Just the way I like. Now, everything's beyond fucking complicated. With her. With me. With the 'us' I can't help but imagine once I get her away from this bastard. Unaware her time's running out, she has no idea why I'm really here. The urgency to recruit a team for her rescue flares inside me. I can't let her know the truth until she's safe.

A few curious glances toss my way from standing guard. The regulars are used to me. I'm no longer of any interest. But the tourists can't help but gawk. Everyone vying for their chance to snag a celebrity photo. Which I guess she kind of is. The beautiful yet reclusive wife of the most notorious crime boss in the country. Garnering gossip enough to spin a reputation of a fairy tale princess. Locked away in a tower with only a few rare public appearances that prove she exists. Except her prince isn't charming. Far from it. Arturo Moretti's a sick fucking psychotic bastard who demonstrates his possession of her through punches and kicks rather than love or affection.

I unfurl my fists when the door nudges me in the back and swing around to jam my foot against the brass plate, offering her my arm. Welcoming a hint of soft flowers wafting over me as she steps closer. Looking up with what I swear is fucking adoration in her eyes. At least that's what I fucking hope. That she trusts in me to always protect her.

In the pew, she slowly glides to a kneeling position again while I sit a few inches away. Another reason I deserve to burst into fucking flames. Powerless to stifle the image of her on her knees for me. Letting me fuck that lush mouth. As tiny as the rest of her, I know she couldn't accept all of me. But it would be damn gorgeous to watch her try. Before I'd lay her across my bed and worship her body the way a princess deserves. The way she deserves.

Incapable of pretending to be anything other than what I am, I remain still while she flows through the motions of the service. Although after all this time, I know exactly when to stand and what to say. I refuse to disrespect her beliefs and act like I possess the same devotion she holds. Besides, I'm no fool. I can steal another opportunity to watch her graceful movements and hear her reverent whispers without her realizing my gaze lies upon her. Only her occasional flinch of pain when she bends and rises ruins my enjoyment.

Usually when we leave, tension returns to her body, coiling tighter and tighter with each step down the aisle. Anxiety stiffening her muscles from the uncertainty that awaits her when we get home. The reprieve from her hell ending almost before she could fully relax and enjoy the peace.

This time though her happy visage remains. Eager to experience my unexpected suggestion, she embodies more genuine joy than I've seen in her since I hired on. After finally passing all of Arturo's rigorous tests to honor the commitment I made to her father long before his unexpected death ruined our thoughtful planning. Taking almost three fucking long ass years to finally get inside the house and to her.

Once we're on the road again, I sneak another glance at her for as long as I can until I have to return my attention to the traffic. "Can I ask you something?"

A curious expectation fills her smile. Wondering what I'm going to say. "Sure."

"What do you pray for? Or will it not come true if you tell?"

Genuine carefree laughter fills the SUV. Damn. I could die a happy fucking man hearing that too infrequent giggle bubble from deep inside her.

"It's not like they're birthday wishes, silly." She leans back against her seat. The humor softens to a wistful smile. "I pray God continues to keep my parents in his love and protection. I pray for strength and wisdom so I can be a better wife."

My fingers ache from clutching the steering wheel so tight. I fucking hate the doubt wobbling in her tone. Absolutely fucking nothing she could do better. She's a fucking angel. He just needs to die.

"That I'll be a good mother someday if I get the opportunity." Bright eyes meet mine again in the mirror. Full of a rare joy that glows bright even within the disillusioned depths. "When I was a little girl, my momma told me prayers of thanksgiving are God's favorite. So I always make sure I thank God for giving me a friend like you."

Friend.

What in the actual fuck? Probably the first time anyone has ever prayed for me, let alone been grateful for me. The irony not lost on me that she's appreciative for a killer who earns his living by ending the lives of others.

A small hand covers her mouth as her face falls. Misunderstanding the horror of my expression. Unaware my furious headshake roots in shock rather than her undeserved label of me.

"Oh, I apologize. I've presumed too much about our relationship." She tucks a loose strand of thick dark hair behind her ear and the wavy tendril slides out just as quickly while she fidgets with the small bag in her lap. Squeezing the short black straps over and over. Laser focused on the smooth leather rather than me. "I just thought…I know how hard you work to take care of me. Arturo and I appreciate—"

"You just surprised me, that's all." Like the bastard I am, I cut her off. I don't want to hear anything about that asshole. Especially his fucking name on her gorgeous lips. This is about her. And me. "I am your friend Viviana."

I speak slowly. Emphasizing each word. Stressing the sincerity of my tone. Even though she sits two feet away, I need to make sure she hears me since she won't look at me any longer. I've hurt her. So fucking fragile, and I fuck up her hesitant attempt at a deeper connection. "Really."

Her head bobs. Slow and uncertain. She doesn't believe me. Thinks I'm just being nice. When I'm never nice. Except to her. Damn I'm a fucking bastard for fucking this up. For fucking *her* up when all she asks is for a genuine friendship while living among a houseful of enemies.

Nothing I can think of to convince her. Or lessen the strain pulsating between us. The silence hangs thick and uncomfortable. A balmy tension stealing my breath and my patience. I need to fix this. The only way I can. Drifting to the curb, I nod toward the side window. Tapping the button to lower the shaded, bullet proof glass. "What do you think?"

She strains toward the fresh air and rising building as far as her seat belt allows. Taking in the first golden rays of the day glinting against the broad stone façade protected by thick white pillars. The hurt darkening her face from our earlier misunderstanding slowly smooths away to a quickening smile that fills my chest as much as her sweet face. Glowing from her plump lips to her almost black eyes. So fucking beautiful.

All the tension melts from my muscles. She's happy. If only for a moment.

With our short leash and tight time, I can only circle the block twice before we have to return to the house. But she doesn't protest when I drive away for the last time. As well aware of our limitations as I am. "Is there any place else you need to go?"

Just a formality. We both know she's not allowed to go anywhere else. But for some fucked up reason I like to make her feel like she has choices. That her entire fucking life, down to the minute, isn't monitored and decided and controlled.

"No, but thank you. Home is fine."

Never once have I heard her complain or act like her situation isn't pure bliss. But I swear I hear a crack in the confidence when she says home. Fuck how much she must hate going back to that prison. The jail her father mistakenly sentenced her to unaware his sudden demise a few months after his agreement with Arturo would ruin her life. Trapping her in a loveless marriage with the only purpose to ensure an heir. As well as a huge deposit into the bastard's bank account.

The quiet between us isn't as stifling as before. Her smile still lingers, with her body soft and relaxed. Even after we return to the compound. Instead, I'm the one full of tension once we circle the drive. God fucking damn. Dante waits outside. With a broad stance, arms folded across his massive chest, and a shit ass smirk on his face, he blocks the entrance to the open bay. Fucking smug eyes bore into mine. Gloating with happiness that I've fucked up, and he's the one to catch me.

Even worse when a broken sigh billows behind me. Fucking destroying me that she knows now too. And, neither of us can do a god damn thing to fix my mistake.

OTHER BOOKS

The Surviving Absolution series:
Wine & Whiskey
Wine & Whiskey: Everything for You
Truth About Tequila
Truth About Tequila: Believe in Me

Suck, Bang, & Blow Series:
Suck
Bang
Blow

Stand Alone Books:
Straight, No Chaser
On the Rocks
Under the Influence
192
Dirty, Bruised Martini
The Last Call
Another Round
Garnish With a Candy Cane

ABOUT THE AUTHOR

Nikki writes contemporary romantic thrillers and admits to a weakness for alpha males and bad boys, especially ones who can't live without the strong women they love. She spends more time in her characters' lives than her own. But, when she's in the real world, her passions include reading, wine appreciating, running, and spending time with her husband and daughter.

Connect with Nikki:

Reader's Group: Nikki's Naughty Tequilas
www.facebook.com/groups/570875083096764

Website:
www.nikkibelaire.com

Facebook
www.facebook.com/NikkiBelaire

Facebook Author Page
www.facebook.com/NikkiBelaireAuthor

Newsletter
www.subscribepage.com/w0h4x2